T0285691

Twilight of Torment

II. HERITAGE

THE FRENCH LIST

Léonora Miano

Twilight of Torment

II. HERITAGE

Translated by Gila Walker

LONDON NEW YORK CALCUTTA

www.bibliofrance.in

The work is published with the support of the Publication
Assistance Programmes of the Institut français

First published in French as *Crépuscule du tourment 2. Heritage*
by Léonora Miano
© Éditions Grasset & Fasquelle, Paris, 2017

First published in English translation by Seagull Books, 2023
English translation © Gila Walker, 2023

ISBN   978 18 0309 154 9

British Library Cataloguing-in-Publication Data
A catalogue record for this book is available from the British Library

Typeset at Seagull Books, Calcutta, India
Printed and bound by Hyam Enterprises, Calcutta, India

I knew life
Began where I stood in the dark,
Looking out into the light.

Yusef Komunyakaa

I am not tragically colored [. . .].
I do not belong to the sobbing
school of Negrohood who hold
that nature somehow has given
them a lowdown dirty deal and
whose feelings are hurt about it.

Zora Neale Hurston

Contents

Principal Characters

Amok/*Dio*

Ajar/*Tiki* (his sister), Ixora (his live-in partner), Kabral (his son), Amandla (his ex), Shrapnel (his only friend, Kabral's biological father, Ixora's ex), Madame (his mother), Amos Mususedi (his father), Angus Mususedi (his paternal grandfather), Conroy Mandone (his maternal grandfather), Regal/*Charles-Bronson* (an old acquaintance)

MoodSwing

At first, alarmed by what he'd done, he'd climbed back into the car, and shot straight ahead. The deluge threatening to drown the world wasn't what had stopped him. It was something else, some unknown force. Without premeditation, without really thinking about it at all, he'd slowed down, turned the car around. He couldn't leave her like that, lying in the mud, under this downpour. His getaway hadn't taken him far, but as he drove back, a hint of consciousness returned to him. Whether or not she was dead, he should be the first to know, to do what was necessary. It was written, however, that nothing would unfold according to his will. Others had beat him to the scene. Not altogether, but all the same. Just as he'd stepped out of the car, slammed the door behind him, a silhouette appeared in front of one the neighborhood's frail dwellings. Wearing rubber boots ill-assorted with her house robe, the woman had rushed over to Ixora, squatted, had seemed to say something. Before he had the time to make a movement she was lifting Ixora by her shoulders, dragging her on the ground. Very soon, someone had joined her, a woman tall as a tree, wearing a white dress, an indigo scarf around her waist. The newcomer was carrying a flashlight, which she slipped under her belt before grabbing hold of the injured woman's legs. He stood there paralyzed, having recognized the first woman. He was a good distance away, but the force of the intuition that had frozen him to the spot was confirmed. The bulb of the last working streetlamp had exploded without a sound. There'd been nothing but darkness, unmitigated, descending on the environs. No one had noticed his presence.

Before restarting the sedan, he'd waited to see the three women disappear. The fury of the storm had masked the roar of the engine, he himself had hardly heard it. He'd proceeded slowly, feeling layers of sludge accumulating under the tires. The rear-view mirror had sent him the image of an uprooted tree, sliding at full speed over the soaked ground, hurled in his pursuit despite the mud. He'd stepped on the gas, before feeling like a fool. He didn't believe in spirits, it was nothing but a deracinated tree, not Ixora's plant double. He'd turned on the radio thinking that would stifle the thoughts assailing him. Maître Gazonga was shouting his head off, calling the whole world to witness his sufferings: *Les jaloux saboteurs aux yeux de crocodile, veulent mon échec et souhaitent ma misère.* The song used to make him laugh until he wept, even though nature had endowed him with no sense of humor. Tonight, the singer's complaint about others wanting him to fail and be miserable had irritated him. There were no *jealous saboteurs* at whom he could point an accusing finger, he had only himself to blame. The incident had lasted only a few moments, less than two minutes, but nothing would ever be the same. For years, he'd built a wall between the world and him, limiting his social life to a strict minimum, guarding against attachments. Then, his only friend had died, in the most absurd way, passing in the metro one night. The man had been a force of nature, sure of his rights over the world, a living god. He'd had to identify the body, bring it back to his native country, face his grieving family.

Even before this, he'd risked opening a breach in the enclosure of barbed wire that protected him. He'd yearned to get close to Amandla. The woman had been the first domino in the line, the one that had toppled all the others. At the sight of her, all the emotions he'd kept himself from feeling, except in his readings, had set him on fire. Their relationship had turned sour. He wanted to be with her but without wanting anything for her. Though he was no specialist in love, life having introduced him only to its disturbing character, a faint voice whispered that this was what it was about: wanting for the other more than for oneself, even if it meant stepping aside. He hadn't been able to resist, to repress his desire to get to know her. Yet, everything spoke against her. The first time he'd seen her, she was standing on a stage in a small theatre, greeting the audience, *in the powerful name of Aset*, before putting her finest qualities to work for a reactionary ideology. Though she didn't necessarily agree with all their positions, she'd joined a group of purported activists whose sole activity consisted in regurgitating the exhausting laments of Negrohood.

The world had no respect for this ancestral mastery of the word that crowned them, wherever they were, kings of rap, stand-up, preaching, or university lecturing. There'd been ample time to observe them. Nothing about the way they operated could be disregarded anymore. It was known that their art of verbal expression went hand in hand with a passion for consumption, that most of these great activists would have killed their father, mother, and their entire community to get their hands on the latest trendy gadget, which owed nothing to the inventiveness of Kemet. Amandla had sparked his curiosity. Even though she wasn't there by chance, her ambitions seemed to lie elsewhere. He'd surprised himself waiting for a call from a *brother* to let him know the secret place where the next meeting would be held. He had to show his black credentials to get past the door, accept to be filmed to prove that he wasn't a mole working for the system, an agent of Babylon. It was a pathetic measure of protection, in reality. Skin color was no evidence of integrity. And potential spies would be happy to smile at the camera, it would only reinforce their cover.

Amandla stood out from the other members of the group. Hearing her speak, he'd sensed deeper aspirations. Something different, in her Uzi gaze, her black-power attitude. Something different: red mixed with blue, a ceaseless wrestling with an old melancholy that often gained the upper hand. She'd moved him, made him reflect about himself, it was the first time he felt so distant and yet so close to a stranger. He'd wanted to see her again at all costs, felt disconcerted by this urgency, incapable of holding it back. Their mutual understanding had been immediate, but what was destined to happen happened, more than once. Amandla was one of those women whose heart beats to some extent between her legs. Her tongue, in love, quickly abandoned speaking for breathing, palpitating, moving. He had to touch her, take her all the time, keep returning tirelessly, like a farmer to his land. Such a task would have delighted many a man, but his capacities in this area had long been atrophied. She was not offended by the first dysfunction, seeing it as the expression of an overly powerful desire to honor her. Then, he'd had to confess, to reveal that he was terrified of conceiving a child, that he refused to give the Mususedi line a descendent. He hadn't undergone a vasectomy, preferring instead to mortify himself again and again. Not reproducing had to be a choice, a decision renewed with each new day.

Naturally, Amandla wouldn't have encouraged him to have the surgery, it went against her philosophy and spirituality. She thought, what's more, that a lie was being told on purpose to keep the Continent's inhabitants from reproducing. That instead of worrying about overpopulation, they had a duty to procreate, that the Motherland had plenty of practically uninhabited spaces. It was known, she said, that the leucoderms had sterilized and poisoned people, sometimes under the pretense of providing medical care. Most of the time, when they said something, it was the opposite that needed to be understood, and, in any case, it was a cultural thing, the Kemites had always revered life. Kemites. The use of this term was natural to her, she said it in all seriousness. Inevitably, whenever the curious word hit his eardrums, he thought of Kermit the frog, Miss Piggy's friend from the

Muppet Show. In the mouths of contemporary Negrohood activists, the ancient language, the medu neter, felt like a big joke to him. All he could do was burst out laughing and tease Amandla, which made her flush with rage. The medu neter, she said, was to the Kemites what ancient Greek was to the Northerners. This made him laugh all the more heartily. The Northerners were also deluding themselves. Never had Greek meant anything to most of them, and to imitate their foibles was problematic. It was like countering a lie with another lie, and then holding out for forty years, as some enlightened ancestors had suggested, and, poof, it turned into a truth. At bottom, it was only fair, after all everyone was lying.

To his mind, it was more comfortable for those who now called themselves Kemites to lay claim to a vanished civilization, with which they did not all have a physical bond, than to celebrate the cultures of those vanquished by colonization. The pyramids looked far grander than the huts of their recent ancestors, whose languages they seldom considered speaking, let alone writing. That the Northerners had wanted to appropriate Kemet, and plaster the features of Yul Brynner or Liz Taylor on it, made it the jewel of *Negro Nations*, a precious object to be recovered at all costs. These Kemites were wrestling with the painful part of their being, where the memory of their fallen ancestors was bound up with a visceral attachment to the material aspects of the very system by which they'd been subjugated. To give up owning the latest smartphone, computer, or flat-screen TV was obviously out of the question. To trade in clothing inherited from the colonialist for a dibato made of barkcloth or a manjua in raffia was inconceivable. So they switched to those wax prints from which Northern industrialists were still making a fortune, having devised the technique to satisfy the populations of the Continent and their taste for gaily colored fabrics. The goose was well cooked, that much was painfully true, history would not be rewritten. Until it was accepted, there would be no moving on, it would be relived, over and over again. When he expressed himself like this, giving vent to his thoughts on the delusions of Negrohood, Amandla would scowl, refrain from saying another word. Frowning, she looked him in the eye, seeming to question the concatenation of arguments that he'd just thrown at her. Then, after an hour or so, her anger dissipated. They had better things to do than politicize their love, it was on another matter that she hoped to make him listen to reason.

Like many women, Amandla had pictured herself curing him of his ills, bringing him to consider his forebears differently. She'd help him come to realize how they'd become who they were. Succeed where they'd failed. That would cleanse the family tree if it was indeed infected. It was up to him to take responsibility for this, since each generation must discover its mission, in relative opacity, fulfill it or . . . Retaining from this statement only the word opacity, which was not there by chance, the man hadn't been convinced of the futility of his choices. Contrary to what Amandla was suggesting, his obligation might very well be to drain the sap of the tree once and for all. They'd traveled to the Continent together for Shrapnel's funeral. He would not otherwise have set foot there again. Then, he'd left her, reason dictated that he do so. The dust of the materials received in inheritance forbade him from imagining himself one day as the builder of anything, be it a couple. Ever since, Amok hadn't lived a moment without a thought for this woman-flame for whom he was consumed with desire until he had to touch her.

Had he been truly surprised to see her on the street that day? He wasn't expecting it, but she'd always wanted to move to the Continent. It was his presence that warranted explanation. Ixora, who was with him at the time, had often heard about Amandla. The two women had said hello, looked at one another, without disguising their curiosity. He'd cut the encounter short, hadn't tried to see her again. Her appearance tonight had been a shock. A facetious destiny had chosen her to come to Ixora's rescue, under the pounding rain, right after nightfall. The man shuddered at the thought that she'd witnessed the scene and his flight. The small house out of which Amandla had sprung faced the spot where Ixora's body lay. The sedan drove on under the downpour, without him having the impression that he was steering it, anyway he didn't know where to go. He heard the first notes of Nico Mbarga's hit song, *Sweet Mother*, and switched off the radio. Thinking about his mother was the last thing he needed, Madame was not sweet and she'd be of no help. The streets of this usually sleep-resistant city were deserted. There was nothing but him, the unrelenting rain, and what it swept away in its path. He needed to think.

The driving was smoother once he'd reached the city center where a few of the roads had been newly tarred in preparation for some international congress. The man parked his car in the lot of a local bank, folded his arms over the steering wheel, laid his forehead against it. He would have liked to cry, if only that, but his anguish was beyond grief. It was too old, too compact. He relived in his mind every moment of the evening, the argument that had started even earlier, as he and Ixora were leaving the great house. Their disagreement, he knew, had preceded this. He'd seen her change without understanding where it was coming from, without having the slightest idea where it would lead them. He was caught by surprise when she'd announced that she was breaking up with him. On top of which she'd made intolerable remarks. This didn't suffice to explain the violence of his reaction. Over the years, he'd learned to control himself, to dominate his emotions. The man devoted the time it took to examine the situation.

When he started the car again, he had a specific destination in mind. Out of courtesy, he phoned the person who must have waited for him at the Prince des Côtes, hoping to leave a message. The one he called Charles to avoid hooting with laughter at the name Charles-Bronson that his parents had given him. The deluge had dissuaded him from going outside, the hotel barman had kept him company, or vice versa, he was too far gone to be sure. A little discomfited after hearing this, Amok heard himself offering to pick him up. As he got off the phone, he wondered why. He could have said he was sorry, after all the man was safe. Never mind. It would be his only detour. Tonight he had somebody to see. The engine seemed to be humming an old forgotten tune, which made no sense. That soppy song in particular. His deceased friend loved this track, the Commodores' tribute to Marvin Gaye and Jackie

Wilson. How he missed him. For years, he hadn't spent time with anyone outside work. Only Shrapnel, that big man with his Olmec head, a god lost among humans, managed to breeze through the enclosure of barbed wire with which he surrounded himself, and force him out of his lair. Only this son of the equatorial forest raised by an old woman in the shade of a centuries-old tree, older, more majestic than a good many cathedrals.

The plant colossus had received a name when the clan had settled in the village many generations ago, following a migration forgotten by history. For this people, everything living harbored a spirit, deserved to be named. They'd called him Shabaka, undoubtedly after having consulted the oracles, to proceed otherwise was unthinkable in a community so deeply rooted in its ancient customs. The world was changing around them, they felt the tremor, without letting it destabilize them. Their strength was internal, relatively undemonstrative, and when modernity would come to scatter them, they met it with silent resistance. The one who'd have himself called Shrapnel when the world was in the grips of hip-hop fever, had had a happy childhood among his kin, deep in a forest that the government would cede to foreign developers. Everything he was had been forged in those early years, the love, the culture, the fusion with nature. He, on the other hand, had experienced nothing of the sort, wasn't complaining about it. He'd had the good fortune to meet this man, the human double of a giant tree. A memory of his friend crossed his mind, he saw him as a teenager here in this country, seeming to defy the sun by his mere presence in the streets. The day star was him, unquestionably.

There was something absurd about his death, in the metro one evening. His lifeless body had been found when the train had returned to the depot, the railway employees had called for emergency medical assistance, too late. The big man with the Olmec head would awake no more.

Shrapnel had told him nothing about the existence of Kabral and Ixora. He understood his silence, he too would not have been forthcoming. The child and the woman embodied one of the deceased's deepest wounds, his failure to build a home. He'd been a happy youngster in his forest, with a grandmother who'd replaced his parents. She'd been his universe, and the whole community had watched over him. Having to raise a son in the North, without being prepared for it, when he was leading a life of precarity, was more than a challenge. Agreeing to raise a Black boy there, even in the lap of luxury, was downright reckless. In adopting Kabral, the man who'd thought he'd hole up in the North until the end of time had had to accept the fact that the child would be better off on the Continent. Before that, he and Ixora had moved in together, it was Kabral who'd wanted them to. The three of them formed a family, in their own way. They'd been happy, until they came here. None of this would survive the night. He'd have liked to reverse course, return to Amandla's house, to know. He felt his fingers tensing. Turning back again was more than he could handle.

The mere thought of a confrontation with these two women, under these particular circumstances, terrified him. It wasn't as if they'd be meeting up for tea, scones, and a chat. Even that, he couldn't have done without being prepared psychologically. Tonight, the beast within had burst out of the cage where he thought he'd chained it forever. He knew it was there, felt it stirring inside him all the time, the cage being a region of his soul, an inner realm. This territory had been bequeathed to him along with the family name, the material comfort, and all the scars left by the dramas that had marked his parents' union. He needed explanations, to have a conversation with his father. He hadn't so much put it off as given up on it completely, walling himself in silence, keeping his distance from the Mususedi family. These measures had not been as drastic as he'd have liked, for his sister Ajar held a key to the cage. There had been two of them in the middle of the battlefield that was the great house, huddled together when blows rained down and screams rang out. Together the two had dared to appeal to their mother, even implore her, to get a divorce, together they'd let her know that they'd be alright. What made them suffer was to see her like that, her face swollen, her teeth knocked loose.

Their father never raised his hand against them. With his children, Madame's husband was all tenderness and laughter. A merry-maker, an expert prankster. Their father was this penniless prince who cared little about his title, but who struggled to have his manly qualities recognized. He was this son of a top-ranking government administrator whose hands trembled when he touched the rifles that had belonged to his father, a war medal recipient, and that he'd hidden under his bed. Talisman or totem, they'd never known the function of these weapons that had protected him from nothing. Their father was this dandy who could only feel good about himself through the envious eyes of his peers, and the admiration and desire of women. With no warning, he'd change into a monster. You could see it in his eyes. All of a sudden something would take possession of him, never to be directed at any other target than his wife. Madame would then sustain a rain of blows, violence that words couldn't describe. That she was still alive, in good health today was something of a miracle. And what about Ixora? What would become of her? Tonight, at the wheel of his car, Amok wasn't hoping to be cured of the atavistic affliction flowing in his veins. He'd always known it. Before putting an end to it all, he wanted at least to learn the name of the wild animal hidden in the souls of the men of his lineage

A deserted road stretched before him, such a thing never happened in this city, no matter the time of day or the weather. The storm being unexpected in this season, there should have been venturesome taxi drivers scouring the streets, looking for fares from pedestrians surprised by the deluge. A perfect occasion to do good business for those who set their prices at will. Fearless carousers should have been defying the wrath of the heavens, showing who was who in this world down below, pledging allegiance once again to partying, as good a reason as any to live. The mad seemed to have regained their sanity. Most unusually, they too were gone, instead of balancing on their heads in front of a woman's clothing store, talking to themselves, or reciting mathematical formulas or biblical verses that had made them lose their minds.

The street was all his. He'd often wished it would be empty like this without imagining how sinister it would actually feel. Every so often, a glow emanating from a house or building, signaled a human presence to him, but mainly there was the coldness of the streetlamps, the flickering of malfunctioning neon signs. If the storm persisted, there would be power cuts in a great many areas, the city center would not be spared. Soon he was in front of the Prince des Côtes. The grand hotel, the jewel of the city, had been built by Conroy Mandone, his maternal grandfather. The establishment was ablaze with lights, its generators ensured that it would continue to shine brightly in case of an outage. There was something unreal about the building's appearance, as if extraterrestrials, equipped with technologies unknown to humans, had assembled it on their planet before dropping it here, for an experiment whose purpose only they knew. This impression was not due to the architecture of local inspiration, designed to honor the memory of a son of the coastal country, hanged by the first colonialists. It was all the light, the flames of a nocturnal fire, visible to the far reaches of the galaxy.

A few streets away, lay the kingdom of misery where misfortune was thriving. Many of the poor would find themselves homeless by midnight. The deluge might destroy the city, but the Prince des Côtes would endure, along with its wealthy guests, and all the freeloaders that hung onto their coattails. As a teenager, he resented belonging to this caste of the privileged whose sole ambition was to remain so. This feeling had grown stronger since his return, given the country's decline, the despair of ordinary people. On the surface this took on sundry forms, but the addictions to alcohol, sex, or prayer often answered the same need. Each person chose, according to their individual temperament, the best way to leave their bodies behind, to die a little in the hope of reaching the part of themselves that was still inviolate, left intact by the ambient rot. It was a faraway place. According to those who had gone there, it was called inner peace. The trouble was that the sojourn was too short-lived, you'd land right back on the ground before making it to the end. You'd have to start all over again, go farther and farther, hurt yourself a bit more each time in order to get out of yourself. Bizarre phenomena could be observed, on the part of people wanting to wrest their due from life. It wasn't so much the ever-increasing number of burglars, forced by fierce competition in their trade to operate in broad daylight, to kill if necessary. The rage of the wretched produced this violence elsewhere, so many films depicted it, scarcely anyone batted an eyelash at the news that so and so died, in his home, at lunchtime.

What was beyond comprehension, his at least, were these women who could be seen, always in crowded places, stripping naked, then getting dressed, imposing such slowness on their movements that it sometimes made them quiver. The ordeal was daunting, yet unavoidable, they had to suffer from it at every moment, to hear their heart racing, to nearly faint, and continue, to exhaust the offering. They had to be seen, to face sneers, insults, curses. Steeped in the bile of invective, they covered themselves with madreporic rock, which made them resistant to lapidation. The cast stone would only bounce off them. You'd have to attack with an axe, boldly, feeling in every gesture their disintegration, then taking that with you, forever. People now filmed these women, the pictures taken on cell phones made their way around the world in a click. You could hear the barbs they received, the mockery they'd prepared themselves to be dealt. It happened, though seldom, that one of them would let the surge overwhelm her, no longer seem so sure of herself. What could the spectators understand? What did they grasp from all this? When he'd ask about it, the answer was often the same, *Can't you see, it's witchcraft.* Victims of a bad sorcerer, the women who stripped like this at street crossings or in marketplaces were seeking wealth, they were just following instructions. What's more, nothing indicated that the calvary was limited to this ordeal, anything was possible, no one knew for sure.

In any event, the crowd had little empathy. They saw these women as devourers of good fortune. Inflicting the sight of their naked bodies on everyone, they monopolized the blessings that others had received when they came into the world. As was apparent to all each and every day, the favors granted by destiny were meager and capricious, you had to work your fingers to the bone to see them materialize. It was out of the question to let them be carried off without saying anything, even if you yourself frequented emissaries of the dark. These indecent women were therefore met with a barrage of insults, but no one lifted a finger against them. No one dared deliver the first stroke of the axe, feel under the blade the thickness of what had reduced them to such extremities, to self-negation as a lifeline. The exposed breasts, the rolls of flesh around the hips, or the roundness of a still-firm posterior that could have easily walked other paths had nothing in common with those of the ancestors, at the time when civilization had not felt compelled to spread to places where it wasn't wanted. The transgression committed by these women in a society that was now Christian or Muslim and, above all, dressed from head to toe annihilated any desire for physical violence. The nakedness they were displaying, you knew deep down inside, was not theirs. They were laying bare the pain, the powerlessness of all, revealing what we were willing to sacrifice, to go to such lengths just to eke out a living, if you could call it that.

Once and only once, Amok had dared make his way through the crowd of onlookers, to approach one of these strippers. The woman was standing bolt upright under the fiery midday sun in a traffic circle, the most dangerous one in the city. The world around her had come to a standstill, halted to look at her, gaping at first in silence. It wasn't her plump flesh, her breasts at once huge and sagging, or her belly covered with stretch marks that made her stand out among the transgressors of moral laws, that crowned her she-devil-in-chief. It was her white hair. That was the telltale sign of experience, of wisdom, it confirmed her status as a library that could burn from one day to the next. More than that, it signaled that she had begun her ascent, her progression toward the noble position of ancestor. No one knew her personally, but all knew who she was. She was everyone's grandmother in this city and beyond, the face of what people believed must still remain intact somewhere, even though they were too busy to really care. At first, passersby had just slowed down to have a look. Perhaps the old woman was losing her mind, which was perfectly understandable considering her condition, the dialogue with the supernal planes could have this effect.

When she'd removed her wrapper, exposing a pair of buttocks that no underwear hid from sight, drivers slammed on the brakes, pulled up short. Then, having removed the top whose puffed sleeves emphasized the curve of her chubby arms, she stood as stiff as a statue. Then, she'd cried out, *Lost children of Katiopa* . . . The doors banged shut, insults were hurled at her, a crowd formed, with the risk of turning, at any moment, into a mob. That one, they were itching to pull apart, chop her to pieces, throw it all in the river that had seen every sort of filth. Not content to defile the universe with her shamelessness, the obscenity of her presence, of her very existence, she took the liberty of opening her big mouth, calling people to account. Anyone still looking for the meaning of the word *witchcraft* had found here a clear demonstration. The fact that this woman addressed the crowd meant that she was drawing to her each of the individuals composing it, which was, of course, the first step in the devouring. She wasn't out to spirit away the blessings intended for others, but to appropriate their very lives: good fortune, yes, but also power. What would be left to face the daily grind? That one, they were itching to shred her body to pieces, eviscerate her, make sure there was no way for her soul to return to this world.

He didn't know where she got her strength, or even if that was the way to describe what drove her. One by one, the man had pushed aside the bodies massed together, in one of the branches of the human spiral now surrounding the traffic circle, to force his way to the old woman. When he'd reached her, he'd looked into her eyes, saw neither madness nor despair, nothing to explain this provocation. She was small, but too well padded for the jacket of his suit to cover her. Having slung it over the front of her shoulders, he picked up the yellow wrapper, the white shirt, dressed the woman who murmured words on which he didn't dwell. *There they are, worshippers of Jesus, disciples of Muhammad. Where is the love? Tsk-tsk.* The only thing on his mind was getting her out of there, and himself too, in one piece. Taking her by the hand, he led her down the knoll on top of which a metal sculpture had once stood, a hideous thing, a kind of one-legged Goldorak, only the framework of which had been installed. Vigilantes had decided to dismantle the horror one night, sell it off or melt it down to its smallest bolt. All that remained was this mound of earth encircled by concrete, with a few tufts of grass, and the four roads that intersected there. Names of birds and wild animals had rained down on them, the crowd had spit as they passed, but no one touched them.

Amok had felt the tension, the fever in the bodies; the strength of a community that knew no better than to lash out at its frailest members. A power that had given up. He'd taken the woman to his car. From the back seat, she'd thanked him: *You're a good man, you could have let me drown in the ocean of lovelessness.* These words had struck him. Was it the truth? Since his return, it felt like he was play-acting, writing scenes to perform every day, sticking to the script. Had he started taking himself for his character? The woman had refused his help, entreating him, as she dressed, to drop her off on the other side of the bridge, on the periphery of a neighborhood he knew only by name. He'd never seen her again. By the time he'd returned to town, the story had spread from mouth to mouth. At the bakery where he'd stopped off to buy pastries for Kabral, he was given a very different version from the one he'd heard a quarter of an hour earlier, in front of the post office where street vendors were taking their lunch break.

Such was the country, such were the people. He'd found himself in the middle of all this, with a child and a woman, without a clearly defined project. In less than a year, his life had totally changed. When he'd met Kabral, the little boy who so resembled his deceased friend, it had been impossible not to embrace him. And having done so, there'd been no question of ever leaving him again. The enclosure of barbed wire had given way. A force had propelled him outside, to a space where feelings dominate you, where people suddenly take on unreasonable importance, without you seeing any reason to object. Amandla had crossed the barrier, with patience and method, hurting herself in the process. Faced with Kabral, the whole thing had collapsed, he'd had to follow the music, even if it meant improvising. Even if it meant admitting that a decision can prove to be as inescapable as it is insane. At a time when hundreds of young men from the Continent were embarking on old tubs to flee at all costs the trouble that was driving women to undress in the streets, he'd chosen to settle here. For Kabral to grow up in a place where nothing would stand between him and the world. Where the powerful and the wretched alike would send back to him a reflection of himself, where he'd know himself to be a man above all. Kabral deserved better, he shouldn't be compelled to find refuge in Negrohood, which was, to his mind, the worst form of alienation. The human being imprisoned in a racial mythology. Life in the North, if you invested yourself in it—which he'd refrained from doing—inevitably led to reckon with the question of race. To situate yourself in relation to it, in one way or another. His son wouldn't live like that.

The thought of the boy's face brought Ixora's features back to mind, the memory of the three of them together, their life, everything they'd gone through until now. Perhaps he should have come back here alone at first, get into the swing of things, understand how this society had changed. Then Kabral and Ixora would have joined him. He'd have welcomed them somewhere other than in the great house with its accumulation of so many bitter memories. Seeing Kabral marveling at the beauty of the place, he'd put off the idea of moving, hadn't even mentioned it anymore. To avoid reliving incessantly the nights of terror when he'd drenched his sheets in sweat, he kept the air conditioning on in the bedroom he and Ixora shared. The bed was big enough, but they hadn't been very comfortable at first, having slept in separate rooms until then. Now it stared him in the face, he should have arranged their move better. When he'd left for the North, he'd just graduated from high school. Thereafter, the only time he'd set foot in the country where he hoped to raise his son was to bury Shrapnel. He could no longer simply sneak away, hang out with the wrong crowd, or arrange to be excluded from all private schools in order to escape being wealthy. It hit him all the more violently knowing he'd have to accept his condition. It was the price to pay to ensure that Kabral, confident of his rights, would not drown his despair at not being able to enjoy them in a bottle or in the ocean. How could he explain all this to Ixora? He'd tried to gain her approval for the only strategy that he thought sound, in such a closed society. Everyone had to keep to their place and, from there, do their best to improve things. What she'd understood was that he was pretending to effect change from the inside while yielding to comfort. She'd thrown that in his face, that and other pleasantries, right after announcing her decision to leave him.

Amok had no desire to go into the Prince des Côtes. From his car, he could make out the silhouettes of customers sitting in one of the lounges. He honked to attract Charles's attention. He saw a bellhop with a large umbrella escorting him to the sedan, noticed his yellow suit, his shoulder pads declaring their love for the eighties, the Kid Creole style hat. This get together would have been a happy occasion, Ixora would have brightened up meeting a man who dressed like this. Too late now. Not a friendly word was uttered to greet Charles, only: *I hope you're not in a hurry to get home, we're going to my father's.* He had only a vague notion of how long the trip would take, the directions he'd been given couldn't be of much value in such stormy weather. He focused on the road, let no other thought take hold in his mind, quickly forgot the presence of his passenger. It was the first time he was going to the place near the hinterland where his father had lived since his wife had thrown him out, after pressing the barrel of a handgun into his belly. Madame had vaguely mentioned her husband's activities on his rural estate, unlikely stories of a plantation that she hadn't bothered to verify.

The news of their separation left him neither hot nor cold, it made no difference anymore. He crossed Plateau Bess, so called after a Northern ship, which may have been named after the owner's mother or sweetheart. Bess, the site of the

Mususedi clan's chiefdom, was one of the city's oldest districts. There were a few colonial buildings of noteworthy architecture, where the independent state had hastened to house its administrative services. Someone had decapitated the statue of the Northern field marshal that used to stand guard in front of the post office, and replaced the severed head with a banner demanding that the country's martyrs be honored. Embroidered on the cloth were the words *the women and men for whose sacrifices we are indebted*. No one had dared remove the banner, but most likely it wouldn't withstand the rain. In front of the chiefdom headquarters, he accelerated without even thinking about it. The high-ranking official Angus Mususedi, his paternal grandfather, had given up his title. So neither his son nor his grandson would sit on the stool of authority. Their name remained nonetheless attached to the chiefdom's prestige. Since he came back, some of the old men of the Coast even addressed him respectfully as *Sango janea, sir chief*.

The chiefdom. In his youth Amok had questioned the sacred character attributed to this institution, the reverence in which it was still held. In the beginning, the coastal peoples didn't have chiefs, each man being his own master and master of his wives and children. When trade with the Northerners was established, it was conducted at first by individuals operating on their own behalf, for personal gain only. Those who were not yet the colonialists they later became, found it more useful to appoint interlocutors whom they selected based on criteria that were by no means random. The chosen had demonstrated their interest in such commerce, but also in the prospects of advancement that fraternizing with the foreigners who'd come over the waters from the North afforded them. After all, weren't their boats more impressive than the commonplace pirogues of local fishermen? Didn't they sport all kinds of accessories and clothing, from head to toe, that drew admiration? Didn't their wives have such graceful names that entire communities had to be saddled with them and thereby brought into existence? People no longer knew what they'd been before the time when the *Bess* had sailed into the estuary. It was in vain that the oldest among them would still mention the clan's totem animal, panthers no longer prowled the outskirts of the city, and the younger generations had never seen any. No one felt bound by the ancient pact with wild beasts, the covenant that the ancestors had honored by calling themselves: *children of panther*.

One day, the man had overheard his paternal aunts, Judith and Sulamite, speaking of the blessed days when the Northerners first arrived, as the story was told in the community. That's when he'd learned the origin of the name Bess, that of the chiefdom as well, invented ex nihilo to better serve the needs of the masters that they prided themselves on having found. Sulamite concluded with words often repeated on the Coast: *The reason we were the first to see them is because we resemble them*. This did not tolerate dispute. It was as clear as could be that the Coastlanders had been colonized just like the rest, all the bushmen from the interior, the tatterdemalions with no manners whom they despised so. The colonialists had had no respect for the descendants of those whom one of their queens had honored with the title of kings. There had been kings galore ever since, in every godforsaken village, satisfied with their lot and making their subjects proud. The colonial state had reduced their position to its most basic expression, which hadn't been difficult given the foundations on which their power rested. However, propriety had been preserved, they had occasions to do their song and dance. In passing, the chiefs didn't refrain from picking up some spare change, especially when community members were finally delivered from life here below. Their families then had to pay a small sum to the *king*, an obligation whose meaning, like the rest, struck him as obscure. With death sparing no effort anywhere in this ferocious age, such a practice was bound to have a promising future, they could export it, reap royalties.

Beyond Plateau Bess, the city looked like a battlefield. The belligerents had all perished, not one had pulled through to relate the events, all that subsisted was the carcass of a housing project over which rust and mold were fighting for control. The buildings along the right side of Boulevard de la Souveraineté looked like they'd survived an earthquake. Tilting at an alarming angle, even more marked in the rain, they seemed perilously close to collapsing at any moment. The city was not even the shadow of its former self, it was a completely different place, the skanky, scrawny sister of its older sibling. People said it was abandoned by the government, which saw it as a stronghold of its opponents. The man was not unhappy to leave behind him the heart of the country's economic capital, one of the most important metropolises in this part of the Continent. Thinking he'd heard Charles humming *Nightshift*, he turned abruptly toward the passenger who smiled at him. He tried to do likewise, then shifted his attention back to the road. Amok stopped at a gas station, jumped out and ran through the rain to the store whose lights were still on. The attendant must be inside, alone with his candy, batteries, and gas canisters. He could have honked, but he had little taste for peremptory summoning, the way his mother had of shouting her domestics' names when she needed them.

The attendant was a plump woman with a mischievous smile, a head of completely white hair, coquettishly braided, a single lock adorned with a silvery cowry falling over her forehead. No wrinkle bore out what the color of her hair indicated, only a taunting crease at the corner of her mouth. Dressed in a white outfit trimmed in gold with her bosom bursting at its seams, she was administering a nice walloping to a steaming dish of mwanja moto, into which she dipped a muna dikabo cooked to perfection. Between her fingers, her thumb, index, and middle finger, the tuber absorbed, without crumbling, the sauce yellowed by palm oil. Each mouthful, slowly chewed, released the flavors of the ingredients one by one. The woman sighed with contentment. Contemplating with enamored eyes the contents of her plate, she took the time to lick her fingers and wipe her lips, before turning her attention to him. Acknowledging him with a wink, she said: *My son, you can see for yourself why I'm not budging from here. This is a rain with no mother and no respect. I'm telling you, there's nothing ordinary about this water. There's even a dangerous wind too.* She punctuated her remarks with a teeth-suck that didn't call for a reply. The man set the money down on the counter, said he would serve himself, she could keep the change.

As he was about to leave, he turned around: *You should close the store. Your customers will knock.* She nodded, yes, he was right, it was nice of him to show concern, it was so rare in this country where human beings had only hatred for their neighbors, he was a good man, one of those who would stem the tide of lovelessness that threatened Katiopa. These compliments troubled him, he was glad to get away from her. As he inserted the pump into his tank, he perceived her out of the corner of his eye. Her plate in hand, she was watching him through the glass pane. Something about her told him that she feared nothing, quite the opposite, maybe she worked for the intelligence agency. Everything was going awry in this country, but the surveillance had always been excellent. Women held choice positions in the profession. He didn't wave goodbye to her. As soon as he got back in the sedan, Charles asked him where his father's house was, he named the place, located dozens of miles from the city center that they'd left behind a while ago. His travel-mate reminded him that the road wasn't paved all the way through, that it wasn't lit either, that it was raining cats and dogs. Whatever urgencies were driving him shouldn't make him lose sight of the unlikelihood of arriving safely tonight, even if he were cautious.

He hadn't thought about it, didn't take the time to do so. Self-propelled, the vehicle took off, careened onto a slippery road. There were fewer and fewer houses, wild foliage grew on either side of the road, this had the advantage of holding back the torrents, thereby preventing flooding. He applauded the pathetic state of the country's urbanization, asphalt and concrete wouldn't have absorbed the rain. Water streamed over the windshield, the windows. He could only see it as a reproach for the aridness of his heart. Maybe Ixora was breathing her last breath, maybe she'd been drawn from the waters only to die in a dry place, between two strangers. In the meantime, behind the wheel of his air-conditioned car, he was on his way to his father's, to stand up to him, to get answers that would in no way alter the horrific deed of which he was guilty.

Amandla may have witnessed the scene. Even if she hadn't, she'd recognize Ixora, head over to the great house, announce the death . . . He felt his jaw clench, his hands clutch the steering wheel. Now that Charles was at his side, turning back was out of the question. His only choice was to take his foolhardiness to the bitter end, something he'd been working hard at in recent years. So he sank deeper and deeper, methodically, with no solution in sight. If he could have plucked up the courage to double back, what would he say to his passenger about the events of that night? Exhausted from being alive, he repressed a sigh. Kabral's voice, inviting him to play a video game, pierced his chest, convincing him once and for all. After having it out with his father, what conversation could he imagine with the son he'd chosen? One could not decently say: *It's not my fault, the men in my family suffer from a nameless affliction that compels them to beat up their women, leave them for dead, take flight. And I didn't really drive off, I came back.* Since he himself had been merciless as a child, finding no excuses for his parents, he wouldn't dare say a word.

And now, it was over, Kabral had no father, no one, on account of him. From now on, the child would have to live with Madame, this woman whose contempt for Ixora was no mystery, this status-obsessed individual who'd want to shape him into an heir according to her own conceptions. This thought almost led him to reconsider his intentions, putting an end to his life would mean abandoning the little one, that would be worse than anything. When he'd reach the land of the dead, Shrapnel would be there, Ixora too. Little did it matter that he didn't believe in the soul's survival after death, in this journey to the afterlife, right now he wasn't sure of anything at all. Kicking the bucket, in his case, could very well be the opposite of a deliverance. But if the decision to live seemed compelling, as absurd as it might be, prison would await him If Ixora survived, she'd press charges, he'd confess, he wouldn't let his family's name protect him. Focusing for a few minutes on this possibility, he gently shook his head. The eternal thrashing that Shrapnel would give him in the land of the dead, the insults that Ixora would throw at him until the Last Judgement, were better than doing time in this country's jails. Then there was Kabral, the most terrifying judge in his eyes. Never again could he look him in the face, be he dead or alive during the confrontation. The more he thought about it, the more he had to accept the obvious: there was no way out. The man felt his flesh turn to ice, all anxiety leave him. From that point on, only the journey occupied his mind.

Charles's misgivings were confirmed very quickly. The road was, indeed, unpaved. It must have been constructed in the colonial period, with trees chopped down, the earth dug with bare hands, lives lost. Ever since, there it was, wrested from the earth, trying to impose itself on nature which was determined to obliterate it. At night and in the storm, only its chaotic aspects were apparent, the thickness of the mud clinging to the wheels, hugging the rims, only coming loose ever so slightly when the car plunged into a crater. There were actual ravines hidden under the torrents of water, the color of which could no longer be distinguished in the dark. The sedan's headlights feebly illuminated the road, with a faint orangey streak ending in a point, as the light stumbled over the shadow that had become compact. Charles suggested that they stop, find a place to shelter for the night inside the car. The man heard himself reply that he'd rather go as far as possible, drive as long as conditions allowed. He refrained from saying the words that his companion wouldn't have understood, the fact that the worst had already occurred, that nothing more terrible could happen. The thunderstorm battered the roof of the sedan while the mud encircled the tires, slowing their progress. Instinctively, both of them leaned forward, squinting in an attempt to see through the liquid barrier rising before them. People appeared on the road, vague silhouettes loomed out of the nearby bush, their shapes stood out against the darkness. He thought he saw a man buckling his belt, the group rushed toward what at first appeared to be some kind of black hole, a gaping jaw in the night. When he saw the doors close he realized it was an opep, one of those vans used for passenger transit. No doubt the silhouettes he'd seen had been passengers going to relieve themselves behind the bushes. The opep didn't move, the driver having apparently decided to spend the night there. His friend advised him to do the same, it was wiser. Even when it didn't rain, once night had fallen, no one took the risk of driving on these roads, abandoned as much by the state as by the divinity.

It wasn't out of sheer contrariness that he refused to park behind the van. There were only two of them in his sedan, he and his passenger, the occupants of the other vehicle could easily decide to take off with everything they had, including the car. They'd dismantle it, if they couldn't drive off with it, and sell the parts, deluge or no deluge. The prospect of making some money would galvanize them, their eyes would become sharper than a microscope, their skin would suddenly have water-repellant properties. When dawn came, not a trace of his vehicle would be found, Charles and he might be dead. He decided to move on, hoping to reach an acceptable place to keep a lookout until dawn, since tonight he wouldn't sleep a wink. He regretted having embarked Charles on an adventure that didn't concern him, but the damage was done, in this respect too. The man did his best to steer the sedan as it pitched and tossed over the bumps and hollows in the road. In all his years abroad, he'd had no need for a car, the metro had sufficed. Here, he'd had to start driving again, it came back to him quickly, and he refused to employ a driver to chauffeur him around 24/7, or nearly, as so many other people in his circles did.

Enoch, who worked for his parents for as long as he could remember, had been offended, seeing his decision as a sign of distrust, an invitation for him to retire. Amok had tried to explain how he felt, adding that he'd lost the habit of having servants take care of him. The driver had looked him in the eye for quite some time, before shaking his head: *I respect you a lot, massa. That's why I speak to you from the heart. You're a boss now. You need to behave. Putting people to work is an act of solidarity and respect. You have the means. You shouldn't be obliging men to panhandle.* Managing neither to *behave* nor to be understood, he'd opted to disappoint Enoch. Until that night, he'd made a point of taking care of the sedan, as his parents' chauffeur would have done. Enoch wouldn't hesitate to berate him if he damaged it tonight, it would be proof of his lack of maturity. No one endowed with reason would have undertaken such a journey at night, at the wheel of a fancy car, even if it hadn't rained.

In spite of himself, the man silently called on some deity or another, an invisible power, to guide them to a place where they could rest. On the verge of making a promise to himself that he'd never put himself in such a situation again, he remembered that it was all over, that there was no more life and therefore nothing to fear, that he was planning to leave this world soon. At his side, Charles was also leaning forward, screwing up his eyes, concentrating on the orangey line traced by the headlights into the thickness of the night. So Charles saw, at the same time as he, what was there, under the sheets of water, in the heart of this night so dense it seemed palpable. A distinct arcade, over which grew a climber with many white flowers scarcely stirred by the violence of the elements. The tufted foliage held the corollas as if they were inlayed. Below, the road was nearly smooth, but there was something even more uncanny. At the end, as if stitched into the darkness of the night, shone a bright glow, a beacon in this tormented hour.

This country had put him in touch with too many bizarre things for this one to impress him. So he simply murmured: *So it's here, the den of the sun.* The old inhabitants of the Coast where he was born, believed that the sun disappears at dusk to embark on an underground journey, where it confronts a monster. Only if it comes out of this struggle victorious will it be reborn at dawn, to illuminate the world, warm the living, ensure the continuation of all life. Since he would soon be going to the land of the dead where those ancestors who hadn't opted for reincarnation were awaiting him, it would be his privilege to bring them the good news: the sun need not exhaust itself in daily battles to take its place in the sky in the morning. It had a hiding place on earth, in the bush, a few dozen miles from the city center. The sedan reared and plunged forward toward the ball of light.

The distance wasn't as far as he'd imagined, a few yards at the most. The road, though it hadn't been paved, was hardly bumpy at all. The mud didn't cling to the tires so much either. As he drove toward the glimmering, the light became soft, welcoming, moonlike. When he parked the car in front of the house from which it emanated, he felt submerged by a flood of melancholy, a cry rose from his belly, caught in his throat, it was a cold lump, an ice cube. He was overtaken by a coughing fit, Charles must have thought he'd swallowed something the wrong way. As his friend tapped his back saying, *Hey bro, are you okay? Calm down, it's okay,* he felt a tingling in the corner of his eyelids. He waved his hand, said it was nothing. He pointed to the house, motioned to Charles to knock on the door, but it wasn't necessary. Someone came to greet them, a gas lamp in his hand, its white light illuminating the surroundings. A tidy, perfectly tended garden, tall royal palm trees, a bamboo fence like the ones that were common in the old quarters of the city a few decades before. The person walked over to the driver, stood there, waiting for him to climb out.

That's when he noticed that it wasn't raining, not at all, not a drop had fallen here for weeks. That's how it was in this realm of the world, he wouldn't have been surprised to learn that the planet's movements had its peculiarities here, that this was the land of the living, but also the afterlife or something else entirely, words eluded him. Amok opened the door, the person stepped back to let him out, he heard himself say, *Good evening*, the other nodded in silence. He couldn't take his eyes off the house, a large conical hut with a round base, as was common in some of the country's northern villages, the region of the savannah that was so different from the seaboard. This was his dream house, the place where he'd have wanted to live, to offer to his son, to his significant other. Two windows in the upper part of the house looked like eyes gaping at the night. The front door led rather unexpectedly to a veranda, whose presence did not disrupt the harmony of the structure. The light that had guided him from the road emanated from the interior. Up close, it was soft, no one could have perceived it from afar, it was the ordinary lighting of a home like any other.

He was invited inside, his host's sex was indefinable in the brightness of the gas lamp. He told himself that this white light was not the sun whose rays had attracted him either, but he suppressed the question that burned his lips. In the distance, a flash of lightning streaked across the sky, thunder made itself heard, the rain did not subside behind the plant arcade whose white flowers still did not stir. He felt heavy as he climbed up the short flight of steps to the veranda, his legs suddenly weighed tons. The sensation of being oppressed, as if he were restrained by a straitjacket, gripped him, he was on the verge of suffocating. Turning to him, the woman raised the lamp she was holding in her hand, cast a mournful glance at him: *It's the weight of your guilt. You don't deserve to be told this but know that the injured woman will live. She will have no permanent scars.* He reeled, his body hit the stone of the small staircase, his heart opened, tears streamed down his cheeks. Amok sobbed as never before, gasping with each breath. He thought he heard Charles's voice but wasn't sure. On the other hand, he could make out the woman's: *Son of Oshun, you must force yourself to carry your body. You have to get up on your feet to enter TaMery. And you will go in alone. The Palace of Shabazz will welcome your friend, the time it takes for you to journey across your night.*

His host's voice came to him like a distant echo, but he heard every word clearly, not that this was any help to him. His vision had become blurred, the world had receded from his sight, there was only darkness, deep down in his pupils as all around. Although he was lying on the ground, Amok felt the weight of his body, about to sink into it. He would disappear noiselessly into the depths of this excavation dug specifically for him, the earth would close up over him, forgetting that he had ever breathed. If the woman was right, could she know that all this weight had not been accumulated in the space of a single night? Old tears mingled with those he was shedding in this moment for Ixora, the tears he'd held back when Madame, beaten by her husband, forbade crying at the sight of her bruises. Those too he'd have liked to let flow every time he'd reproached himself for not having the courage to defy his father, to defend the abused wife, if only in words. He'd stay in his bed, paralyzed, sweating through all his pores, so frightened he nearly pissed in his pajamas. He'd resented Madame for not demanding a divorce, for accepting the humiliations, such as the day when his father, under the spell of who knew what dark power, had seen fit to chase her around the garden. They were both naked, in one hand the husband held the bath towel that concealed his genitals, in the other, he was waving a thick piece of wood. The wife, stark naked, ran from the man who threatened her, as their servants looked on dumbfounded. This was one of his most horrible memories, one of those shameful images that had haunted him incessantly, no matter how many years went by.

At times, when Madame would start scoffing at Ixora, *that woman you brought back from the North, that lineageless person who grasps nothing of our customs,* he'd picture her again naked, looking back over her shoulder at her husband running after her, picking up speed to keep out of his reach, her hands over her breast, two soft balls that didn't stay in place, averting her eyes from the household employees who stood frozen with stupefaction. That, and the impossibility of intervening. Doing something meant not only confirming that they had witnessed the scene but also passing judgment on the actors. The alternative was not moving, almost not seeing, banishing it from their minds, silently but firmly promising themselves that no matter what happens, this collective hallucination would never be discussed. He and his sister Ajar were in the big living room whose windows opened onto the front part of the garden, with its white gravel paths. Rooted to the spot, they observed their progenitors, wondering once again about the implications of such a phenomenon, the consequences that it could have, to come from such madness. What they knew about other families did not comfort them. On the contrary. One day, going over the couples in the high society coastal circles notoriously beset by similar violence, they came to the conclusion that their parents' entire generation suffered from mental illness.

Among the men, this took the form of sundry disorders, including mindless domestic violence. So-and-so had become famous for not hesitating to hurl the burning lid of a cast-iron pot at the face of his dear, sweet wife. Another, bent on rivaling his friend, had broken several of his better half's vertebrae. A third, eager to outdo the others in the championship, had used a razor blade to carefully slash his beloved's veins. They were legion, roaming freely the streets of this country that granted husbands the right to punish their wives as they saw fit. The women seldom left them, finding nothing appealing in the prospect of the social downfall that would ensue. Given that the skirt-chasers made offerings of their semen whenever possible (the occasions presented themselves not frequently but all the time), staying married was the surest way for women to protect their children's inheritance, at least the house where they'd raised them.

Madame, who was wealthier than her husband, didn't have this excuse. She could have asked for a divorce, left her spouse to his own darkness, saved her children from the turmoil, aspired to something else for them and for herself. She'd done nothing of the sort. His sister could find all kinds of excuses for their parents, he refused to do so. They were the elders, in a society where such a position placed you almost above all else. The least they could have done in such circumstances was to . . . What exactly? It was too late to ask for forgiveness, too late to give to each other the fondness that had frozen in their hearts, too late to heal the wounds, simply open up their arms, cry, then laugh together. He didn't choose the stony character of his relationship with his parents, it had taken hold as the only way to ward off the onslaughts of madness. You never knew when it would strike, when the fragile harmony of the playful moments with his father would burst asunder. He'd had to establish a reasonable distance between himself and his parents, try to survive the mechanism they had set up under the name of a family. What did he care about how other people lived in big houses with swimming pools or even in hastily built shacks in poor neighborhoods. If the family was this lethal institution, why would anyone want to start one? He preferred by far freely chosen ties, like those that bound him with Ixora and Kabral until, in a single act, he destroyed it all. The mire from which he was born, in which he had been formed, flowed in every cell of his being, forbidding him to imagine anything beyond. Thinking that he could escape it since Kabral was not of his blood, and because of the platonic relationship that he and Ixora had opted for, he hadn't been chary of the power of the land. Never would this country be a place like any other for him. This ground was not neutral. The generations that had preceded him on both the Mandone and the Mususedi sides, plunged their roots into the depths of this soil. He was made of it, had been fed on it, long before walking it.

He had more than good reason to leave the North to rescue his son from Negrohood, from its pathological relationship to the self. His mistake had been in coming back here, to this childhood home so unconducive to his growth. He should have embarked on a real adventure, dared to go elsewhere, provide himself with an unknown destination, give himself to it too. Something had kept him from doing so. The duty, the responsibility that falls to men ever since they stopped approaching women for the sole purpose of copulating, then leave them to cope with life by themselves. One day, no one knows exactly when, women had started yelling that it was too easy for men, to do their business, then turn away with no concern for the consequences growing in their wombs. And the men had heard them. One day, the men had understood that only women's bodies made sons, so to ensure their progeny, these had to be appropriated, taken away from other men. One day, the men had fallen prey to a storm, an inner swell, even more powerful than the fleeting tension between their legs, the burning in their loins. They no longer wanted merely to possess women's bodies, but to take refuge in them, more profoundly. The men had discovered the need to look after women, so as not to be homeless. Ever since, the nature of the foundations that underpin couples hadn't changed the problem in the least, men had to fulfill two specific functions: that of protector and of provider. Proposing that they pick up from one day to the next and move to the Continent implied that he was up to the task of offering Kabral and Ixora a comfortable existence. Straightaway. Wild adventures in unknown destinations, of the kind organized for celebrities on the TV show *Rendez-vous en terre inconnue,* were out of the question.

In real life, you didn't know when the rough ride would be over, you'd get no help from a cohort of people ready to leap to your side to resolve the slightest problem, which obviously would not be filmed. In real life, the contribution of so-called indigenous peoples to the beauty of the world now resided in Northern museums where, deprived of speech, it served only as a vestige of prelogical thought. It was just as well. The people here no longer knew what to do with all that old stuff, the money would be better used for buying mansions, and enjoying the benefits of barbarism—for the North, which had only ever managed to destroy, had corrupted the term civilization, no turning back on that one. In real life, people of sub-Saharan African descent didn't dream of immersing themselves in these primitive existences that would have required that they ignore having been inoculated, through the colonial channel, with new desires and practices. When they promoted a return to ancestral values, it was understood that these would henceforth embrace all sorts of products of the Northern mind. One could try to dismiss the pain this caused by asserting, for example, that Northerners had done nothing but perfect the creation of the eldest sons of the world, those ancestors whose names were proclaimed to make sure that their echo was still perceived. The improvements to which one reluctantly paid lip service from this North, which was all the more reviled in that it was impossible to extricate it from oneself, were nonetheless the fruit of its conception of the world, and it was well liked by all and all were eager to become its minions. Whether it was jeered at or celebrated, it had become the sole reference, the ultimate anchor.

Unless the woman demanded it, it was thus excluded that the man take it into his head—if it wasn't an outing to an amusement park—to suggest an exploration of some unknown destination. There were, of course, a few oddballs, often artists or social misfits; those women would sometimes set out on precipitous paths, searching for the meaning of their lives in this world. They could end up at the bottom of a cave, on the flank of a cliff, or even swept away by the wind, it didn't worry them. Amandla was one of those women whom no man could protect or provide for, the material question being resolved in advance by this capacity they had to rush headlong into what mattered to them most. It was something else that would have to be shared with them. Coming from a very different mold, Ixora's energy didn't manifest itself that way. She'd have denied ever having had such expectations, but the men in her life, whether or not they were her lovers, had to provide more than the basic necessities. It wasn't money that interested her but presence and stability.

At first, after moving into the great house, she'd await his return to come back to life and get moving, like one of those old-fashioned dolls with a windup mechanism, or like a flower opening its petals at the sight of the sun. When Amok was not there with her, even her son couldn't cheer her up, she'd barely see him, remained sunk in a place where no one could reach her, where the little girl couldn't stop wondering about the absence of the father, her existence in relation to his other children. This didn't escape Madame's attention, who was quick to rail against *the gloomy temperament of that woman you brought back to us from the North* . . . He'd had to endure these scenes often, he'd respond with the coldness he'd inherited from her, keeping to himself the bitter memories that flooded him whenever Madame opened her mouth. He never threw in her face the words he was itching to speak, the question about the respect due a mother whose nudity had been exposed.

The stranger's voice brought him back to the present, to the weight of his body, to the sobs swelling his chest. She apologized for hurting him, she had no choice. Being incapable of lifting him, she was going to pull him by his shoulders, which would be painful. He couldn't answer to reassure her, but his body wasn't suffering, the pain was elsewhere, in that area of his being where he thought he'd imprisoned the atavistic madness. The woman said she was called Ayezan, adding that this was her nocturnal name. If things went as expected, he'd only retain a confused memory of their meeting in this place. This wasn't the time to delve into these considerations, there was much to do. An odor of smoked wood with whiffs of spices floated around her, like out of one of those old kitchens where the embers of the fireplace merged with the earth. Her energy was powerful, tranquil, it was palpable in the loving inflections of her voice. This was not the softness that is regarded as the special preserve of women, but rather a force. The allusion to his crime pushed him over the brink, made him cry even more. She pulled him onto the veranda, left him there on the ground, spoke once more, *You must get up.* To make this possible, she was going to give him the care needed to begin to purify his energy, but there'd be more to do later. What was critical at the moment was to get him to stand on his feet. *I have to undress you.*

Steeped in negative elements, his suit, and everything in it, had to remain outside the walls of TaMery. The house was meant to be a sanctuary, a place devoted to providing spiritual weapons to those in need of renewed strength. People came here when they'd lost their bearings, when they no longer knew the reason for their birth among the living. Ayezan couldn't delve into details, it was not the time for that, she repeated, they had to hurry. She went to get her lamp, put it next to him, thereby bringing light to the veranda. Repeating that his friend was no longer by his side, the woman continued: *He'll be well treated, the Palace of Shabazz is a nice place. That's the name the youth hereabouts have given it.* At least, those among them who were looking for the path, the way back to the kingdom of their fathers. They hadn't found it, still hoping it would come from outside themselves, desiring to settle in a place that others would have built. All they'd have to do then is stretch their legs out under the table, snap their fingers to have their needs fulfilled. A man had appeared one day, had his house built there, and because they'd never seen anything like it, the young people of the area had decided it was a castle. Amok would have time to discover the place once he'd returned to the material world. Of all this, he grasped at most every other word, sometimes less, the sentences followed one another, as if recorded on a tape that was being played without releasing the button.

Amok had stopped crying, but the stiffness that kept him from moving persisted. Kneeling at his right, the woman placed green stones in a row on his chest, malachite, she said, a mineral with the property of restoring the *ka*, the vital force. This would give him back his ability to move. His love force was damaged too and had been for a long time. His flesh had become stony, and no longer knew what love was. She pronounced incantations, perhaps in medu neter, he thought they might be because he'd recognized the name TaMery. Having had a good education in this area from having fallen in love with a champion of Negrohood, Amok knew that the term meant beloved land, in the dead language of a people that had been extinct for thousands of years. What eluded his grasp more than ever was why such hogwash kept crossing his path. The man found nothing particularly appealing about this mythology, the lost glory of his people mattered little to him, history was full of defeats, they came in all colors. His grief had no political coloring, and he yearned to drown himself in it once and for all. The idea of taking flight took shape in his mind. As soon as he could get up, he'd run to the sedan, in his underpants if need be, since the guardian of TaMery had consented to let him keep them on, even though this transgressed the mores of the beloved land.

Silently, Ayezan looked into his eyes, applying her hands to his chest. She raised eyes to him brimming over with pity,

which was unbearable. He'd have rather by far heard her protest, reproach him for his deed. Feel her contempt, wait for
the well-deserved punishment. The woman did not grant him
that. When she expressed herself again, it was in an affectionate tone: *Son of Oshun, now you can enter your home, your
heart. You cannot escape yourself, don't think of it. If you let
things unfold, the morning dew will come to fortify you. You'll
find the answers.* She got up, signaled to him to do the same.
The man stood up as a child would, first kneeling, then pressing his palms to the floor. Standing was uncomfortable, his
head was spinning, his vision was blurred at intervals. He
stayed like that without knowing what to do, he wouldn't
have the strength to rush to the car. Charles was gone, how
could he try to escape and leave him behind? The stranger ges-
tured to him to move forward, led the way into the house. He
couldn't help shooting one last glance at the car, imagining
what he'd have to do to get there, evaluating the distance to
cover. He searched for the flowery arcade that marked the
entrance to the estate, but didn't see it. There was only darkness, and the sound of pounding rain in the distance. It felt as
if he'd fallen to the bottom of some abyss, a pit in which this
uncanny place was found, along with the woman who spoke
to him. She repeated, *You cannot escape yourself, don't think
of it. Son of Oshun, don't take advantage of the leniency of
the One and Only. You have gravely offended the Universe.
Follow me.* She added that he'd be served a meal, they mustn't
tarry.

There was no entrance as such. Having passed through
the door, he found himself immediately in a circular room that

seemed quite large to him. It was divided into half-moons. Decorating the floor, a long strip of boutala fabric delimited the two spaces. On one side was an altar to honor the ancestors, various elements allowed him to identify its function. Raffia mats had been rolled up in a corner near a section of the wall covered with a shoowa cloth, it was the first time he'd seen one that big. Bottles set on a caryatid stool displayed stoppers made from banana tree leaves. On the other side, the wall had been left bare, it was ocher in color, like the earth in this region. A royal palm was flourishing in a pot, there was nothing else. His host drew him to this spot, asked him to wait for her before disappearing through a door at the rear that he hadn't noticed. The man kept on asking himself where the light was coming from. There were no candles, no fireplace, no light bulbs of any sort. The gas lamp had been turned off, he thought, when the woman had preceded him inside. Ayezan, who'd left him for a moment, was soon back, holding a folded cloth. She handed it to him, almost reverently. It was a bogolan tunic, a fabric that passably pleased him, this Amok kept to himself, merely asking, in a low voice, if she'd forgotten the pants.

By itself, the tunic looked like a dress to him, he didn't emphasize the point, to what good. Ignoring his question, the woman urged him to put on the garment. The technique used to dye the cloth made it a symbol of the earth, his ka needed this grounding, she thought it helpful to let him know. He complied, he was having difficulty thinking. The woman nodded in satisfaction, bid him welcome home again. She took him by the hand. They walked across the room, through the door at the rear. A staircase descended into the bowels of the dwelling, this was the image that came to him when he had to make his way down. Suddenly, something became clear to him. All this, Amok thought, didn't exist, his sick mind, the anxiety plaguing him, from which he was tried to escape, was fabricating this unlikely situation. Because he was incapable of turning back to see Ixora, because it was too late to question his father, because he could not bear Kabral's look, because he would have put an end to his life years ago, if he could have. This madness was born out of the contempt he felt for his own life, his inability to end it all. Running away had become his way of living. Where was he right now, where was he really, if not in the depths of his own inner darkness? The confrontation with himself had triggered a flight mechanism, plunging him into this illusion. Some people took drugs to achieve such results. All he had to do was be in the world.

The low-ceilinged basement to which he was led was the same size as the upstairs room, where he'd changed his clothes. Two carved doors, pieces from the Baule country, had been mounted on the wall. Recognizable by the simplicity of their motifs, he considered them more elegant than the busier designs on their counterparts from the Bandiagara escarpment. He thought that TaMery was decidedly a surprising place, for its medu neter called for a different type of decoration entirely, at least a djed and an ankh somewhere or other, but there were none. The keeper of the place didn't have a name that connected her to the defunct civilization of the Nile Valley. A low coffee table with a big top occupied the center of the room. It was set with glasses, napkins, and cutlery, a jar too, but no plates. The woman indicated where to sit, near a window whose wooden shutters had been closed, there was no curtain, simply this solid wood, it must have taken two people at least to push the casements. Slipping his legs under the table, since he wasn't about to sit cross-legged in a tunic that came down just above the knee, the man let out a deep sigh. He'd heard of that strange disorder, sleep paralysis, when the person has a waking dream, or something of the sort. The situation he found himself in wasn't comparable, he could move, utter intelligible words. Whereas the paralyzed dreamer endured events, often threatening, without being able to react. So what was happening to him? He hadn't fallen asleep. There had been that light, the sun in the middle of the night, and then this. This woman, this house, her incongruous language, this surreal situation. Revising his earlier analysis, he said to himself that nothing of all that was here could spring from his own imagination. It wasn't his. He'd been very close to Amandla, but at no point had he ever let himself be swayed by the twaddle of Negrohood. If there was one thing that his mind would always oppose, it was this identity-forming mythology. So, how could he explain what was happening to him? It made him queasy to think that all of this was simply happening and didn't mean a thing.

After making sure he was comfortably seated, the woman left him alone again. She soon returned, carrying a large steaming dish, set it on the center of the table. Her eyes met Amok's: *Son of Oshun, rest assured, I've done what was needed. I invoked the ancestors, served them their portion, implored their support for this journey through your night.*

She sat down, admitted that she hadn't actually gone all the way back to the Kandakes, she'd have had to start at the break of day, for there were so many valiant foremothers. Moreover, as sometimes happened, she'd only concentrated on a specific area of memory, limiting herself to Mari Jan, Toya, Sesil Fatiman, and Anakaona. To them in particular, because they were all too often forgotten. Having evoked these honorable figures that, despite his erudition, he didn't recall having heard mentioned before, she raised her arms, closed her eyes, sang the litany of their names as she must have done during the invocation, punctuating her appeals with a long *mwen rele ou koulye aaa*. The woman was now completely relaxed, in excellent spirits. She let out a joyful laugh, clapped her hands, seeming to invite the invisible ones to the festivities. The man finally took the time to really observe her, she had the face of his inner turmoil. From exactly what part of his mind was she springing? He couldn't tell. She interrupted these questions: *Come now, let's eat. Given what's raining down on us, we need to gather strength.*

Without another word, Ayezan dug her spoon into the dish. She took a bite of the big ek<u>o</u>ki at the center, closed her eyes and chewed slowly, slowly, slowly. He didn't know who'd prepared it, but it was the finest ek<u>o</u>k'a mbasi, made with vegetables called bel<u>e</u>mb<u>e</u>, shrimp, and pieces of smoked fish. It was presented in the pouch of leaves in which it had been cooked, accompanied by a variety of tubers. The dish was one of his favorites, one of those he'd sometimes missed over there, up North, without admitting it to himself. The woman feasted on the meal with obvious delight, as if they were there under ordinary circumstances, just a cordial get-together sealing a pact of friendship. He, on the other hand, having just recognized not only the gas station attendant, but also the grandmother from the traffic circle, said he wasn't hungry. It was true. The memory of this old woman stripping in the middle of that roundabout when the sun was at its zenith had haunted him for a long time. That didn't explain why it was preoccupying him so tonight. Ayezan had frizzy hair, as white as cotton. It was tied in a bun with a golden ribbon. Her dashiki was yellow, with white embroidery over the chest and on the bottom of the sleeves. Whenever he'd seen her, these colors were there. Did it mean something? She answered him, arguing that he was annoying her, all these questions were saturating the atmosphere. The fact that he hadn't formulated them aloud didn't change a thing, she could hear them anyway, it was oppressive, it spoiled her appetite.

This then was what he wanted to know: she had the mission, in Amok's life, of guarding passageways, that was why he'd encountered her in specific places. Since the task had to be accomplished outside TaMery, she'd taken on appropriate identities. Apparitions of this nature were only initiated under exceptional circumstances, they'd occurred because he was in grave danger, long before this night. Lowering her head, the woman sighed, never had she imagined he'd commit such an act. The colors he'd noticed were those of the principle that she obeyed during this diurnal work and which were his law too, in the incarnation he'd chosen. She'd come back to that later. None of their encounters had been by accident, they'd been warnings to help him get back on track, but Amok had not understood these messages. Ayezan could not have prevented the events of this night, that wasn't her role. Everyone had to know the reasons for their presence here below, and act accordingly. Anticipating the question that occurred to him about Charles, the woman indicated that he had no reason to worry. Unlike him, his companion hadn't been injured, he just had a little mud in his shoes. *They'll give him another pair at the Palace of Shabazz*. Amok wondered whether he should try to understand what was happening to him or wait, as if it was just a sleepless night, for his anxieties to dissipate in the morning. He liked the decor of the room. He'd become acquainted with local crafts in the Prince des Côtes gallery, where his father had an antique store. The objects in TaMery were his favorites. Only the bogolan tunic bothered him, he preferred the Northern clothing he'd always worn, the rest felt like a disguise to him. Amok didn't touch his food, his host commended him for this: *You're not eating, that's good. The woman will be back on her feet, but right now, she cannot move. If you still have questions, now is the time to express them. Soon it won't be possible.* He wasn't sure what to ask. Everything was so uncanny. He'd have liked to think he was dreaming but when had he fallen asleep? He was sure that he'd driven to the Prince des Côtes, picked up Charles who'd been waiting for him, then stopped at a gas station, filled up the tank . . . What could Charles be doing now?

The Palace of Shabazz. That name. Shabazz. Another emblem of Negrohood. Some crank preacher had come up with the fable of an original community of Blacks named Shabazz. The myth provided answers to the thorny questions that tormented that breed of people. It reassured them: once upon a time, they had silky hair; once upon a time, their cultures were refined, and they themselves were the most delicate creatures in the world. Then, bad times had come, they'd had to face challenges. That's how they found themselves in the heart of the Continent, in hostile places where they had to feed themselves as best they could, lose finesse, become savage. Their features thickened, the texture of their hair changed. Shabazz, a fabricated glory, a name invented to have a clean one again, to remember that one had once been human, and could be human again. Shabazz. Just another magic formula, because Black had not always been beautiful, and one had to learn to see it that way, to design corrective mirrors, stare at oneself in them to the point of trance, until the stigma was erased, at least on the surface. These incantations, these talismans, these legends, this eagerness to like being oneself again. And that's where one still was, imprisoned by pains that didn't go away. Perhaps it was simply impossible to get beyond having been, for a time, banished from the human family. Men had passed sentence, there was every reason to doubt their mental health, but that wasn't enough to solve the problem. And so there were followers of Shabazz just a stone's throw away, but in what way did this concern him? Amok would have given everything not to have made the decision—but had he really?—to leave Ixora in the hands of strangers. That was what tormented him, right now at least. His deed deserved punishment, he conceded. What he was experiencing at the moment was surely not punishment enough, which brought him back to his initial supposition: his mind was attempting to escape.

Amok kept silent for a moment, then said the first words that came to mind: *What was that light?* In the rain, in the darkness, that light. The woman shrugged. The light, to him, was this house. Many people had visions during their passage on the road that had led him here. Everyone projected their own images onto the luminous screen that appeared to them. She had nothing more to say. The woman spoke again of their daytime encounters, stressing his kindness. He'd always had a caring gesture, a kind word for the poor sufferer whose face she'd assumed. When he'd climbed out of the car, he'd been floored by the pain of the woman abandoned in the rain, because his heart was not closed. Amok kept his eyes fixed on the stranger. All this had to mean something, even if it was only a figment of his sick mind, a materialization of his anguish, his guilt. This stranger took up so much space in him that she obliterated all tangible presence of Ixora, whose face he could no longer see. Only the name remained, three syllables whose music was gradually fading. Every so often, though more and more infrequently, as if the events of earlier that night had taken place in the remote past, he would see her body in the mud and one woman, then another, racing to her side. The guardian of TaMery grew irritated: *She's unreachable to you now. It's within yourself that you have to look. She doesn't need you at the moment.*

From his mother, he'd inherited at least one quality: her clear-sightedness. Making up stories to fool himself had never been his style, he was not about to start today. He knew deep down that he didn't want to see Ixora as long as she hadn't recovered, as long as she still bore traces of his blows. That didn't suffice to account for Charles's absence, nor the fact that he'd projected himself into such a place as this house. He associated the Kemito-Nubian coloring of his thoughts with Amandla, whom he'd seen running to help Ixora. But he'd already crossed paths with Ayezan well before tonight and this he couldn't comprehend. Oh well. Lifting his hands, he tried to wave away the keeper of TaMery, who didn't move one little bit. *Leave me alone*, he hissed, *leave me alone*. She answered him in a distorted voice, whose accents were those of the sandman. Amok shut his eyes. This time, he did so willfully. If he was to look within himself, he'd have to close his eyes first. Stop wondering about the purpose of a window, even unopened, in the basement of this unreal dwelling. Stop looking at the woman sitting in front of him, and heed her recommendation to delve deep down inside. He didn't see the approving look on his host's face, nor did he feel himself gently sinking, overwhelmed by fatigue, all these unanswered questions.

II

When he opened his eyes, the woman had vanished, the house itself was gone. He found himself in the only room of a crude hut, with the early morning light filtering through cracks between the poorly assembled planks. The foam of the mattress on which he lay was so thin he could feel the hardness of the wood under his back, its roughness too. Judging from his sensations, he pictured a base made of a tree split in half, that nobody had bothered to plane. There was no sheet or pillow. As a makeshift curtain, the corners of a frayed wrapper had been nailed over a window, which meant it couldn't be drawn. It was one of those cheap wax fabrics, with a mauve print. The blue background, which had faded, imitated the hue of a peaceful sky. Opposite the bed, a mat had been unrolled, with another wrapper on it, one in better condition and folded in four. The mat had nothing traditional about it save its shape and use, the raffia had been replaced by threads of citrus-colored plastic. This created something electric in this bare setting, a screech in the heart of silence. He saw no other furniture, a large area of the room being out of sight, there may have been other shrill notes, other discordances in the harmony of old things thrown together, other striations on the surface of this way of being. A rooster in the yard launched into his morning lamentation, reminding the living that it was their responsibility to honor the additional time granted to them, a day at least. According to his father, roosters never sang, their cry was more of a warning, that's how the people of this country used to understand it. Their concern was to bring the best they could offer to the new day, so as to permit the advent of another morning. Living to avoid leaving the world to darkness. Living to confront the return of darkness. Amok didn't know if he'd slept, he saw himself closing his eyes to escape the turmoil, within and without, that was his last memory from the night before. He'd had no dreams, the hoped-for descent into himself had not taken place. Or maybe, yes that must be it, what he'd encountered there was a vacuum, utter bareness, something against which he'd crashed, before opening his eyes here. This time he didn't accuse himself of creating another hallucination. Real or not, the situation was palpable, he'd come to be here one way or another, so it was a truth. It was the day to fill, the day to usher in. He hadn't seen Charles, but he could hear a man's voice outside, speaking in hushed tones, so as not to disturb, or perhaps to seal some conspiracy in a word. Despite himself, apprehension assailed him, the fear of having been moved from TaMery to the Palace of Shabazz, a place that logically would be as unrefined as where he now was. Hadn't Shabazz, the first with this name, led his disciples to the heart of what the myth described as a jungle, in order to toughen them by an existence so rough that it would change their appearance and lifestyle? It was through trial that the Black being had been engendered, all of the stories told on the subject bore this out. Those who were now claiming to be descendants of Shabazz might find it necessary, still today, to submit to this ascetic imperative, for everyone could see that the battles fought until now had been merely a warm-up before the final fight that would bring victory. To die so as to be reborn, to die relentlessly, obstinately, to exhaust death's duration, to journey through it as you'd progress through the meanders of a subterranean passage. Perhaps imitate in this fashion the sun that descends, at twilight, to the depths of the abyss from which it will emerge victorious, without this glory being a triumph, because it will have to sink anew, be hurt again, risk rising nevermore. No. Shabazz was the name for those whose trajectory was no longer modelled on the star of the day. For them, the journey must have an end, a definitive resolution, that would be in their favor. Living in this expectation alone, they'd created an experience of death unhinged from life, no longer its disagreeable twin but its enemy. The Shabazz myth had not been created in these lands, it came from another source.

Silencing these reflections, Amok thought of getting up to look around, not letting himself be buffeted by circumstances, doing something on his own initiative. The day had dawned for him too, requiring of him that he make an offering to life. What he wanted to do, even more than finding Charles, was to take the road that had led him to this hut in the other direction, go back to see Ixora. He didn't have even a hazy idea of what he'd do then, but he would no longer shrink from it. He tried to get up, it proved impossible. The upper part of his body hurt when he moved, only his head did not suffer from neuralgia. The smell floating within the sickly walls struck him, the smell first, then he discovered that it was coming from him. Looking down, he found that all his clothes, except his underwear, had been removed. His torso was bare, a cloth, tied around his waist, covered his lower limbs, he could see his toes. Poultices had been applied to his arms and to part of his face. A kind of clay that didn't dry out completely, most probably a paste made from some plant or other, he preferred not to delve into the question. At least, the paste was not causing an epidermal reaction, the smell was quite pungent as it was, he wondered why his nostrils hadn't been attacked earlier.

He didn't dare touch the ointment, moving could release its charge, intensify its stench, the pain too. All the same, he wanted to know if Charles was indeed there, outside, this would dispel the delirium of the night once and for all. He called out several times. A pudgy woman entered, wearing a yellow robe, and, on her feet, white *sans confiance*, plastic sandals that owe their name—French for unreliable—to the fact that they break without warning, leaving the soles of the feet defenseless on rough roads. An immaculate scarf concealed her hair, but he recognized her. A smile on her lips, she drew near, put her hand on his brow, said a few words in the torn language, the one that should have been transmitted to him. The woman was talkative, her tone kindly, but he didn't understand the idiom, the right to it had been denied him. Why was she suddenly speaking to him in it? Last night, they'd no trouble communicating. Amok pronounced her name: Ayezan, but she shook her head no, she didn't understand, signaled to him to wait, dashed out, came back accompanied.

The man who walked beside her had a coppery complexion, long hair pulled back in a ponytail, his torso was naked and he was barefoot. He was young, tall, athletic looking, wore black jogging pants, held a straw hat in his nervous hands. When he neared the makeshift bed on which Amok lay, he looked deep into his eyes: *My name is Continent Noir, welcome to my humble abode. They say that I'm crazy. I don't know if that's true. People say a lot of things, they talk all the time. Let's say I'm crazy. But this here is my place.* The man swept his arm through the space. An epicanthic fold gave his eyes a half-moon shape. He had Asian features, a pronounced local accent, and spoke haltingly. Continent Noir declared that he'd found Amok on the road of dazzlements. He'd lost consciousness but was breathing calmly, so he decided to carry him here. When he'd arrived home, with the unconscious man over his shoulders, he'd met this nameless woman. Sitting in front of his hut, she'd pointed to Amok, saying she'd come to watch over him. Continent Noir had accepted her help, she'd taken care of Amok, who'd slept an entire day.

The man fell silent. Amok asked about Charles. Continent Noir shrugged. He'd found only him. On the passenger side, the door was open, the window down. Since Amok claimed to have had a companion, he was willing to go look for him, but it wouldn't be easy. The storm had flooded the roads and, although it was the dry season, it would take a day at least before you could get around easily. Continent Noir didn't own one of those huge motorized beetles, that gutted the earth as they passed. Neither could he rely on the residents of the neighboring village. He'd been born there, but they'd chased him away years ago. He was crazy. It came from mixed blood. His head swayed, his eyes saw too many things, his mouth couldn't stop talking about what his eyes had seen. Amok kept quiet. So it wasn't the day after the stormy night, as he'd thought, since he'd spent at least twenty-four hours here in this hut. Continent Noir had mentioned a dazzlement, which suggested that the road was known for this. That was already what Ayezan had said, but he didn't understand. There had been that light in the darkness, a fiery glow, looming large over the deluge, as if in superimposition, but it hadn't blinded him.

He remembered perfectly the arcade studded with white flowers under which he'd propelled his car to land amidst palm trees, in the TaMery garden. He said nothing of this. What worried him most was Charles's disappearance. He recalled the conical house, but the idea of a Palace of Shabazz seemed far-fetched to him. What good would it do to ask a man who described himself as crazy? Continent Noir looked like he was in a world of his own. Twitches convulsed his face. When he wasn't talking, his already slanted eyes narrowed, half-shut. Amok thanked him for getting him out of the vehicle and sheltering him. He'd decided to engage fully in the reality unfolding before him, to believe that it was true, to make it tangible through his will. Yet, he had no impulse to smile anymore and couldn't get rid of a certain mistrust. His eyes riveted on the man's face, he listened to him say goodbye. *The mother has done everything for you since you've been here. She'll take care of your meal.* He took three steps back so as not to turn his back on Amok abruptly, and withdrew.

Alone with the woman who was the spitting image of Ayezan but with whom communication remained rudimentary, Amok closed his eyes, showing in this way that he was overcome with fatigue. She left him to himself, went over to a corner of the room, where he heard her busy herself with something. Careful not to make too much noise moving the things she needed, the stranger began humming a song so tenderly it almost lulled him to sleep. Before leaving, she removed the wrapper nailed over the window, folded it, put it on the mat, opened the shutters. Daylight poured into the hut, a breath of air too, bringing with it whiffs of the still-damp earth. Leaving the window wide open, the woman stepped out. He saw her outside, in profile, her head bent over a table or a bench, her working area. Every so often, she looked at him, with laughing eyes. He didn't deserve her kindness, but she offered herself to him with such generosity that to push her away would have been an insult, the mark of unbound egotism. So he smiled back, it was like standing at the edge of an immense plain whose bareness was not a void but an invitation. To sow something, to believe that one had something to grow and sustain. Amok was not yet there. He contented himself with smiling at the intimate stranger, this woman he'd already seen, the mother he'd never had, the grandmother he'd never thought to get to know. His tears surprised him, he let them flood his face, made no move to dry his eyes.

The return of the stranger calmed him. She'd brought warmth into the space, this overflowing fullness of love, forming a magnetic aura around her presence. Continent Noir whom she'd called on to translate her words stood in the doorway, one foot in the hut, the other outside, ready to help, then slip away. The old woman was holding a slightly dented tin cup in her hand. She spoke to Continent Noir in the language that Amok couldn't understand, but he knew they were talking about him, the woman never took her eyes off him. Continent Noir explained: *The mother says you must drink water and go outside. The light will help. The wind will help too. So we have to carry you, the two of us. At first, we're going to* choke *you, but you'll be alright.* Amok laughed, nodded with difficulty. He'd never known how or why *to choke* had become synonymous with inflicting pain. It was used to apply to a specific case, when the *choked* person had already been wounded. *Choking* happened when the sensitive area was touched or brushed against. Any pain thus inflicted was seen as a strangulation which, even very briefly, obstructed breathing. For years Amok had heard this expression. It brought other, equally odd expressions, to mind, with which he and Ajar, as children, with the help of their father, weaved outlandish stories.

He'd forgotten about that. All the laughter. In the great house, in the midst of all the devastating grief, they'd laughed and laughed, until they split their sides. And nobody had seen the laughter shooting from some distant star. The outbursts of joy had been born right there, nuggets in the peat of which they were a part. Under normal circumstances, he would have shunned the memory of these blasts of jubilation pried from the pain, for they weighed little in comparison with the rest. The violence. The silence that came after, denser and denser, until there was no way to bridge the distances its thickness created. On the cusp of adolescence, the age when *children of the barrier* didn't leave their protected homes to wander the streets like ill-bred underprivileged kids, the love that he and Ajar felt toward their father was mixed with terror. Since it was impossible for them to resist his affection, not to give in to his tenderness on days when the darkness chose to spare him, they preferred to steer clear of him. To rush up the grand staircase when they heard him honking his horn, suddenly having homework to do, anything to avoid seeing him, touching him, responding to his love, and betraying their mother. She didn't let them cry over her bruises, her loose teeth. She wouldn't be prodded to divorce. But distraught as they were at the time, they needed to do something to break free, or at least to start filing away at their chains.

Madame had been oblivious to their state of mind, their outcry against sufferings that she wasn't complaining about, the indications of their bewilderment too. Their existence was a rent, a breach to return to again and again, since they would never pull themselves out of it. They could flee, but their escapes were merely physical, and deceptive. Inside, deep down, the trauma had set up its nerve center. The comfort and beauty of the great house, that some called the Mususedi castle, were the inverted mirror of reality. The house was as solid and imposing as its inhabitants were frail and breakable, ever on the verge of disintegrating. Had they survived? Had they managed to create a protective shell over the breach? By the age of twelve, his sister had started drinking, first liqueurs because she liked their sweetness, then the hard stuff for which she still had a taste. No one had ever seen her drunk, any hint of disgrace had to remain private for someone who'd come into the world with a name, prior to having an identity. To begin with she'd practiced domestic transgression, before later moving on to courteous misbehavior once she'd been granted permission to go out. She was fifteen at the time, their father had handed her the keys to the great house, Madame hadn't disapproved.

It was a symbolic gesture after all. *Children of the barrier* lived in guarded homes, hidden behind walls, commonly topped in those days with glass bottle shards to dissuade criminals. Sometimes, there'd be a hound barking behind the fence, and a small *Beware of Dog* sign on the metal gate. The key was superfluous, the house was only locked when they were gone for some time. Faithful to the practices of her milieu, the teenager had exercised her freedom with discretion, intent on not embarrassing their parents. He'd done just the opposite.

This morning, after the rooster's lament, thoughts of the family quartet took hold of him, which was not in itself an unusual thing. But this time details surfaced, tiny treasures buried in the rubble, delicate cantilenas amid the din. An emotion suddenly gripped him, that did little to change the mess he'd contributed to perfecting. He didn't accuse himself of anything, to what good. What he hadn't managed to retain in his memory forced itself on his conscious mind, without affording a remedy for the disease that consumed him. A gloaming was in him, standing in the way of any impulse the morning might have had to emerge in its turn. In the great house, it was dark. When a laugh burst forth, it was spawned by darkness itself. You lowered your guard because you couldn't do otherwise, that's how you explored a form of joy. It left a bitter taste. It was a dirty joy, you knew where it came from, it was only good in the moment. An unavowable pleasure, that was why he'd suppressed the memories of it. Joy in the great house was glitter not diamonds. The treasures buried under the ruins of their souls were not even stardust, they were nothing but sand. He'd had the good fortune to receive genuine gems, he knew the difference. The man saw Ixora again in the mud, in the rain. The day turned dark, he shut his eyes.

At the woman's request, Continent Noir signaled to him that a chair had been placed for him in front of the hut. They intended to set him up there, which meant he'd be *choked* for his own good. He could drink, have a bite to eat if he wanted, spending the morning outside would speed up his recovery. He'd stay seated today, and by tomorrow he'd be able to walk. His legs hadn't been hurt in the accident, the injuries on his arms didn't mask fractures, he was lucky. Was he ready? They'd take him out when he was. Amok had no desire to experience again the pain that had whipped through him when he'd tried to get up before. Yet he decided to let them help him. Slipping one arm under his legs, the other under his back, the woman lifted him up like a wisp of straw, without any assistance from Continent Noir. He had just enough time to see the hard base on which he'd been lying that had hurt his back. It was not a tree of unsmoothed wood, but a bed of ancient manufacture. Narrow and made out of solid wood, it displayed a series of finely carved figures under the poor-quality foam mattress. Long ago, not far from the grasslands, dignitaries had had beds like this on which they rested, marrying their skin to the sculpted flesh of a carefully selected tree. That a piece of this value could be found in such a desolate place conversing with a synthetic fiber mat under the gaze of a vulgar wax wrapper was baffling. The man yielded to the embrace of the old woman who carried him without seeming to strain her muscles. Her body kept its softness, holding him effortlessly as she would a baby. Surrendering to this solidity, Amok let himself become the child he no longer knew he'd been, a trustful being because no fear troubled him, a powerful being because he drew on the forces around him rather than imposing his own.

Maybe he'd never known such trust, nor such power. This knowledge, it seemed to him, might have kept him from behaving as he had, especially when he was younger. Makalando, the woman who cooked their meals in the great house, had reprimanded him one day, incensed by his extreme acting-out as a teenager in crisis. She was an employee, but first and foremost an elder, which gave her the right to put him in his place. That day, he no longer remembered what he'd done, but she'd grabbed him by the arm, pulled him to a corner of the garden where fruit trees grew. There, under the thick foliage of a mango tree whose branches sagged under the weight of the fruits—some of which, still green, had been gnawed by bats—she'd unleashed a shower of flames on him. It was not just in words, it was the red flashing of her eyes, the scornful twist of her lips, the fist she restrained from hitting his skull, his impudent face. She had to keep herself from touching him, from even brushing against him, lest the unworthy son be reduced to dust. There she stood, torso leaning forward, fist trembling. *You, you might not have been born. They did everything they could to keep your mother from giving birth. But she wanted you. She wanted you so much, and when you came, she gave you a name that you don't deserve. Tsk. Asumwe mba boso, get out of my sight.* Makalando had paused between each sentence, choking back her rage and her tears too, he sensed. He hadn't replied, hadn't asked who'd spared no effort to prevent Madame from becoming a mother, what they'd done. He'd never brought it up with her, it was the period when they no longer said anything of any importance to each other. For a week, no more, Amok had behaved himself, trying to grasp what was behind the words so bitterly uttered, imagining a time when Madame, fearing that she'd lose her first child, had clung to him. Her anchor. That was what she'd wanted him to become. How was this a mark of love? Was being brought into the world to save his mother from drowning worthy of gratitude? She'd wanted him more than anything. For whom had she desired him? What had she wished for him?

The culmination of his reasoning having hardly proved satisfactory—in fact, quite the contrary—Amok had continued on his course, with increased frenzy and evermore pronounced determination. Whenever the birth of her first child came up, Madame would insist on one thing only, the vivid memory of her suffering. The tone with which she recounted the experience was enough to plunge the listener into the agonies that the young woman had endured. She'd dragged herself on the floor in the dark, at a time when young wives had the right to expect that they wouldn't be left alone. Her husband was out whooping it up, which was the phrase he himself used to describe this activity, an expression that wiggled its behind and stripped life of its gravity. This was not dancing; dancing was deep, sometimes serious, it was an act of self-elevation and self-expression. What Madame's husband did was whoop it up, proudly so. Everyone recognized that he was more than just competent in this area, that he had a kind of expertise, a capacity for innovation too. Monsieur gave the best of himself to levity, right when Madame, her water having broken, was struggling alone in the darkness that had invaded the house due to a power failure. She moaned for herself, and for the child who heard her. The young woman writhed in pain, swearing to herself that one day she'd have an anchor to hold on to.

Crawling as best she could to the chest, whose massive shadow loomed at the other end of the room, Madame had groped for the candles kept in the bottom drawer. It would have been better to leave one or two in one of the night-table drawers, but it was too late to think about that now. From what depths had she garnered the strength to dominate what threatened to tear her insides apart? Had it crossed her mind that she'd been thrust into a tropical adaptation of *Rosemary's Baby*? Had she massaged her belly while humming, teeth clenched, murmuring to the child in hushed tones because it was together that they'd make it through the night? It was said that intrauterine life was the real beginning of the one that would unfold later. He didn't know what he and his mother had shared in that special intimacy, what had been imprinted in him. *Rosemary's Baby* . . . The movie had terrified Ajar and him, despite the precaution they'd taken not to watch it at night. They'd shuddered with fear for days on end, his sister refusing to sleep alone in her room. In his childish imagination, he'd associated certain scenes with the way Madame talked about her first pregnancy, that thing inside her that wouldn't consent to be born without first tearing her belly. Very young, he'd thought of himself as the offspring of some sickly force, a raft that had begun drifting dangerously well before it was put into the water. He was the one who'd have needed an anchor. He'd denied his mother what she hadn't given him.

When he was born at the crack of dawn, at the time when the rooster wails and those out whooping it up become men and fathers again, the young wife, exhausted from her long battle through the night, had barely looked at the infant. She'd held out long enough to hear him cry. When they'd tried to give her the baby to hold, she'd lost consciousness. The husband had often told this part of the story, the one in which he had the leading role. He was the first to embrace his son. He'd come home just in time to drive Madame to the clinic, he liked to recall the color the sky had taken as the rooster let out its melancholy cry, the mauve streaked with dark blue, with stars still ablaze here and there. The ideal dawn to celebrate the birth of the first child, the awaited son. People of the coastal country said that the eldest child chose his siblings, that he knew them from the reservoir of souls, summoned them when the time came. Even more than the parents, he was the one responsible, he had to set the example. Fortunately, his sister had known how to do without a model. They'd grown up sticking close together, supporting each other as well as they could.

Their adolescence had separated them somewhat, but they both knew what bond united them, what painful secrets, what disappointed hopes. He'd pretended to ignore the things she didn't confide in him, but the city had eyes and ears everywhere. And the high society of the Coast was a microcosm whose practices were tied to consanguinity. Amok had made it a point of honor to dissociate himself from it, but it was hard to escape it totally. The employees of the Prince des Côtes, whose company he preferred to that of the sons and daughters *of*, with whom he should have been keeping company, whispered to him about the comings and goings of the young Mususedi daughter. She was not really hiding, since operating openly was, in certain circumstances, the best way to divert attention. No one would have imagined that she went prowling around bars and swimming pools, looking for poor young guys who came there to sell their bodies. Anyway, the people telling him these things laughed in the middle of their confidences, saying that it was just the impression she gave them. They couldn't be sure.

Amok shrugged his shoulders, not having seen her operate, not having heard a word of complaint. He wasn't too worried about his sister, she was more grounded than he'd ever be. Ajar had been born at the day's end, when cocktails are served and life is sweet, shortly after the star of the day had gone underground. She'd come at evening twilight, when swarms of birds invaded the coastal sky, spreading their dark silhouettes over the mauve veils unfurling up above. Madame hadn't suffered, the already kindly girl had come out without a hitch. Their parents, who alone kept the memory of their early childhood, had described the attitude of the elder. Usually so capricious, he'd stood there, gravely, by the cradle where his younger sister lay. Hypnotized by her delicacy, he hadn't taken his eyes off her, holding out a chubby little hand to caress her cheek, her already full head of hair. When mother and daughter had stepped through the door of the great house, he'd wanted to take the child in his arms and had given her a frangipani flower. As a child, there was nothing he loved more than flowers. He and Ajar had wandered around the great house, discovering there what others learned in the street, pornography, the crude words of erotic poetry. There'd been mornings, there'd been nights, they'd grown up. Pragmatic, his sister had remained a daughter of her caste, a specimen of a species whose faults she neither ignored nor renounced. It was her world, her place in the world, she made do.

Amok had wanted something else, without knowing what or where to find it. He'd struggled to tear himself away from the clan, abandoning, as soon as he could, the well-born boys with whom he was expected to associate. This hadn't been enough to free him from his chains. Knocking at other doors, he'd been bitterly surprised to see them open only because of his parents' social status and the acculturation that made him pronounce the words of the coastal language with a strange accent. Bambaata, a friend of his from the slums, had once called him a muna mukala, a white boy, without meaning to insult him, far from it. His attempts to master the ancestral idiom had stopped there and then, his yearning had been mocked instead of encouraged. He was seen not as a lost son looking for the way back to his birthplace, but as a foreigner putting on a disguise, a traitor perhaps, guilty of entryism. Those who felt honored to know him liked what he detested in himself. Those who looked up to him from below confirmed that there was indeed something hateful in him. Nowhere could he escape his name. The people of the Coast felt no friendship for those who aspired to rid themselves of their ancestry, its legacy. Who could they possibly be in that case?

Now in this new dawn, in this unfamiliar place, here's what he knew: the rooster had sounded its lament, and he'd discovered a mother's roundness, thickness, and strength. The nameless woman, by offering her support, becoming an anchor in his stead, wasn't healing the wounds caused by the car accident. At present he was suffering only from a slight shooting pain between his temples. The stranger sat him on the high-backed reclining chair. The nightwatchmen, in residential neighborhoods where the moneyed live, used seats like this. Throughout his youth, he'd seen these pieces of furniture in the guarded homes where they were the sole local elements of a Northern décor. That was how it was. The Chesterfield sofa, the solid-wood coffee table copied from a model in a Northern catalog—when it was not imported—the bar in the shape of a globe and the carpet, all tolerated the proximity of some pieces of sub-Saharan craftmanship. There were plenty of them in the hotel lounges and bedrooms of the Prince des Côtes, where the onslaughts of air conditioning enjoined them to keep silent once and for all.

These decorative masks, unlike the antiques that his father would unearth when he was selling them, did not object. Their status as imitations prohibited it. Anyway, the people who carved them, polished the wood, and covered them in earth to give them a false patina expected nothing from them except a bit of spending money. The high-backed chairs were among the few pieces of old-style furniture whose daily use had been preserved. It was the first time he'd had the opportunity of sitting in one, and he was surprised by the comfort. Amok immediately understood why so many nightwatchmen, who were supposed to be kept on alert by the hard seat, were frequently caught snoring. Continent Noir, who hadn't needed to *choke* him, checked that his posture was good. Then he left him in the company of the nameless woman. Using a damp cloth, she removed the poultice. Then, she went inside, came back with the tin cup, filled with cool, clear water, from which he took a sip. The stranger smiled. He did too. When she stepped aside, he beheld the world stretching out before and around him.

The chair had been placed by the door. The hut was part of a compound that was quite big for one man alone, and a madman to boot. Royal palm trees had been planted in the garden, where they grew next to fruit trees. Amok didn't see any flowers, but it all exuded a sense of opulence that contradicted his initial sentiment. The road where they'd found him extended to his right, but the entrance to the estate was not there. He couldn't have sworn to it, but he seemed to discern an arcade along which a leafy climber studded with large white flowers could have run. Looking at the stranger, he said once again *Ayezan*, but she shrugged her shoulders and laughed. An agama scampered between his legs, over the red earth. It was rare to see one after it had rained. This one's body was both bright and dark blue, its head was purple, as was the tip of its tail. The lizard was now clinging to the trunk of a palm tree, its body adhering to the material. It raised its head, looking for a ray of sunlight. Lifting his eyes to the sky, Amok discovered the colors of daybreak, a mauve veil with blue stripes. The rooster wailed again, he asked what time it was. The woman didn't reply, she hadn't understood him, he didn't insist.

The colors of the sky caught his eye again. The mauve was slowly dissipating, withdrawing from the blue, like a lover tiptoeing out of the bedroom. The analogy was odd, but he saw a kind of tenderness in it, a profound sentiment whose worth resided in the acceptance of separation. Maybe the mauve had no desire to go away, but that's how it was, it had to. These nuptials could only be brief, to be renewed ever and again. Nothing was embedded, nothing entrenched, everything passed, the days resembled one another in appearance alone.

The stars his father had described so often did not grace this break of day. If this morning's twilight imitated that of his birth thirty-four years before, it was also to remind him that it had taken place. As if from a distance, Amok saw himself, examined himself from every angle.

Countless sunrises had come to pass, and just as many roosters had cried their lament, their invitation to take one's place in the light, not enter it empty-handed, or at least come to it with the intention of contributing something to life. He'd refused to be the pillar on which his mother could lean, the understanding son of a father possessed by the spirit of a beast, the serene grandson of a man whose distinction came from having collaborated in the colonial enterprise. That's what had occupied him most, the reluctance to come into the world, to take a step outside the womb. At times, he'd heard life fluttering outside, had moved forward to capture its rhythms. So there'd been Shrapnel, his only friend. There'd been Amandla, his too-sensual, too-embodied lover. After the loss of these two, life had not turned away from him. Kabral and Ixora had appeared and, for once, he hadn't stayed only on the receiving end. They'd been happy. Ixora was not his lover, but his feelings for her were not merely fraternal or friendly. In the great house they'd slept head-to-toe, each turned away from the other. The music of her breathing had become indispensable to his well-being. The warmth of her body comforted him. It was also because she was there, with him, that he'd been able to consider returning to his parents' home. Her presence, and Kabral's, helped him project himself into the future.

But something had changed. Madame was no stranger to this, in his opinion. He'd been wrong to leave her so often to face his mother, she was a fearsome woman. Yet he alone had singlehandedly dealt the blows, he alone had left her lying in the mud. If the night at TaMery had any reality to it, if he could give credence to his strange host's words, then Ixora had survived her injuries, would not suffer any physical consequences. Would she still want him? Would she be ready to follow him out of the great house? He would throw himself at her feet if that would help . . . The day had now separated from the night, the sky was clear, as cloudless as his mind was cloudy. He wanted to hear news of Charles, but didn't sense that he was in danger. On Ixora's side, on the other hand, the horizon was murky. What could he say to her? Amok did not intend to bring up his atavistic insanity, the wild beast that he'd kept chained for so many years and that had broken free from its bonds. What had happened could happen again, he hadn't seen it coming, but he wanted her to stay with him. Was it possible to say this? That all he could do was make a pledge, promise, do his best, that she had to believe in him for him to succeed? There was something between the two of them that did not fit into the usual categories, they'd brought each other too much to let go now.

It had started almost like a joke, they'd seized on the pretext of pleasing Kabral, when they were the ones who'd benefitted most. The boy had wanted them to move in together, to have them every day within reach of his affection. Amok jumped into the newly opened space with both feet, heeding for once his intuition when he was usually paralyzed by reason.

So the three of them had combed through the classified ads, visited apartments, looking for a nest. A vitality had come over him, an ability also to organize his schedule according to the needs of another, he'd done all this with joy, he'd felt alive, after so many years spent trying unsuccessfully to evade the shame of being in the world. Shrapnel was dead. He'd needed this new, unlikely adventure, to keep from following him to the grave. The apartment they chose was the one that Kabral liked most. He'd loved the sunny living room, its old-fashioned parquet floor, its fireplace, its moldings. The potted shrubs in the courtyard that the living room and his bedroom overlooked delighted him. He immediately saw himself in the semi-open kitchen, with its central island, whose pale gray countertop went perfectly with the sliding panel. They'd been lucky.

The owner, a foreigner, had no racial prejudices. Their two modest but regular salaries had suited him fine. And he thought their faces inspired confidence. He was a wealthy libertarian who delighted in renting his beautiful old apartment to Blacks. There was no dearth of occasions to revolt against the system, but people could only do what cost them the least. He'd been happy there, with his live-in partner, a Mediterranean man from the peripheral zones who'd macerated in the rumba sung in Lingala, and who swore or exclaimed only in this idiom from Katiopa. The couple had decided to move to the seaside in the south, as Malik no longer tolerated the dreariness of the capital, the bitter cold winters, the very idea of this climate. They left some of their furniture, the new residents could help themselves, give the rest away or sell it off.

In the south, their decor would be very different, they'd have no use for these drab things: *We had all we can take of taupes, grays, and beiges* . . . The house in the sun would be colorful, there'd be blues, yellows, it would be warmer, more alive. There'd be a garden, perhaps a swimming pool, if Malik would listen to reason and let go of his ecological precepts. The negotiation wouldn't be easy, given that the protector of nature had already had to give up on the idea of dry toilets. Kabral, Ixora, and he soon found their bearings. Little by little, they'd decorated the place to their liking, leaving the natural beige and taupe colors of the wall which easily accommodated whatever they wanted to hang there. The organization of their everyday life had required no effort, things had fallen seamlessly into place.

With Ixora, he'd found the perfect relationship. She loved him without being in love, had no need to copulate, would never be pregnant by him. This had allowed him to loosen up, even relax. He'd felt his shoulders unwind, his whole body give up its defensive posture. Before, every so often sitting at his desk, he'd realize that he was holding his shoulders up a bit, that he'd kept them like that, as if in a vise or a strait-jacket, while his arms were rigid and barely detached from his body. He was permanently tense, that was his normal state. Before Kabral and Ixora. Had he wanted to punish himself, to keep himself from tasting such bliss? Was he bent on wrecking it all, because he had no right, was not made for this, that he'd persuaded them to follow him to the Continent? In the North, racism was their daily fare. Prejudices, refusal to identify with this portion of humanity that had been brutalized, thinking that in this way they could avoid sharing its fate. The impossibility for some to make their voices heard, unless they were specifically solicited, and then only on stipulated subjects and in a prescribed tone. Amok had always known what some people were thinking and saying, because they couldn't do anything else, but think and say. For a long time, the acrimony slid off him like water off a duck's back, he didn't worry much about it.

In the low-income neighborhood where he'd lived when he first enrolled in university and even later, he'd rubbed shoulders with poor ignorant devils who hardly knew their own language, who couldn't read it. People who'd missed every boat and were busy keeping several wolves from their doors. Their rotten luck occupied them full time, it was their only companion. White privilege did them a fat lot of good. Wasn't it legitimate that they reject change, the boundless expansion of their identity? Wasn't it natural, after all, that they should want to recognize their own face wherever they looked? Wasn't it understandable that their belonging to the nation never be questioned, that the criteria of beauty be defined according to their appearance, that they not be denied jobs or housing on racial grounds? This and more seemed to make perfect sense to them: after all, this was their home. And until recently, their need to have people who were smaller than themselves had been fully satisfied. But those days were over. Now, the nigger-trash no longer tolerated being used as door-mats without hollering, though still practically apologizing for feeling pain. They sounded off, asserting their rights in the country, their refusal to be chased out, their intention to shape its future. The nigger-trash now displayed the insolence of graduate, master's, and doctoral degrees, and professional experience that sometimes authorized their admission into the closed circles of the global elite. The nigger-trash could now make a show of their possessions, whip them out to show that that they too counted among the top performing agents of the gentrification industry that would boot the poor devils out of city centers to forsaken places whose names did not even figure on official maps. Somewhere outside this world. Some of the wretched of the earth had managed to extricate themselves from their material condition.

The political hegemony of the majorities may not have been undermined, but their methods were known. Many had acquired endurance and dexterity from having slipped again and again on the banana peels that they enjoyed scattering along the road. More than that, they had managed, through observation, to ferret out a few circuitous byways. The most popular allowed, incidentally, for mixing business with pleasure. All they had to do was make the appropriate love choices, so that they didn't have go by themselves to visit the properties they were about to appropriate. Being in the company of a partner of local color had the effect of relaxing the interlocutors, opening up access to networks. Not too broadly, but sufficiently to fill the poor moneyless whites with bitterness. The descendant of Vikings would bristle with rage at the sight of these Black bodies leaning out of balconies in buildings whose front doors he'd never pass through except to put unwanted flyers in the mailboxes, after having put in time at the employment agency. It was all he'd found to avoid starving to death, there being few opportunities for the jobless whose benefits had come to an end. And so, while he was holding the wolves at bay weighed down by all this unsolicited paper barely even good for wrapping fish or household garbage, the apes were kicking back. And not discretely either, it wasn't their style.

They had to be seen: they chose cars and clothing to this end. They had to be heard: they laughed loudly, spoke loudly, turned up the sound of their huge TVs and their car radios. They had to be smelled: they were not averse to a good cigar, they didn't turn up their noses at expensive perfumes. The penniless whites did not intend to take this lying down, they had a ready weapon to counter this invasion, this colonization in the etymological sense of the term, this racial decline. Previously uninterested in elections, they found their way back to the voting booth, threw all their weight behind the far right which would rid the world of vermin. Something had to be done. Just look at how the already hardline right, which had just been elected, was trying to run with the hare and hunt with the hounds, to give a good impression. It had understood all too well that it was being asked to wash whiter, its words and deeds showed that it had, but it wasn't going far enough, or fast enough, was still talking about assimilation, when eradication was what was needed. If only one could . . . At least send them back where they came from, they were everywhere, this human swarm was downright unbearable.

Amok had observed the changes of society, seen it standing at the crossroads, undecided about what to do with its recent past, with the imprint that this had left on it. Before Kabral and Ixora, the despondency of the once powerful didn't bother him, the agitation of internal colonialism didn't concern him. His life unfolded in an interstitial space, a non-place between being and nothingness. This suited him just fine, he expected nothing from life. He had something of a yellow streak that kept him from putting an end to his days, and then, although he was the one who didn't cling to this life, Shrapnel was the one who died. Adopting his best friend's son brought him new preoccupations. It seemed to him that the deleterious atmosphere that had enabled him to maintain his hatred of the world, the burgeoning expression of previously inhibited racism, would have a negative impact on Kabral. Like a great many other children of his country, he knew all about race. It didn't put on kid gloves to introduce itself into people's lives, as early as possible. He knew what effects this would have later. Kabral deserved better. He'd wanted to show him a wider world, to transmit to him such a natural sense of his humanity that he would need neither to assert it nor to defend it.

The appeal of Negrohood was unquestionable, the comfort it provided, the sense of belonging. But it was inseparable from the circumstances of its creation and could only be conceived, especially in the North, in terms of permanent opposition. Constructed as a binarity that was itself fabricated, Negrohood could not break free without breaking down, coming undone. Negrohood didn't transform the face of the world, though this was its aspiration. Yearning for this metamorphosis, it prevented its advent. Change had to continue to belong to the realm of dreams, a mirage ceaselessly approached but never reached. These questions became an obsession as his affection for Kabral grew. Previously, he examined them from a distance, out of habit. Paternity plunged him in right up to his neck. The look in people's eyes on the street, their attitudes, the words they said, nothing escaped him anymore. The equanimity that had let him go through life without attaching importance to the world's troubles was disappearing. His private torments themselves were taking the back seat. The last thing he wanted was for his son to learn to stay in line or watch his step, in a vain attempt to reassure the nut jobs on the verge of a heart attack at the sight of a kinky head of hair. Nor did he want to inculcate in Kabral the obligation to do at least twice as well as others in all areas, to sell him a dream of conformism that would end up deadly. What he needed to do, above all, was to take Kabral to a less hostile country, a place where he'd encounter who he was, who he wanted to be, before being assigned a place by others. To offer him a place from where he could enter the world without having to ask permission. Not having to conquer what, in principle, belonged to one and all.

Ixora was readily persuaded. The idea of moving to the Continent had somewhat surprised her, at first. Then, for a variety of reasons, she'd been enticed. It would be an adventure, it was time to have one. He'd been close to Amandla, the memory of each one's wounded childhood had strengthened their bonds, to the point that he'd thought it would be impossible to be so close to anyone again. Yet his relationship with Ixora was equally strong, healthier he thought. Their intimacy was not physical, but they told each other things that many lovers don't share, abrasive stories from their past. He especially, for he had quite a few of those in his baggage. For the first time, he'd recounted his introduction to sex, the cruel games that the youth of his caste played, with girls who couldn't complain, no one would have believed them. The gang rapes that the perpetrators presented as orgies were known, at the time, as mp_oti, he'd never learned the origin of the term. Did anyone know? The technique was simple, as old as the world, that's what the tough guys would say. One of them would seduce a girl, break down her resistance, persuade her to come over to his place alone, at a time when his parents were out. She'd show up, smartly dressed, often with a home-made cake in hand. In those days, young ladies were raised to think that femininity was demonstrated over the stove. Bringing a pastry was the least they could do, given that the date was at snack time, a common practice among the wealthy. Some girls were curious about what two naked people do behind closed doors, and hoped to lift the veil at least, when they weren't bold enough to take the initiative. They were never the ones to fall into the mp_oti trap, for the predators were methodical and instinctively honed in on prey. They were intent on remaining in control of the situation, committing the act in a group allowed them to do too.

The popular girls were confident and naive. They'd go bouncing around, enjoying their budding breasts, accentuating the arch of their back when they were no longer scampering about, when they began playing at being women. None of them imagined what would happen, the intrusion into the bedroom of one, then two, then three buddies, just when their bra had been unhooked. The curtains would be drawn to hide from the light of day, the gardener or the laundryman still at work. The girls sometimes struggled but they never screamed or called for help. They had names. Family names as respected as those of their assailants. They were girls, keepers of the morality of whole families. Anyone who dared talk about it, even to a friend—who would hurry to spread the word— would still be at fault. What were they doing alone in a boy's house? They had it coming. And those Madonna-style skirts, those low-cut tank tops. Invitations to fondling, to penetration. Their behavior was in itself an authorization. Everyone knew, girls, women practice a non-verbal language, an ancient form of speech. To decipher the morphemes, you had to interpret gestures and attitudes. To learn to read the person's sexual temperament from their face, from their curves.

Amok was thirteen years old when he was invited to enjoy the presence of a teenage girl in a boy's bedroom. Sex was one of his main preoccupations, and he sought the company of older boys who'd describe their experiences. The coarseness of their language desacralized an area reserved for adults, and this he liked: no reason to get into a tizzy about something so basic. He memorized strategies of approach, technical details, saw himself in these guys, in the place where they had their sexual adventures, and in the sometimes-fabulous situations in which they found themselves. Sex was a compelling power, its commands must be obeyed without fail, and with a submission that led to defying circumstance. Their inquisitiveness of parents, especially of mothers, made it impossible for them to do as they pleased. Mothers would be blamed for their offspring's misbehavior. Boys had to become men, but in their instruction into the great bewilderment of masculinity, they also had to safeguard the honor of the woman who'd given birth to them. You'd feel your member swelling, it risked imploding behind your fly, because you were obliged to behave yourself. A girl had stopped by to say hello, and all you could do was sit with her in the living room, watch a video over a glass of Sprite, and walk her home.

That was usually a good time to make a move, when *rythming* her back to her place. So you'd chat her up. You didn't know you could talk so much, but the sense of urgency was such that the words came of their own accord, sweet and spicy, to persuade her to spread her legs behind some hedge. To get right down on the earthen classroom floor in a nearby school that would be empty at this hour. No, no danger of sliding down the steps if she gave herself to you on the staircase without a railing that ran along the rear wall of the church. No, no, she wouldn't get pregnant, it didn't happen so easily, don't listen to what people say. Okay. Alright. Since she refused to do this hastily, would she at least agree to take it in her mouth, huh? That wasn't the way babies were made, she had nothing to worry about. Yes, you talked and talked. Until your mouth was dry, and you had no words left. You'd be smoldering inside, but you had to remain gentlemanly, overcome resistance with patience, create an opening and be ready to dive in, always make her think she was the one who made up her mind. Who decided in good conscience. You kept talking, your lips on hers, your hands on her buttocks or under her blouse. You didn't give her much of a chance. The girl's precociously well-developed body was all astir with new sensations that these caresses enflamed. It was the hormonal age, the years of being on fire. All these stories opened a continent for him to explore, possess, dominate. He couldn't wait to be there, and it showed. That's why he'd been invited into this room.

That afternoon, one of the older boys whose company he sought had given him a few coins to buy sodas at the local take-away. Amok saw himself traipsing merrily down the street, passing the shoemaker with the wooden sign *Shoe Meka*, hard to tell whether it was the Mecca of shoes or the man letting everyone know he was a shoemaker. Probably a bit of both. He'd turned at the corner, in front of old Anti Sue's yard, where chicken was smoked from daybreak on wooden worktables covered with banana leaves. When he got back, he'd found two of the guy's friends, boys he knew. The three always hung out together, out of both habit and affinity. Their parents invited each other over, the kids had gone to the same schools, what they had in common was a question that never came up. He was too young to be admitted into this circle, but he'd acquired the status of mascot by rendering minor services, accepting the role too of a zealous supporter, cheering them on from the sidelines of the basketball field. He made them laugh and he flattered them. The ones who'd just arrived drew him into the guest room, signaling him to keep quiet. One of them, the gang's technician, had turned on a radio station, but it wasn't to listen to the news or to music. He said, *Bro, ya hear me?* Left alone in the living room where one of the key scenes would be played out, their host had answered: *Hear ya loud and clear bro.* From there they could prompt him, if he happened to forget his lines. The only window in the guest room faced the garden in the back. There were tools there, but no one to look in, one of the boys smoked a cigarette, threw the butt out the window. They didn't have long to wait, they'd turned up right on time, the girl would arrive a quarter of an hour later.

He'd puked his guts out. His eyes had met the girl's, and he'd puked. He hadn't asked the others to stop, he'd run away, leaving her to the three boys who took turns getting their rocks off inside her. They didn't look at her, didn't see her, she was just a hole between legs. She wasn't in his class, but he saw her in school the next day and every day thereafter. Every time he found himself in her presence or simply saw her passing by, he threw up. And each and every time, he felt her come undone. Humiliation was a corrosive bath. Before the end of the term, the teenager had tried suicide, no one around her understood why. Amok had been incapable of telling her that his shame and disgust was at himself, not her. Ixora, upon listening to him relate these events from his past, had wanted to know the girl's name. He'd never divulged anyone's identity, it was astounding, for his silence protected no one, exonerated no one. Silence made the acts committed by those once-admired boys weigh on him all the more, and on him alone. Silence turned the victim into an unreal figure. Yet all this had happened. *If you pronounce one name only, let it be hers.* He'd done so crying, imploring forgiveness, years later, too late.

Her name was Jóng. Paula Jóng. She'd died one night at a party in celebration of her graduation from the Fine Arts school. Paula had thrown herself out of the window while her guests sat around sipping cocktails and champagne in the living room of her parents' apartment up North. Everyone thought it was sad, such a tragedy. At bottom, it wasn't so surprising, was it? She drank too much, took pills, her parents didn't know what to do, didn't understand. She'd lacked nothing. Paula had seen a psychiatrist for a while, she'd seemed to be doing better, but it hadn't lasted, no one knew why. Her body had been brought back to the Coast. Paula had never said anything. Because it was her fault. That afternoon, she'd worn a short dress that showed her legs, she'd put on make-up, a little too much, like fourteen-year-olds do. It was her fault. The fragrance of Ombre Rose perfume had wafted from her skin. She'd sat down in the living room of the villa, with the self-confidence of someone who feels at home everywhere. Because that's the way she was, Paula, before. At fourteen. A protected child, who'd been taught that the world wished her well, that it couldn't be otherwise.

She'd brought lamingtons with her, laughing as she explained that it took three tries to get the sponge cake right, that she'd never be that kind of a woman. The boy had laughed, too. Did she want to show him what type of woman she thought she'd be? Paula couldn't have guessed that there was sometimes an auditory lead-in to the mpoti. Through an elaborate radio system, networking two devices, the boys heard every bit of the conversation, the courteous opening of preliminaries. From the bedroom, they listened to what their friend and the unwary girl were saying to each other. They laughed, imagining what they would do to her, one after the other or at the same time. They were going to kombo her like crazy. Shove their ndeng in all her holes. Take her doggy-style, make her fart. Djo, *if you make her fart, she'll never forget you.* So that would be the goal of one of them. To make her fart loud and clear. They repeated words they'd heard, got themselves going. But he, he wasn't laughing. His blood was curdling. In the moment, he'd hardly believed it. For him too, the mp<u>o</u>ti was new, the boys had never described the practice in his presence.

He'd heard the word pronounced among terms for known positions. He'd thought it was a code name for one of them. *To take the girl in mp<u>o</u>ti,* was what they said, and nothing in the speaker's voice indicated clearly what it meant. Nothing indicated that the room would be bathed in half-light, that the drawn curtains would be thick enough to keep daylight out of the room, that they'd listen to *Woman Is a Wonder* by Maze, Frankie Beverly's group, that Paula would be bare chested, the boy kissing her would have slipped his hand down her panties, she'd moan, clumsy fingers would play with her clitoris, it would be unpleasant, almost painful, she'd get up to tell him, shaking her head, poking a little fun at him, the older guy, soon to be a high-school graduate.

That was when she'd seen them, shadows moving in the room, heading to the bed. Paula had wanted to scream. All she did was open her mouth, while one of the boys, the one who planned to make her expel gas, tried to persuade her not to resist. It would be alright. She'd have four times more pleasure. Paula had shaken her head. But it was all her fault. She'd come alone, to a boy's house. Good girls didn't agree to such things. Good girls didn't chase after older boys. Good girls knew how to be discreet, bow their head, wait to be chosen. Paula whistled at guys on the street, it made her laugh, she hit on them outright, took phone numbers, called them. All the guys were talking about it. No one behaved like that. A brassy one, she was. At fourteen, she was already hot, perfectly ripe. From her way of walking, of swaying her hips, they could guess she was no longer a virgin. The one who'd just thrust his finger in her slit before rubbing her clitoris confirmed: the way had been cleared. Why was she acting snooty? She'd have four times more pleasure, that's for sure. Amok had no longer been admitted into the circle.

After Paula had tried to put an end to her life, horrified by what happened but still unable to say a word, he'd repeated a grade for the first time, losing the year he'd skipped. He'd arranged to get himself thrown out. To change his environment. No longer hang out in high-society circles, find another world. It was the age of black or white, a time with no nuance, when one sees the good guys on one side and the bad on the other. To his mind, the bastards were there, behind the high villa walls, around pools, in these schools to which they were chauffeured in air-conditioned cars. Doing his best to get himself expelled from all the private institutions that would have clapped him in bourgeoisie irons, he'd engaged in an ongoing conflict with his parents and his social rank. It was when he'd ended up in a public high school that he'd made Shrapnel's acquaintance. They'd been inseparable, but to him too, he'd said nothing, about Paula. Only Ixora knew the story, he'd never seen any of the boys involved again. All of them lived somewhere abroad, holding positions in the international public sector or in finance. He'd finally pronounced their names. One of them had taken a more unusual path, since he was now an evangelical pastor, at the head of a church founded by him in a neighboring country. His congregation had a website, videos showed him bouncing around in the midst of fiery preaching or dancing, all to make prosperity rain down on his flock.

Ixora had watched some of these short films, scrutinizing the individual's face, trying to find traces of guilt, of torment. Nothing. The man was joyful. If the memory of Paula had troubled him at some point in time, all was now forgiven, the rhythms of redemption carried the minister, high, very high, as the Word ran through him. It was spectacular. Ixora had described all this to him. Amok hadn't seen these images. Once he'd moved up North, he'd put even more distance between himself and those people, had made sure he was never in places they might frequent. He'd never crossed paths with any of them, he'd been granted this at least him. He'd heard their names pronounced only by Ajar. His sister thought it was indispensable to share news with him that he'd never asked for. She spoke to him of so-and-so, you know, the son of, or the brother of. She was the one who'd told him about Paula's suicide. Ajar had been right there, in the living room of the apartment, downing her first shot of *sky*.

He'd pictured the scene from her description. Paula's red dress, a light, slinky, short summer dress. Her face against the asphalt, she could have been asleep if it wasn't for the pool of blood, a dark halo around her head. They'd tested her blood. She hadn't taken anything. She was sober. In her right mind. She hadn't screamed. If a guest hadn't seen her leap into the void, it would have been some time before anyone would have noticed her absence. The festivities were just beginning, no one was tempted to step out on the terrace in this late-spring drizzle. The walls were vibrating from new jack swing music, the catering staff hired for the occasion were passing around with canapés. There were more people than Paula even knew, that's the way it was at these parties, there were sometimes more crashers than invited guests. Paula had had cards sent out, but she wasn't the type to have them check at the door. He hadn't gone to her funeral. Ajar had dragged him to a service in a Protestant temple, before her body was sent home. He'd sat in the back row, left before the end. Paula wouldn't know he'd come. She'd never know what had made him vomit. That was the memory he'd left her, the image of herself that he'd given her.

To Ixora, and to her alone, he'd also told about his first time. There was no better expression to describe the ghastly experience that, in the comfort of the great house, was indeed an initiation. For a long time, his mind had camouflaged it behind indistinct images of a childhood nightmare. Then he'd recalled what happened and, once the clarity of the events had taken hold of his mind, the memories had never left him. Added to those that had already piled up inside him, they'd intensified the presence of the past. Amok had ended up dwelling in these remembrances, passing through the present as if through a hallucination. Only memory was tangible. With it alone, he couldn't cheat, couldn't play a role, as he did at his job. The past stood fixed, immutable. He'd spoken of it in a flat tone, Ixora's attentive listening echoing back to him his neutral, controlled voice.

A relative, on his father's side, was staying in their home for a while. Tall and spare, she looked like a dead borassus palm. Her turbaned silhouette moved without a sound through the corridors of the great house, so that she'd always creep up on you by surprise. Expressing herself in refined, sometimes abstruse terms, she had strange ways, not hesitating, on hot days, to lie half-naked on the marble floor of the vestibule. The coolness calmed her, she said, from the burning sun, but also from her inner fire. The woman's voice was husky yet soft, and a child's laugh shook her startling body. Like Sulamite and Judith, his father's sisters, she relished beer, with a prefer-ence for the brown ales that were becoming popular in the country at the time. She'd had several professions, lived on three continents, bringing back nothing from her travels besides tall tales and a scrawny body. No one had had any news of her for years, they'd hardly known where she was, and then only because someone had happened to bump into her. She'd been seen, at least six years before her unexpected return, in a clandestine casino, on a coast in the Pacific. The person who'd encountered her there had not dwelt on the sub-ject, but it seemed she ran a bar in the city, this had been said reluctantly. In the telling of these events, the word bar had a metaphorical function. What she was really doing would not be divulged. The woman was a disgrace to the family, but they had to put her up, Madame murmured in conclusion. These words had seemed absurd to him, the Mususedis were noble in name only, none of them were respectable. The Lady of the Pacific could not besmirch their honor, no matter how hard she tried. The man hadn't been able to pronounce her name the night he spoke about her, calling her only *my father's aunt or cousin*. She was unnamable.

They'd gone out to eat at a restaurant as they often did on weekends, after a show. Ixora loved the theater. This time, the play hadn't lasted for hours, and they hadn't had to go to the other end of the universe to see it, then take a shuttle back to familiar territory, wait half an hour for a cab. On evenings when attending a performance involved an epic journey, they left Kabral at Odetta's, their downstairs neighbor, an elderly woman with whom they'd hit it off. That night, they'd been able to go out together, all three of them. People took them for an ordinary family, and nothing about them belied that impression. Kabral still wanted to be read to at bedtime, the man had discovered this pleasure with his adopted son. Having put him to bed, he'd joined Ixora in the living room, to prolong these sweet moments together. It was often like this, they were happy to have found each other, and showed it with silent gratitude. It was all in their attentiveness, in the way they listened to each other's voices, to the silences too. Ixora was talkative, especially when her heart swelled with joy. The words came pouring out, with no restraint, she couldn't stop interrupting him, that was how she showed her excitement, the pleasure being only that of conversations. She lowered her head, apologized, she'd been alone for so long. It was in his presence that the lack, that the need she'd had for company became manifest. A logorrhea came over her, with words tumbling over one another, spilling out in an effort to regain lost time, reputed to be inaccessible. One secretly hoped to find it again, to plant there the seeds of rare species.

Amok laughed, he didn't mind her cutting him off. He knew what it was like to have only yourself to converse with, to spend time asking and answering one's own questions. Ixora said, *When are you going to stop being just like me?* It was all good. Them, together, it was good. Two misfits capable of inventing something livable, sustainable. Something that wasn't limited to railing about misfortune, to nursing one another's wounds. He bought flowers to sow smiles around the apartment, to thank life. He spent hours in the store before making up his mind. In winter, he usually chose hellebores and cyclamens. He felt it was important to respect the seasons, even though you could find everything nowadays, at any time of year. When spring came, he wanted to know if the nearly white, pale pink peonies would please Ixora, or if she liked the carmine color better, the ones that shed their center petals as they died. They'd drop on the table, around the vase. This melancholy sight moved him as much as an old blues tune. He bought this variety for himself, to see the opulent corolla open, watch the special way it has of losing its bloom, the last graceful act of a tragedy. After he'd bought himself a bin to grow a few of them on the balcony, he'd continued to buy cut flower to watch them live and die.

Ixora had given him back his forgotten love of flowers. Their relationship ignored the voraciousness set off by carnal desire, that craving to incorporate the other in oneself, that way of opening one's arms only to imprison the other person. Theirs was based instead on accepting the effort it took to reach out to the other, constantly, especially for loners such as they. Outside professional circles, they'd been rather unsociable.

He'd cut off all contact with his parents, receiving news only sporadically, through his sister. Ixora went to visit her mother every other month, some distance between them had become necessary. Ever since she'd left her childhood home, shortly after passing the state exams to become a teacher, she'd lived in the company of books. For his part, Amok had spent more time listening to music than breathing, of this he was convinced.

Without Kabral in her life, Shrapnel in his, their existence would have essentially unfolded within the confines of their inner worlds. This form of seclusion had suited them, and so the decision to share the same space required an initiation into relationships. They were not roommates, living together so they could have a nice apartment without breaking the bank. So, they'd told each other things. Without expecting a remission of sorts from the confession, they'd believed in the liberating power of words. They wouldn't heal, but there would be someone who would know everything about them and, even so, would not turn away. This commitment had not been formulated, no vow had been uttered. They'd taken the risk of trusting.

That night, Ixora had asked him if he'd like a cup of hot milk. He'd teased her. Did she take him for Kabral's twin? She too had laughed, her son would make a face when she proposed to give him that almond drink masquerading as milk. Only mammals lactated, and he knew almonds were oil seeds, not cows. It wasn't bad, but the child preferred what he'd always known, the thing that contained lactose. What about him? Would he like to taste her almond drink? She'd serve it with waffles made of kamut flour, a new product she'd found on the shelves of an organic store near the high school where she taught. He'd tell her what he thought. Warily, he'd taken a few morsels, then thought better of finishing his plate. It wasn't food. He didn't live to eat, far from it, but this was too much. Anyway, he wasn't hungry. Luckily, they'd eaten in a normal restaurant, where you could still find dishes on the menu that humans in this part of the world had been cooking for centuries. Potatoes, roast chicken. He and Kabral had eaten with gusto. They'd pitied her with her lentil salad.

Ixora replied that her body was a temple. Okay, so she didn't fuck, that wasn't the only source of pleasure, there was true pleasure in being attentive to what you ate, discovering new flavors. *So you get off on kamut, if I understand correctly.* She'd given him a vigorous nod of assent. That's right. He'd replied with a long teeth-sucking sound, but she'd remained unflappable. Seeing her devour her so-called waffles would have made anyone want to partake. Refusing to be impressed, he'd gone over to the turntable to put on a Curtis Mayfield record. Instead of *Roots*, which had the song *Beautiful Brother of Mine*, that made him think too much of Shrapnel, he'd opted for the melancholy *Sweet Exorcist*. Stretching out on the sofa to enjoy Mayfield's smooth soul, Amok had started thinking. The idea of deriving pleasure from kamut had been a wisecrack, at first. As Ixora brought her empty plate back to the kitchen, and he heard her running the water to wash the few dishes she'd just used, he wondered about what form his own pleasure now took. What he felt listening to music was intense, but he didn't associate it with bodily pleasure, not since the feverish days when he and Shrapnel had had so much fun. It hadn't lasted long, he hadn't been the best dancer. Even though he'd remained attached to foods containing masses of gluten and had no intention of giving up meat products on the grounds that they were full of toxins, he wouldn't have described himself as a gourmet.

Amok ate little, had no fanciful expectations from his meals. Certain dishes from the Coast brought back the atmosphere of places where he and Shrapnel ate and drank, and the high-spirited women who prepared them. He didn't feel he'd suffered much from having to do without them up North. Ixora had rejoined him in the living room. She'd flopped down on the kilim covering the parquet floor, turned over on her stomach, hugging the floor cushion like a child her blankie. Before they'd moved in together in this apartment, she almost never listened to music. Now she was discovering its interest. This didn't stop her from talking in the middle of a piece, which was precisely what she did straightaway: *What about you, where do you get your pleasure from?* Questions that were benign led to confidences that were less so, and the tranquil evening suddenly took a serious turn. No, Amok didn't think he felt sensual pleasure of any kind. He experienced desire. Hunger. Satisfaction was not deep pleasure, as he imagined it. It didn't wrench you out of yourself, before restoring you, as if you'd been resurrected. Ixora was sorely mistaken, the pleasures that she gave to her body could not replace sexual pleasure. It was something else entirely.

Sexual pleasure sometimes involved pain and did not always exclude shame. The deranged devouring by people with eating disorders was different. He'd observed both processes at work in Amandla, whose carnal existence was complex. That night, they hadn't talked about her. The question Ixora had asked had sent him traveling back in time, to a place that had been occulted since childhood. His father's relative, who they'd had to put up in the great house because the doors of the chiefdom had been closed to her. Given her temperament, the fear was she'd cause a scandal. She'd have had no scruples about letting everyone know that the Mususedis had turned their back on their blood relatives, that they'd refused to give shelter to their own kin. So the woman had come, with her weapons and luggage, literally. Amok's father had waited for her at the airport, he'd gone there in person.

The aunt had arrived at night, he and his sister were in bed. A noise had alerted him, outbursts of voices in the hallway. At first, he'd thought it was just another argument, it had become his parents' favorite pastime. Cracking open his bedroom door, he listened. His aunt's voice came to him, ordering Madame to lower her eyes in a sign of respect, *You are not my equal.* She did her too much honor in accepting to spend time under this roof. Madame had turned to her husband. *You have nothing to say? My house isn't your garbage dump.* Then she'd left them, her husband and his relative, there at the entrance. Monsieur had settled his cousin in the bedroom set aside for her. Their voices had receded, but for a long time the last words of the woman had resounded in the great house, words spewed out in a raucous roar. *Is it really Makake Mandone's descendant who speaks to me like that? I'm the one who should be complaining about being tossed into the trash by my kin. It's your presence that turns this house into a garbage dump.* For the first time, Amok had heard the name of the founder of the maternal line. It took years for him to grasp the implications of such ancestry, what it meant, on the Coast, to have the blood of a captive in your veins.

For him, it wasn't an issue. It hadn't weighed on him as much as Angus Mususedi's involvement in the colonial enterprise. When the Lady of the Pacific had arrived, he was going on eight. The cries hadn't woken Ajar, and he'd seen no point in telling her what had been said. The next morning, at breakfast, he'd discovered the aunt's face. A turban with a complicated tie accentuated the angular character of her features. She wore a black shirt with a jabot, and a burned-sienna skirt. The toenails on her naked feet were painted bright pink. Her long, curved fingernails were brown ochre. She was balancing on her chair, occasionally sinking her fork into a plate of Exeter Corned Beef that had been filled with garlic, onions, and chili pepper at her request. His father's relative hissed as she ate the dish, to get some air into her mouth which was on fire. The burning was part of the enjoyment. At its paroxysm, one of her feet, the left one, tapped to the rhythm of a song known only to her. Sweet potato fries and a bottle of brown beer accompanied the salted meat.

His sister was following him, he recalled, trailing close behind when he'd entered the dining room. The aunt had responded with silence to their greeting. Shooting an enigmatic look at them, she'd stopped eating. Viennoiseries and tartines were already set on the table, hot milk would be brought to them to pour over the cocoa powder. He and Ajar had thrown themselves on the pains aux raisins. The aunt had sucked her teeth. There were no values anymore. Now children were eating at the same table as grownups. What would come of such an upbringing? Things were out of control. *We were colonized, nde nika e titi pula kwala na di ma timba nde bakala, that doesn't mean that we've became whites.* With a gesture that she would have used to chase a fly away, she told them to clear out, to go have their morning meal in the kitchen. Diboti, the young man in charge of the service at that time of day, came upon the scene with a song in his throat, a smile on the lips. He loved the little ones. Seeing them leaving the dining room, he questioned them with his eyes, understood from their faces that Monsieur's relative had struck. He put the milk jug on the table, signaled to the children not to move, he would go at once to notify Madame. Stuck between two contradictory, equally binding injunctions, the children froze on the threshold. They owed their elders respect, regardless of their social status. Only Madame could settle the issue.

Left there with the aunt, they'd kept silent, avoided her gaze. Striking the palm of her hands together in amazement, the Lady of the Pacific exclaimed: *With a mother like yours, it's not surprising that you obey the employees.* They'd both raised their heads, staring at her, as it was forbidden to do at their age. Grabbing hold of the milk jug, the aunt had opened the window and emptied it on the hollyhocks growing outside. The viennoiseries and tartines were thrown to the birds. Satisfied, the woman had returned to her corned beef, hissing all the more, tapping her left foot with joy. It was not Madame who'd rescued them but their father, who had a conversation with his relative that Amok had not forgotten:

—Bana bam ba, They are my children.

—How can you be sure?

—I repeat: They are my kids.

—You speak of them as if you're the first to have any.

She didn't understand how the family reproached her for not doing what was expected of her. Here was her cousin who'd committed the worst transgression, and was boasting, to boot, about having produced offspring. He'd dragged his forefathers' name in the mud, all for a woman who didn't even deserve the status of concubine. Monsieur had slapped the harpy, with two sharp smacks, with an open palm then with the back of his hand. That morning, when it came down to it, they weren't hungry.

The Lady of the Pacific had kept a low profile for a few days, chewing over her rage, taking her meals alone. They found themselves left more or less in peace. Then she'd come to see him. The household was sound asleep. He hadn't heard her. Turning over in his sleep, he'd seen her, a shadowy silhouette leaning over him. He'd reached to turn on the night-light, the woman had grabbed his arm. The air conditioner had blown the acrid smell of the intruder into his nostrils. He'd rubbed his eyelids with the back of his hands, hoping it was a figment of his imagination. This hadn't made her disappear. He'd felt her climbing onto the bed, she was humming something that sounded like a nursery rhyme in an unknown language. Open vowels were repeated, always the same, again and again, there were only two or three lines. The aunt had a long dress on, maybe a kaba. She'd lifted it to straddle his body, without touching it. With her vulva against the child's mouth, she ordered him to lick it. *At least you will know how to make a woman come. Lick.* In that magnificent country on the Pacific where she'd come from, little nippers like him made their living doing this. He was no better than them. They were poor, but they had clean blood. *Lick, don't suck. I'll tell you another time how to suck. Now lick.* Of course, he wouldn't tell anyone. Of course, he wouldn't presume to repeat these gestures with a girl. *Leave other people's children alone. Do you understand me?* Stunned, he'd remained there motionless. The tall silhouette of the aunt, the turban with fringes tied around her head, formed a strange picture. He hadn't understood right away what she wanted. She'd let go of her dress to take his head in her hands, guide it between her legs. The fabric had engulfed him, he'd found himself under waves of cotton, all he could do was swim. The Lady of the Pacific held his head. The slow to-and-fro motion of her pelvis made his tongue slide from the clitoris to the slit as it got wetter and wetter. It had an acrid, salty taste and a pungent smell.

It wasn't until a year of two later that he and Ajar would discover their parents' porn video collection. None of those films showed the act forced on him by the aunt. The women didn't come like she had that night, in a muffled yowling. It was his first time. That was how he put it, in spite of the repulsion, the shame. He hadn't said anything. Children know when they can talk. In the great house, there'd been no one to receive his distress. The aunt returned, on several occasions, throughout her stay. The eve of her departure, she'd wanted to prolong what she called a game. As usual, she'd insulted him between two sighs, two moans. That's all he was good for. He was clearly his mother's son. Unbelievable that his father had married a Mandon*e*, a woman of tainted blood. It was said that he beat her. She'd have liked to see it for herself, hear the female scream, count her bumps, pick up her teeth from the floor. While his relative was around, the master of the house had decided to play the model husband, so that Madame wouldn't lose face. *Why protect her? She's impure.* He was too. Those things were in the blood. He hadn't defended himself. He hadn't denounced her. Because he knew, at bottom, what he was. *I would have denied it. I'd have called you a liar, but you'd be a little higher in my esteem. Just a bit.* She sat on the edge of his bed, legs spread apart. She was naked under the flounces of her skirt. *Come here. Take off your pajama pants. And not a peep out of you.* The aunt had wrapped a thick rough rope, smelling strongly of camphor, around his neck. She'd laughed, that was how his grandfather, Makak*e* Mandon*e*, had come to the Coast. Shackled in restraints. Like a goat that you sacrifice on New Year's Day.

She'd pulled on the rope so that he'd feel it, know the risk. She had laughed again. Her laugh was light, full of mischievous joy. *Come now, on your knees. First, lick. When I say, inside, insert your tongue slowly, turn it around inside. Come out when I pull the rope, then back in . . . You're eating me out good, little sheep. I'll let you live, but at a price. Every life has a price, even yours.* The rope had tightened around his neck, without strangling him completely. The aunt had leaned forward, had felt his buttocks first before smacking them at regular intervals, with the flat of her hand. She didn't want to dirty her fingers, she said. He probably had some leftover pieces of shit in his butt crack. She'd thought of everything, racked her brains to figure out how to proceed without leaving obvious marks, nothing that couldn't be mistaken for irritation due to constipation. All Amok could say about the thing inserted into his anus was how cold, thick, dense, and stiff it was. It wasn't metallic. It wasn't wood. He never saw or knew what it was. The child had sobbed, while she'd toyed with him, pushing, pulling, pushing, pulling. He'd left off licking, it hadn't changed, hadn't stopped a thing.

The Lady of the Pacific went wild with excitement. Many times he'd swallowed her secretions, but never had they been as abundant as that night. *To give yourself like this, you must love me in your own way. Like a dog. You know who the master is, you know it's not you* . . . He didn't sleep a wink that night. The dawn had found him feverish in bed, the nursery rhyme running around his brain. His sister informed him of the aunt's departure, shortly before the rooster's lament, while the sky still wore its nocturnal attire. He'd listened without reacting. For him, the aunt was still there. All night long, he'd wondered what she'd used to penetrate him. He'd thought of a green plantain, peeled, cut in two. She'd pressed on the round, flat end, where it had been sliced by the knife. It went nearly all the way in. From one day to the next, he'd stopped eating bananas of any sort. Without being able to say why. His mind was a blur of images from that night, from all the nights he'd been raped.

He'd relived them only in dreams, in snatches, without identifying them as memories. The face of his assailant didn't appear to him, ever. He heard girlish laughter, the tune of a nursery rhyme without the lyrics, saw himself on his knees, a rope around the neck, and woke up. Sometimes, there was no face, no voice, only a presence resembling that of an animal, a yowling that opened his eyes before the nightmare ended. When he and his sister had discovered the pornographic films, he'd watched them with interest, without questioning his fascination. He was just a child curious about the secret world of grownups. Watching these films, Ajar and he didn't express what they felt deep down. The comments barely scratched the surface of things. For reasons he couldn't explain, his desire to be the triumphant male with a horse cock delivering pleasure to women was confused with a craving to feel the effects of a correction. Coming like these men did, out of natural exhaustion from such intense physical exercise, seemed insufficient to him. He soon grew weary of watching these movies, but an obsessive curiosity had taken root, he couldn't wait to actually do it.

Now he thought his mind had come up with this as a means of defense, a way of getting past his wound. He'd had a period of amnesia regarding what the aunt had done and, from the fog of his memory, a craving had welled up, which he disguised behind good manners, an appearance of discretion. Without making things happen, he waited for the opportunity to satisfy his still-immature desires, leaped without a moment's hesitation on any chance that came his way. He'd rubbed against girls when blues were played at birthday parties. At the time, blues was the name for every slow song, and the grownups liked encouraging their children to dance in couples. Reluctant as they tended to be to mix with the other sex, most of them gave in grudgingly, making sure to leave enough room between them for a bus to pass through. The unwilling partners held each other at arms' length, on two distant hemispheres, staring off into space, waiting for the song to end.

Amok seized these occasions to discover the girl's body and his own sensations. The exercise required application, so he clung to his dance partner, it was the only way to get an emphatic result. Since the instruction to dance the blues came from above, it was hard for his partners to escape his embrace. His eagerness earned him amused, somewhat bawdy, compliments from the women dictating the rules, the older cousins whose responsibility it was to look after the little ones. Nevertheless, by the age of thirteen, he still hadn't made love, and surely wouldn't have imagined the mp_oti as a first step. It was not what he wanted. Neither the talk of older boys nor the porn films seen as a child had prepared him for it. In the movies, when the number of protagonists exceeded two, it was usually a man with several women. They appeared to be willing, even thrilled. When he'd met Paula's gaze, something had come back to him. A flash. One of those visions that he still thought, at that time, came from some murky dream. It made his stomach turn.

Later, Amok had had an intense sex life, exploring this sphere as far as he could, often with girls who were a little older, students who'd been held back several times because they'd failed the qualification exam to get into the last year of high school, or those taking their graduate exams for the third time. He waited to be chosen, let himself be courted, gave in to their desire, surprising them with his fervor, his ability to push the limits. He'd had an ardent affair with one of them, Katie, verging on the role switching that was his fantasy. Her generous curves, light complexion, and gray eyes, which made people call her a white woman of color, drove men crazy. Some had asked her for her hand, pointing to the material benefits she'd derive from such a union. Others, the less wealthy teachers, let her know that her marks would improve significantly if she treated them well. Katie turned a deaf ear to all these propositions. She wasn't interested in the men who chased after her; she preferred to choose her partners from among boys who wouldn't have dreamed of catching her eye. Sometimes she saw several at once. Who'd want to eat rice day in and day out, variety was good for her stability.

The way Katie had of declaring her intentions pleased him. *I have time Thursday at around 4 p.m., you can come by.* In a few words she'd extended both the greeting owed to a stranger you're approaching for the first time, and the invitation to get to know each other, and more. He'd smiled at her. She'd gone on, *I'm staying in Merry Widow. Go straight, after the temple, just past the fountain. Ask anyone, they'll point you in my direction.* She hadn't bothered to return his smile, this didn't unnerve him. Some young ladies didn't see why they should impose on themselves the needless lassitude of stretching their lips out and upward. Subjecting their body to too much agitation was not advisable in such a hot country. So they wore an utterly expressionless face. This attitude presented several other advantages, such as not giving the impression that they were easy, but also not betraying their thoughts.

Katie was like that. A distant observer couldn't possibly have imagined what she was saying.

Merry Widow was so named in the early sixties, when the district's residents had seen Tute show up, or at least that was the name that the woman had chosen for herself. After the burial of her husband, who'd been struck by a deadly disease, she'd refused to wear mourning clothes. The very next day, she'd put on a red dress with a bare back, her prettiest shoes, tucked a gold clutch bag under her left arm, and set off to see what life had in store for her. She'd barely taken a step when abundance came to meet her, ready to unveil its multiple faces and secrets. The woman had not repressed her curiosity.

Her in-laws hadn't understood this explorer fever, and it had upset them. Her own relatives hadn't accepted her eagerness to devour life, her repudiation of the education she'd received. The woman had gathered the two clans together and provided them with the necessary explanations. They should all keep in mind that the marriage, from which fate had liberated her after twelve years, had been imposed on her. At twenty-eight, she was determined that the mourning would not be. Her clothing would be in all colors, except the navy blue which widows were expected to wear. She had no intention of moping around for weeks on end in that house with its accumulation of bad memories. She belonged to herself, she'd waited all too long to stand up and say so. She hadn't come into the world to watch others live but to have her own experiences, which was precisely what she now planned to do, this was her last word. From then on, the doors of the former marital home had been shut to her. Her own family, who'd been forced into debt to return the dowry, let her know that she was banished. She could go wherever she damn pleased. That was how this woman, who then called herself Tutè, had shown up there. The name that she'd given herself meant *abundance*, and destiny would provide for her needs.

A man had taken pity on her and granted her the use of a few hundred square feet of land on the edge of a cornfield. At the time the city was still struggling to pull itself out of the countryside. To show that she didn't own the land on which her house would be built, it had been made in planks. With this roof over her head, Tutè had lived life to the hilt, not letting even the tiniest of joys with which life gifted her slip away. She hadn't remarried, it had brought her the first time nothing but bondage, and she regretted not having broken free of it earlier. Women had loved her because she kept secrets, paid back the money she owed, borrowed husbands only with permission and never for too long. Children had adored her, because she never held back when playing mbang, she shamelessly cheated at cards, threw the jakasi pebbles up high, and made the very best hush puppies. The men had wanted to unite with her in holy matrimony, because that's how men are, they run after what resists them, are ready to get the moon for the woman who's not asking for it. They'd had to accept her conditions. It was to them that she owed the nickname Merry Widow which wasn't a compliment. Only a murderer, only a witch would rejoice in the loss of a spouse. She hadn't cared. The creative power had covered the earth's surface with an abundance of men. There was always one in working condition when she needed company.

When she'd gone to join the ancestors, her hut had not been demolished, the women of Merry Widow hadn't allowed Kambon, the owner, to have it razed as he'd intended. The elders had threatened to show their naked behinds to anyone who'd dare, so other plans were soon found. The spirit of Merry Widow still resided there, you could hear her laughing when the sun set, crying out in pleasure when the night was past the midpoint of its journey. Some saw her often, they swore they did, in a red dress, a clutch in her hand, hailing a taxi to go dancing. In Merry Widow, the city hadn't won the battle. There remained a village atmosphere. Middle-aged women were not embarrassed to be seen in a bra. The cooking was done on makeshift hearths, for the most part three cinder blocks, set in a triangle before adding the charcoal. Meals were eaten from a single platter, a custom that was seldom practiced among Coastlanders anymore. So that was where Katie was living, that's where he'd gone to see her, that Thursday afternoon when she had some time.

They'd see each other in the room where she was staying, in a backyard of the house of an uncle who lived in the city. The room was just big enough to fit a bed, underneath which a suitcase served as a wardrobe for her clothes. Textbooks piled up high on the floor served as a support for a shadeless lamp connected to a crank battery. There were no windows, no other source of illumination, even in broad daylight. The installation worked poorly. But he wouldn't have insulted Katie by replacing it, she asked for nothing, and would have taken it badly. One afternoon of exceptionally stifling heat, while she was prolonging the pleasure of a meticulous blowjob, her tongue had grazed his anus. Had she licked the orifice inadvertently? Amok hadn't said anything to avoid shocking her, hadn't dared suggest she continue her exploration. He'd confined himself to returning the favor, hadn't asked her what she meant when she murmured, *You lick me better than a woman.* With Katie, as with the others, there was nothing sentimental, that wasn't the point. Any attempt to understand what she'd had in mind could have led him to reveal himself in return.

Amok had kept his emotions to himself, the excitement he felt performing cunnilingus, something someone had forced him to do in his boyhood nightmares. A faceless woman crooning a nursery rhyme whose words he couldn't understand. The taste, the smell of a woman's wet genitals electrified him. It all started in his head, before spreading throughout his body. He saw Katie for quite some time, nearly an entire school year. Sex with her was complete, that was the term she used, to let him know that pulling out before coming was out of the question. Sperm, as she saw it, being an essential food for a women's well-being, it mustn't be wasted. On this subject too, he hadn't asked her whether this was an ancestral belief, knowing that societies in the past attributed particular virtues to human fluids. When she'd thought she was pregnant, his panic had made him desire her less. Then, after a medical examination had confirmed that it was a false alarm, Katie's family had packed her off to their village, hastily arranging a wedding with a man who was not very fussy about her chastity. He was willing to turn a blind eye, for *the white woman of color.*

That night, he hadn't said anything to Ixora about it, but something had suddenly struck him. Amandla's physique was similar to that lover from his youth, that girl with whom he'd never been in love. And like Katie, Ixora was two years older than him. He'd never wondered what had become of her, but she hadn't disappeared completely from his life. His sexual frenzy belonged to a time long gone. When he graduated high school, Madame had congratulated him, saying that his rowdy teenage behavior had reassured her. She'd feared she'd never see him become a man worthy of the name, he'd been so taciturn as a child, so withdrawn and overly emotional. All it took were those few words for him to feel dispossessed of the freedom he'd conquered. The nights sleeping away from home, the pleasure losing himself in a girl's body, all this turned out to be a family affair. The first years in the North had been trying. First because he'd gone there against his will, then because Shrapnel, his partner in crime, had not been able to leave the country. He wouldn't rejoin him until much later, after a perilous journey that forced him to cross the desert and to reside for varying periods of time in different regions. Deprived of Shrapnel's presence, haunted by his mother's discourse, Amok had quickly opted for a different way of life. Of the insipid adventures he'd had with girls he'd met at university, he retained very few memories.

Only the time spent with Laurette came back to him occasionally, she was the one who'd vaccinated him against an ongoing relationship. Having come from a place that was exotic to him, where a few humans kept company with herds of dairy cows, she was the first in her family to go to a university. Laurette did not intend to stay there long but simply to increase her market value a bit. The young woman's single aim was marriage. A whim to find an educated spouse had taken hold of her, a man whose job wouldn't involve getting up before sunrise to milk the cows, someone who could take more than a week's vacation a year. This desire for something else, coupled with a need not to be dominated, had prompted her, due to preconceived notions, to set her sights on sub-Saharan men. At first, her sexual availability had suited Amok. But on her good days, Laurette confused love and appropriation, demanded explanations, imagined things that made her cry. On bad days, she remembered that the inequality of races was a historical given, a fact that there was no reason to question. Of course, she never uttered a word about it, it was all in her attitudes, in some allusions too.

History was thus invited into their sex, and Amok's organ was expected to feel honored to penetrate a light-brown-hair pussy. History dined in their company, especially when he took her to what she called canteens. Believing that she was living at a time when the most insignificant sub-Saharan student could become president of some new republic after completing his studies, Laurette felt cheated, and found a way to remind him that here, in her country, white woman remained superior to Black man. It was untoward—that was the word she used—that, not having understood this, he'd taken the liberty to bring her to such lowly places. Ultimately, when they'd settle down in his native country on the Continent, they'd fortunately have an altogether different lifestyle. She wouldn't work, neither outside nor in their home. An army of servants, who'd come into the world to anticipate her needs, would scramble to satisfy her. Convinced that someday soon she'd rise to the place that was hers, Laurette condescended to take a bite of her battery-raised chicken, tilted her head to the side, pouted her lips, and asked, *Will we see your parents this summer? Isn't it time for you to introduce me to them?* Taking to his heels, Amok had left the lovely lady alone to visit those olden times that shaped her outlook on the world. One day, he'd seen her sitting at a table in the campus cafeteria over an unrefined meal, showing off her engagement ring to a friend. Laurette, who had stars shooting from her eyes that were visible even if you approached her from behind, had succeeded in hooking a guy from her hometown, one whose family was comfortable and owned land, and he had studied too. Older than she, he held an executive position in a public works company. The following year, no longer engaged but most definitely married, Laurette had said goodbye to the university, without bothering to take her exams.

For a while after that, Amok had gone to prostitutes, to satisfy his hunger for sex. It hadn't been what worked for him, he didn't like paying. What he was looking for was a surrender of power. Not submission but a relinquishing of the self, a letting-go of one's identity. Madame's words that day had made it clear that it would always hunt him down, that nowhere would there be an abyss deep enough to devour it. His recourse to sex workers had confirmed this, especially when they came from the Continent. He could read their story in their eyes, he'd end up having it told to him, leaving without touching them. The young man hadn't given up, he'd explored other possibilities, notably those available via the Minitel, a forerunner in the field of online dating services. This hadn't worked out so badly for him until the day when, thinking his fantasy was coming true, he'd exposed himself more than he should have. He'd talked to no one about it, the whole thing had been so disturbing, he was in no hurry to open up to anyone. Ruling out a dominatrix promising strap-on dildo humpings that would leave him panting, he thought he'd found just the right balance with a shemale, they still used the term in those days. They'd had a few conversations via Minitel before arranging to meet up.

Amok had taken care not to share his phone number, fearing that he'd be pestered if he decided not to follow through. He showed up ahead of time in the cafe they'd chosen, hid in the shadows, waited to see her appear. She'd described herself in great detail, giving precise information as to what she'd be wearing that day too, an electric-blue dress, bright yellow sandals, she liked *flashy* colors, she'd said, using the English term. He'd had nothing against that. The taste for such colors was shared by many sapeurs but it was particularly common among women. Mabel—that was her name—turned up on time, looking exactly as she'd described herself. A real beauty. Her dark skin, narrow hips, and firm rounded rear end made her stand out. She was tall and slender, she didn't wear a wig, false nails, or lipstick. Under her bodice, her breasts looked supple and mobile. Mabel had sat down, back to the wall, to take in the room at a glance, and see him appear in turn. He'd waited for a waitress to approach her, distract her for a brief moment.

When she'd smiled at him, the room had lit up. He'd liked seeing this smile as a way of designating him as the object of her desire. The Minitel didn't allow for this, he needed contact, needed to perceive approval and consent, in the eyes and gestures. Women's desire had always aroused and fed his own. Amandla had been the only exception, a one-off anomaly. Despite Mabel's qualities, she had a disturbing particularity. Her deep voice was unmistakably masculine, and every time she spoke, Amok was so struck by it that the meaning of her words immediately escaped him. For a moment, he'd thought he'd leave it at that, sensing that the shemale would not be the creature of his fantasy: a woman with a penis. He'd let himself get carried away by his imagination, by his lack of knowledge too. Amok had pictured a perfect hermaphrodite, a body with the fully developed attributes of both sexes. In reality, he didn't care so much about the presence of testicles, having no plans for them. What he needed was a vagina whose flows would intoxicate him. What he was hoping for was a well-formed penis, so that he could experience role-switching, without further delay. To penetrate his partner and be penetrated by her in turn.

He'd seen this in a movie, one night, when he was looking around a sex shop with no intention of buying anything. The image had been a rare source of excitement, before becoming an obsession. The store clerk was watching a video while nibbling on his cold fries on top of an old sandwich. Two women, straight out of his fantasies, were giving themselves to each other, exploring all the possibilities. They were perfect, they seemed to possess a knowledge acquired from the Theban oracle, of which the gods themselves had been deprived. Their experience was undoubtedly more intense than that attributed to Tiresias by the myth, since they manifested, simultaneously and continuously, the masculine and the feminine. That was his idea of the shemale, a living miracle, a replica of the divinity. Under the images of their double genitals, without testicles, was written, in bold type, the explicit reference: Sexy Hermaphrodites. His whole being had been inflamed. It was the first time that a pornographic film had aroused a genuine emotion in him, a desire that was not the pull to crash at the bottom of the ravine he could feel yawning inside.

Until that night, he hadn't had the occasion to watch, in reality, these bodies that had often peopled his imagination. Such visions formed in his mind when he masturbated, muttering under his breath unusually crude words meant for his virtual partners, unpronounceable when fully conscious. It was always in solitude that they visited him, vanishing as soon as he'd come, and the question of knowing why came to mind. Why this desire? Why this attraction to the freaky? What he thought he knew about hermaphroditism derived from an incomplete version of the bodies seen in the film. The individuals concerned did not have two equally well-developed genitals, such figures existed solely in myths. This was apparently not the case, he'd wanted to explore this area at all costs. No doubt he'd poorly formulated the wording of his ad, but he couldn't see himself writing, *Young sub-Saharan man seeks woman, preferably of same origin, with a vagina and a penis—balls optional—for role-switching.* So, he'd pussyfooted around somewhat, evoking a gender disorder, something in-between, he wasn't sure anymore. As a teenager, he'd liked to hear crude sex talk, but he'd never had much of a talent for it. The person's origin had mattered to him. The journey being quite unorthodox as it was, he'd preferred embarking on it with a partner whose features would be those of humanity, as he'd come to know it in opening his eyes to the world.

Of all the responses he'd received, Mabel's had seemed to correspond best to what he was looking for, he'd questioned her as a matter of form, to confirm her phenotype, age, availability. Amok hadn't seen the point of asking additional, deeper questions, sitting behind the small Minitel screen. At Mabel's place, after taking a seat on a crimson armchair, over which hung an astonishing polyptych portraying sub-Saharan representations of Christ and the apostles, he'd found his fears confirmed. Mabel's penis was clearly from birth, and it was in perfect working order. The size of her testicles was such that they couldn't hide a vulva. The growth of her breasts could have been stimulated by hormones with no effect on the timbre of her voice, or, for that matter, on the small ball that made the choker she was wearing rise and fall. Amok hadn't paid attention to it right away, the tiger's eye adorning the gem at its center. You saw the stone, not the projection it masked. Confronted with the truth that was revealed to him, as Mica Paris sang *Young Soul Rebels*, Amok quickly assessed the situation, wondering how far he'd be willing to go. Mabel was standing there before him nude, a nudity that was not only physical. In her eyes, highlighted by a thin line of kohl, he could read the pain caused by the incomprehension of others, her familiarity with rejection. The world was not kindly toward her peculiarities, it felt threatened by her sensibility. But this was her. This non-compliant body was the dwelling of her spirit. Whether or not she'd had recourse to medicine, her choice had not been a matter of appearance. Her decision had been to live, to make this possible.

Mabel's beauty was not limited to the symmetry of her features, their delicacy, the harmonious whole they formed. The narrowness of her hips. The length and curve of her legs. The roundness and firmness of her behind. It was also this non-conformity to norms, the unexpected balance of primary sexual characteristics. The tip of the circumcised penis looked like the point of a weapon whose blade had been polished by use, without blunting its lethal capacity. The softness of her breasts made the promised death even more desirable. Amok had been deeply stirred, he hadn't wanted to be the cause of new injuries to someone so exceptional. After all, he'd been the one to turn on his Minitel, write this ad, say, *No, not Wednesday, more like Friday.* Knowing that he too was a freak of nature, a probable anomaly, he'd refrained from hurting her. He'd had to put his cards on the table. *Limitations free,* proclaimed the singer of *My One Temptation* and *Breathe Life into Me.* In the maid's room Mabel rented in the attic of a building on a street lined with clothing stores, two altars faced each other. One had been built to honor the sub-Saharan ancestors, the other declared her closeness with Christ, who died on the cross to redeem the sins of all. That this was not a place for banter was evident from the biblical scene in which the protagonists, wearing adire textiles, looked down at him. Without beating around the bush, Amok spoke his mind.

Mabel's male voice rang out, *No, no, no, tsst, tsst, absolutely not,* she didn't do penetration, *No way.* She was willing to suck him off, was planning to do so, and since they were talking about it, what could she expect from him? It would be hypocritical to pretend that he'd taken no pleasure in the sex, Mabel's knowledge of the male body surpassed the abilities of all the women he'd ever been with. The combination of delicacy and passion that she'd put into the slightest caress had transported him. It was firstly to express his gratitude that Amok had wanted to give her a blow job, ignoring that in doing so he'd reach a form of bliss. Mabel's skin had a sweet, tangy scent, a subtle flavor of oyster. It was especially the shape, the thickness, the reactions of this member in his mouth that had made him almost lose his mind. On the brink of inebriation, Amok had only stopped when he heard her beg him not to make her come like that. He'd turned her on her side to see her face, kiss her cheek and her temple. Then, with all the gentleness of mounting an untamed horse, he'd ridden her to the sound of *Chris'Tal*, a forgotten hit by the Parisian band Dis bonjour à la dame. Mabel had a body with perfect curves. Her breasts had reacted as expected to the touch of his hands.

Amok had noticed some light stretch marks on her rear end, which made him smile. In the old days, the Coastal People of his country sought women with such marks on their skin, seeing this as a sign of fertility. Mabel's breasts may have been genuine, one couldn't be sure, nature did troubling things at times, it was its privilege. The nape of her neck, bared by her short haircut, had responded warmly to kisses. Velvety-skinned Mabel had, moreover, the good sense not to be a talkative lover. Discovering the incomparable sensation he had in this narrow anus, the impression of drilling the perfect well,

Amok had closed his eyes, imagining himself in his lover's place, trying to discover the mystery of this other satisfaction, without losing anything of the pleasure that was his. The conjoined efforts of mind and body had brought him close to the outer limits of well-being, until the moment when, feeling her pleasure swell, Mabel had yelped before ululating in a language that sprang from the depths of Katiopa. It was at that instant, while he himself was coming, that the aunt's face had come to him, the headscarf with fringes covering his head, the flounce of her dress, the already wet vulva that she'd pressed against his lips the first time.

He'd collapsed on top of Mabel, who was disconcerted by his crying. Several minutes had passed before she dared to gently push him off her back, onto the side of the bed. Looking at him silently at first, she'd risen to go over to her altar to Christ, where she'd taken hold of a rosary. Then, she'd come back, taken him in her arms: *I know what it feels like the first time. We are God's children* . . . When she'd begun singing a hymn, her deep voice filling the small room with its sky-blue walls, Amok's sobbing intensified. It had taken him a while to calm down. Mabel had dressed, warmed something up, set the table, a wax tablecloth folded in two, which she'd placed directly on the floor. In the center, a dish contained pieces of kwanga, another some salted fish. *Come. Let's eat with our hands. When you're in pain, you need a little warmth. The cutlery is ice cold.* She'd have liked to serve him a fresh emperor bream liboke, it would have made him feel better in no time. Occasionally she made some, but never when she was seeing a stranger. The room would reek of fish for days on end, not very sexy.

Amok had put his pants back on, washed his hands in the sink, eaten without saying a word, not knowing if he was hungry. Mabel had put on a blue bazin dress, the top part embroidered in mauve. Her legs were crossed to the side, as girls are taught to do. The red-polished toenails of her bare feet gleamed like small jewels. Her short, cropped hair brought out the shape of her features, her Nubian profile, her fleshy lips. She'd said grace before inviting him to eat, smiled when she saw him examining the scenes of the polyptych on the wall: *A Black revolutionary, that Yeshua was. They're the ones who die like that.* She wasn't that much older than him. He hadn't sought to find out what she didn't say. How she'd come to this country, what she did for a living, when she began taking hormones. He hoped she wouldn't have surgery, it would be a shame for her to fit in, but he couldn't say so. Not without promising to love her as she was, every day that would follow. He had no plans, at the time, to love. Mabel didn't have any facial hair, but no conclusion could be drawn from that. Maybe she'd always be like this, a divine union of woman and man. He wouldn't know. Mabel was on her path, she was advancing, one step at a time, with more courage than he'd ever have. She might fall at times, the road to oneself being fraught with obstacles, but she'd get up, keep going. It was simple. To live. It could be as simple as a dish of salted stockfish, accompanied by kwanga.

As she washed the dishes, she softly sang *Mama Said* in a low pitch that let the high notes through in a way that revealed her range, easily four octaves, like Sarah Vaughan. Even quietly like this, she sang better than the original singer of the tune, who wasn't bad at all. Knowing the lyrics, Amok had seen a message in it, felt like a monster, even though there'd been no mention of feelings between them. He'd had the urge to defend himself with irony, to say that, according to his mother, his misbehavior was a sign of healthy masculinity. She may not have imagined that he'd take such a leap, but she'd encouraged him, something she rarely did. Amok kept his thoughts to himself, the joke didn't even amuse him. Mabel turned to him, looked him in the eye: *The thing to do first is to cry until there isn't a tear left to shed. Then, to keep still and think about what hurts. And finally, to dance, at home or elsewhere, but to dance because you're alive. That's how to chase away the pain or make a partner of it, because it always comes back. Now go.* They said see you to each other, though they didn't expect they would do so. He'd walked for a long time through the city streets, lost in thought, in exile in this world. Without reproaching himself, he'd wondered about his deeper motivations.

Amok didn't know what emotion had him in its grips, how to speak about the chill that froze every cell in his body. He'd stepped into a brasserie, ordered a sole that he didn't eat, examined each of the mental images that sprang up. That final night, the eve of the aunt's departure, he hadn't stifled his cries. He'd screamed, he'd called out. The silence of the great house had answered him, followed by the laughter of the Lady of the Pacific. *You're waking up a little late, they won't come, you know they won't come. There'll be only me.* Leaving the restaurant, he'd hopped on a bus to go home. In the elevator mirror, he'd looked at the reflection of his face only to find the combined traits of his parents. The very people who hadn't heard his cries. Who'd praised his misbehavior. In the solitude of his apartment, he'd spent a long time thinking about his presence in the world, about what he should do with it. Some questions had met with nothing but silence. Others, with answers that seemed obvious, had severely shaken him. Little by little, he'd taken the path of abstinence, which for him was not about asceticism, not a means of purifying himself, but quite the opposite. Sex had entered his life without being invited, without giving him time to understand. The episode of the mpoti which he'd wriggled his way out of without denouncing it openly, had been a warning. Incapable of interpreting it as he'd have needed to do, he'd ended up sinking deeper and deeper into an inner abyss. Amok had nonetheless come to a conclusion that what was dark in him had been consigned there by his family. That's when he'd begun to harden. In his fourth year of university, while he was completing his studies in finance purposely undertaken in one of the less highly rated schools, he'd turned himself around.

The man Amandla met jogged to control his impulses, shooting up with endorphins as if he were taking a detour, the last emergency exit. He'd been unable to resist the desire to get to know her, still blamed himself for having wasted her time. How could she have understood and accepted his neurosis? This disorder born of a long conflict with his ascendants, and therefore with a part of himself? His personality was singular, to be sure, and he thought he'd escaped any social determination. Yet the ties were there, unbreakable. Refusing to see them could not wipe them out of his memory, give him another past, a different story. There was nothing else. Nothing that he could build that would be totally disconnected from that. So, he wouldn't build a thing. He'd thought of what his sister would say, every time he criticized their grandfather, the colonialist. Ajar would shrug. Angus Mususedi may have made the wrong choice, but it was his affair, humans had the right to make mistakes. Pro-independence fighters and other pseudo-revolutionaries, she observed, would hide in the bosom of the former colonial power whenever they felt threatened. Their shame at having deserted the battlefield is what drove them to recreate it wherever they were, to try to impose elsewhere what they hadn't had the courage to build at home. At least Angus's behavior had been coherent. He was no longer of this world. Those who thought they could do better were free to do so. On this point, Amok couldn't disagree, but that didn't help him make peace with the figure of his grandfather.

Sexual pleasure, the life of the flesh, were distant memories by the time he'd met Amandla. It pained him to think of the efforts he'd made to satisfy her. He had no trouble with cunnilingus, but she wanted something else. For him, it took superhuman concentration to make her climax, pulling out without having come, which was also a problem. Like Katie, she wanted to receive her partner's semen, to feel the seven or eight spasms of the male orgasm run through her, and then both their fluids flowing out of her. Whereas others inspected the bridal sheet for evidence of purity, she liked to feel the wetness under her bottom, as the mark of what was, in her eyes, a spiritual act. It was too much for Amok, this sacralization of fucking, even though he was madly in love, he couldn't get it. All he'd managed to confide in her was his refusal to be a father. There was some truth to that. To quench his inextinguishable thirst for Amandla, the man had had to simulate once or twice, she'd left him no choice, he was sure she'd noticed, though she hadn't said anything. Most of the time, he couldn't keep an erection. That evening, the conclusion of his confession to Ixora had held in a few words: his flesh was dead. When he listened to music, the groove went to his brain, to his heart perhaps, in a metaphorical way. The rhythm didn't go down into his limbs. He didn't miss sexual pleasure, not anymore, he'd done without it for so long that he wouldn't know how to find it, where to go looking. On the other hand, he didn't intend to live without Ixora. With her, he hoped to see Kabral grow up. Without her by his side, fatherhood seemed an insurmountable challenge. Sharing the education of his son with Madame was inconceivable to him. Alternating custody, in addition to being disturbing for Kabral, didn't appear to be an acceptable way of life in this country.

He also needed her for himself, for what she now represented. Of all the women he'd known, Ixora was the only one with whom he could be intimate without any question of sex. Their affection for each other would not be threatened by the pull of the flesh. She'd never experienced the pleasure of an orgasm, had no idea what it meant, since she imagined it was comparable to the pleasure she had from her kamut waffles. Once she starts her job teaching at the Northern high school, everything could fall into place. For this, he'd need her forgiveness and to leave the great house without delay. It had been madness to go there. His childhood home couldn't accommodate the new life that they'd promised each other. It brought him back to the past, kept his head under the cloudy waters of the family's history. He'd have to try his luck. But what if Ixora rejected him . . . Seeing his father didn't seem so urgent anymore, it wouldn't change what he did, wouldn't erase the blows to his partner. No matter how hard he tried, Amok couldn't see what words he could pronounce to convince a woman he'd beaten and left for dead in the mud to stay with him.

The men of his father's generation, who brutalized their wives, kept a hold on them in various ways. Ixora owed him nothing. Their son was hers to begin with, even though he'd adopted him. And to him, to little Kabral whom he cherished, what would he say? Out of all people, he knew from experience that violence within the couple destroys the children. Admittedly, Kabral hadn't witnessed the scene. The child hadn't experienced the fear and terror that gripped children whose parents tore each other apart in the adjoining room. This was cold comfort. Even if Kabral's mother survived her injuries, there may be scars. He wouldn't lie to him. He would ask for forgiveness from Kabral too. The child had chosen him. It was thanks to Kabral that the prospect of a peaceful, even happy, life had taken shape. The mere thought of these conversations made Amok's heart beat wildly. Not from nervous anticipation or anxiety, but from terrifying lucidity in face of his responsibilities. There was no way out, the stakes were dizzying.

The sky had the white hue that the sun bestows on it at noon. Voices reached his ears, whispers, like when he woke up. He looked around, saw only the garden with royal palm trees, and, quite close to each other at the back, two outbuildings that might serve as sanitary facilities and a tool shed. Maybe one of these shelters was used as a granary or pantry. Judging from the layout inside the hut, Continent Noir's madness did not preclude order or logic. He knew how to live in this world. Maybe he simply had a foot in the other, and the oscillation between the two made him hard to grasp for those who'd banished him from their midst. At least they hadn't made an attempt on his life. Amok remembered the stories his father told, after playing seesaw with Ajar and him, and giving them ice cream and pastries. Nodding his head while his children ate their treats, the man spoke of yesterday, of today, of times that you wondered whether they had been or would ever be. His imagination was as fertile as his memory was true. As a child, Amok loved listening to him. His father's voice, a weave of silk and leather, was reassuring. It contained a softness that soothed, a strength that protected.

As a boy he hung on his father's words, let his voice penetrate him, nestled inside it. In the memory that came to mind, his father talked of life in days gone by, the way punishment was inflicted on perpetrators of acts that seriously threatened the group's cohesion. There were no prisons to lock them up for life, such a practice was unknown. And for crimes that were considered unpardonable, there'd be neither remission nor a death sentence. The person who'd been found guilty was led out of the village, where he was given a ration of food. Then, the direction to take was indicated to him, he was to walk until his steps could no longer carry him, and never again appear among those who had been his people. This banishment, serving for the group as a symbolic execution of a harmful creature to which it had given birth, left the offender a chance to redeem himself. If he survived the journey, the outcome of which no one knew, he could choose to make amends.

Continent Noir had not gone very far from his birthplace, since what he'd been accused of was not a major offense against the divine. In the past, he wouldn't have been banished at all. People were not driven away simply because they were not quite right in the head. Amok's thoughts circled back to his father, this great thwarted love. What could they say to each other? In the end, he didn't want to question him, ask him what had poisoned the sap of the family tree. Doing so came down to regarding his ancestors as more than merely humans who preceded him on earth. Genealogy became an ontological reason, a power in its own right, which cleared individuals of their responsibility. The bad blood inherited from his fore-fathers hadn't done a thing. Amok had struck Ixora because he'd lost control of himself. He'd abandoned her there in the mud because he'd grown accustomed to withdrawing into himself to avoid conflict, pain, and shame. He didn't know exactly where he was, but the time had come for him to leave this place. Return to life. He still felt that there was a monster dwelling inside him, but he no longer saw it as being born from the silent experience of the men in his family. The animal was him. It was his aberrant double, conceived by his morbid melancholy. Would Ixora accept to share the life of this other inside him? If she consented, would he be able to get rid of the beast once and for all, and be simply a man who loves flowers and music? Something was missing in his reasoning, he could sense it. His thinking went one way, then another, came back to the starting point. This confusion would persist until he got moving.

Without conscious thought, he stood up. The wooziness that had compelled him to stay in bed was gone, he felt no shooting pains. As he was about to take a step forward, to go find the nameless woman whose features were those of Ayezan, Continent Noir sprang out of one of the huts at the rear of the garden. The man came running, stood right in front of him without a word. Amok kept his calm. Dressed in black sweatpants, bare-chested and barefoot, Continent Noir held an old ghetto blaster on his right shoulder. No sound came out of the player, but Continent Noir was bobbing his head to the beat, looking Amok in the eye. He introduced himself again, saying that this house was his, that he'd built it with his own hands. It was his father who'd given him his unusual name. He hadn't really known him. The man, who'd come to the region with a group of his compatriots, had returned to his country once his work in the mines was done, leaving behind a son whom he wouldn't legitimize. As long as he'd stayed here, the community from which he'd chosen a concubine had not mistreated the child. There'd been whispering in the huts when the father, refusing to declare his son's birth at the registry office, had settled for an improvised ceremony, during which, officiating alone, he'd given the child the name Continent Noir. The foreigner had laughed, was what people said, presenting the baby to the earth and the wind, they'd smiled to accompany him, to share in his joy, without really understanding. One morning, he'd packed his suitcase. A family far away was awaiting his return, it was out of the question for them to hear about the existence of a child of impure blood. He'd be dishonored, over there, in the land of the rising sun.

The mother had been lucky. A man from the village, who was sensitive to her disgrace, had taken her as his fourth wife, the family hadn't asked for a dowry. The child, whose father had deemed him unworthy to bear a name from his nation or follow him there, had become a burden for his loved ones. Continent Noir had not gone through initiation with the young people of his age group, since knowledge is not passed on to degenerates. They'd tolerated him until he was fifteen. *The first thing, when I got here, was not the house. That I did afterwards. To begin with, I circumcised myself. As I healed well, I stayed here. The place where I buried my foreskin is my home. This is the land of Continent Noir.* He never felt lonely. Sometimes he walked around aimlessly, for no other purpose than the walking itself. That was how he'd discovered that other territory, the State, the one he would have been a citizen of if his birth hadn't been hidden, the one where his home and his meager possessions were found. He'd always come back here. Buried, in the earth, his flesh called out to him. He wasn't ashamed, neither of his name, nor of his history. It was his destiny.

Continent Noir sat down, all the time holding the huge boombox on his shoulder, his hand clinging to the handle. *I told you, you had a dazzlement. You weren't the first, you won't be the last, it's the road. It was carved out at the center of the masked village. Previously, when there were still people and life, I mean before before.* With his free hand, the man indicated the distant past to which he was alluding. *Before, when they were taking people like one picks ripe mangoes, the village disappeared. The elders of this area held the secret. A light shone so brightly that the manhunters were blinded. The village went into hiding. So that was where the colorless put the road. In the middle of the village. The people went away, they left the light.* Amok remained silent, the man stopped talking. Pressing a button on his ghetto blaster, he began to speak again, trying to cover up Bobby Hebb's voice singing *Sunny* with his own. *We don't know. We've lost the secret of the old fathers of before. But sometimes, we hear things, spirits send messages. They can also send someone. You know this song, don't you?* He said that he was listening to this song, playing in a loop on his radio, when the invisible one had spoken to him. The words had crept into the lyrics, that's how speech went about addressing him, because he never listened to anything that wasn't musical, what's more it asked him not to reply, it was pointless.

About the dazzlements, Continent Noir had still more to say, before coming to the reason for its presence. Now some claimed that these luminous manifestations had only started after a famous singer's ashes had been partly scattered here. The diva, who'd died seven years earlier, would come back to life during storms in dry season, when an unexpected downpour pummeled the Coast. The radiance you perceived came from her and her music, she and her music were what you gazed upon behind a curtain of rain. Seeing the music could no doubt disturb unwary drivers who ventured here at night.

Some versions of the fable said that she played the piano standing up while spinning around naked in the rain. That was utter nonsense. Continent Noir gave no credence to such gibberish spread by the women hereabouts. They said they'd asked the ngambi. The oracle had revealed the name of a singer they'd never heard of, which should be proof enough that they were telling the truth. The artist had requested that her ashes be scattered in three specific places in Katiopa. The ritual should have been performed in the big city, but local dignitaries, some of whom remembered the lady's lack of restraint, had feared that, even from the other world, she might upset the established order. Just think, she'd been seen, this sister from the other shore, dancing naked on tables. Nevertheless, they were not about to violently offend her by refusing to receive her remains. So they threw her here, in the bush, without beating the drum or singing a song. According to the women, Eunice Kathleen Waymon, also known as Nina Simone, projected her blinding light so that she could be seen in the places she loved, at the risk of killing the reckless who drove their cars when the rain came down in torrents, right in the middle of the dry season.

Women today would do anything to draw attention to themselves, give themselves a sense of importance. He, Continent Noir, knew the truth. His ghetto blaster was a direct line to the invisible one. Bobby Hebb's tune was ending on a riff lifted from the James Bond theme, when he decided to deliver the message of occult plans. Continent Noir stood up, took a step forward, put his player down between Amok and him. After this solemn gesture, the man retreated, held himself bolt upright. The voice of a radio show host announced the next track, *A special piece of funky music that I've held in reserve just for you, music lovers will appreciate it. Here's Come On Down, by Greg Perry.* The very first notes brought tears to Amok's eyes. Obviously, given that Continent Noir had introduced himself as a madman and never stopped confirming this diagnosis by his behavior, nothing justified such an emotional response. Moreover, Amok didn't believe in the invisible, in the dead who, having never departed, resided as much in the brightening darkness as in the gathering darkness and, no doubt, in Continent Black's ghetto blaster. And yet, if Shrapnel had wanted to signal his presence to him at this moment, he'd have chosen *Come On Down*. First of all because he loved the song so much, and then because the lyrics contained an exhortation to get his two feet back on solid ground and face reality. It was a song of manly love.

Knowing that his love is attracted to another man, the lyricist tries to remind her of a truth that she's neglecting to take into consideration. This woman belonged to him, maybe she'd taken drugs, was having hallucinations, whence his exasperation: *Get your feet back on the ground, Stop your fooling around.* Amok also loved the groove of this forgotten song, the pleas of a man who, fearing he was losing his heart's chosen one, would never utter words like: *Laisse-moi devenir l'ombre de ton ombre, l'ombre de ta main, l'ombre de ton chien, Ne me quitte pas.* If Shrapnel was really there, they would have had one of their interminable conversations about the history that led Blacks to inhabit their masculinity in such a loud way. Everything had been taken from them, they possess only their bodies and souls, and their women less and less. Amok would have answered that history had nothing to do with it, that men everywhere were phallocratic, that they were set on remaining so, that masculinity undid most men. He felt heavy-hearted yet had a mad desire to laugh, and say, *You're such an idiot.* But Shrapnel wasn't there. There before him, Continent Noir, imperturbable, hadn't budged an inch, and in the sky, where the sun's radiance had obliterated the blue, no cloud had taken the shape of his brother-friend's face. The radio host didn't announce the next track. Before Amok had time to say a word, Continent Noir had turned around and ran back from where he'd come, the ghetto blaster pressed against his ear. There was nobody but him, alone under the colorless sky, amidst a silence so great that he thought he could hear the blood flowing in his veins.

Royalty Jam

Chorus

He'd tried several outfits before settling on this pastel-yellow suit Found it gave him a Luther Vandross look The soft tone brought out the black of his complexion Mahogany brown with red undertones

Wearing colorful clothing was not especially daring Witness the elegant *ambianceurs* rivaling each other with outrageous attire

Bwana had imposed his clothes But his idea of good taste had not taken The ancestors had not been defeated They had left their mark on souls Love of finery and perfumes An innate talent for flamboyance Dress as language

These traditions were being revisited Reinvented Identity shifts expressed in styles of dress They were not stated quietly

Sometimes there was nothing to say Sometimes dressing seemed less an art than an expression of mental illness Regal did not like judging He refrained from it Absolutely Cherished liberty

But all the same

The spectacle of those who called themselves *lookers* plunged him into a bafflement verging on anxiety No doubt he was old-fashioned Appearances notwithstanding A bit classical

The looker made a point of pushing the limits He had to shatter the three-color scheme That inescapable rule of elegance It did not concern him

All that mattered was the look

A beyond down here below Mismatched shoes over printed socks Striped tie over a diamond-pattern shirt A polka-dot jacket to top it off More than four colors without counting the pants And toting a heap of jewels Gourmettes Chains to boot

Especially chains

Then there was the hairdo It defied description A shriek too shrill to be understood It just attacked the ears Like the bewitching rhythm of certain local bands

Regal preferred the smooth sound of Luther Vandross

Forever living

His gaze drifted about The modesty of the apartment The computer that would be outdated before having been paid off The desk taking up the entire living room The spartan furnishings of the bedroom where he was A futon on top of a tatami A ndop for a blanket

He folded it every morning Used neither sheets nor pillows No one was inconvenienced He never had strangers over

Only a few of the locals were given permission to enter his place Little Jamika would draw in a corner while he read Her mothers would come pick her up Then there was old Kambon who rented the place to him That was about it His apartment was his private space

The place held his precious and abundant wardrobe His research work It didn't earn him a living Hard science was not popular in this country It was white man's business People who said such things knew nothing of themselves He didn't waste time contradicting them

Their ancestors had invented nothing Of this they were convinced

He understood the misgivings The expression of uncon-scious wariness Science had played dirty tricks on the people of the Continent It had fabricated race and eugenics Sterilized women Inoculated the sick with dubious remedies Viruses that appeared only in them As if by chance Experiments conducted Under cover of vaccination campaigns

White man's science

His magic

Regal taught at the university to support himself He'd been hired after completing his thesis A miracle in a country where everything was secured by cooptation His meager remuneration was seldom paid on time He loved his research Speaking in public was not his forte

He spent many hours preparing his courses Wrote them out so he could distribute copies Made himself as available as possible to his students Saw himself at their age Doing his best to look well-kept Concerned with his image It was important The way one had of carrying oneself In front of the youth of this Bruised country The words that one used To speak of oneself

He didn't think of himself as destined to make good triumph in the world Far from it Took his part in the chaos Some of his colleagues were simply imposters Others evinced impoverishment elevated to a system In the ever growing ranks of poor wretches cheated by the regime A dictatorship so sure of its power that it no longer silenced the press

Recent protests that swept the country had been brutally repressed The faith of the people in a future had been undermined

Broken

Now everyone inhabited the narrowest Possible view

Of oneself

The look signaled an awareness of this

All Regal could give his students was an idea of dignity He possessed nothing but himself His head held high His straight back His impeccable suits with their somewhat outdated cut Tailored from old patterns Outfits from the time when he dreamed of buying such clothing It was his only folly Luckily his rent was low Basically a contribution to the functioning of the community

The inhabitants of Merry Widow had formed a non-profit Everyone gave what they could afford They trusted each other more or less on that count The money collected served for cleaning common areas Transportation for schoolchildren

Medical care The elderly women always had something to eat Even when their salaries were held up Nothing was lacking

He'd lived for a time in Old Country Another district of the city But Old Country was not for him Men were welcome Contrary to what people said The women who founded the community had one demand from people of the masculine sex That they should live in agreement with their *other side*

That's what the elders told him when he arrived They provided him with the necessary details The man's agreement with his other side did not mean that he took himself for a young lady It was not a matter of such trivialities Their concern was with inner harmony

The soul that had incarnated in a masculine body had come into the world to have the experience of a man's life They made no objection to that It was the law Yet it was important to understand what a man's life was What it meant to be a man Not a male The other side was the power that made men

The matriarchs refused to use the expression feminine force Rejected this term as misleading The energy in question did not belong to women They did not always manifest it in the best way They had not been its most discerning guardians

Males hadn't given birth to themselves They were born of women's authority It was sacrificed to the sons they'd raised They were given as husbands to other women Males had come into the world when women had accepted to be men's property Fathers or brothers who swapped them for possessions Husbands who bought them They were now the zealous minions of the power that oppressed them They'd perverted the name of woman

Regal was but a young adult at the time Not understanding a word of what the elders were saying Too exhausted by his worries to decode their language He came from a different world From a down to earth concrete life A world that had little use for the principles evoked by the Old Country matriarchs

The old women had put him to the test before approving his admittance They'd observed him Probed him One of them had come to see him at the end of nine weeks

He was waking from a nap

Sisako Sone's silhouette had appeared The door frame turned this sight into a pictorial work Strange Uncanny Shapes made her recognizable

The contour of her body

The flounce of her long skirt

There had been no color

Her clothes must have been red or blue

The acting nganga had declared *The matriarchs decree that you are a whole man You are at home in our home*

So Regal had lived there Sheltered There'd been children's laughter Circumcised youth wearing a wrapper tied at the shoulder Young girls with belts of beads around the waist Infants whose hiccups were calmed by placing a piece of white thread on their fontanel

There were women everywhere That's what made tongues wag most Out there In the city And even in other regions

People talked and they talked gibberish about the women of
Old Country

Word of the legend had been sown throughout the city
Had sprouted in the red earth of back alleys The brown dust
of beaten tracks The thin layer of asphalt of the main arteries
It had grown Produced robust trees The legend was what was
known of this community It was told with pinched lips While
spitting on the ground While repressing the urge to retch

Hmm the gynecocracy of Old County Oh the deviancies
of Old Country They regretted the good old days of punitive
excision That would have made them stop these perversions
Those women of Old Country It would have relieved them of
an all too prominent clitoris That thing that thinks it's a ndeng

Regal never said he'd been a resident of this village of she-
devils That it had been a haven of peace for him A paradise
conquered by individuals bold enough to shape a universe to
the likeness of their dreams

He'd left Old Country for reasons of profound incompati-
bility It wasn't obvious to anyone He alone knew it He said
nothing because he did not want to appear ungrateful Old
Country was too regulated for him Too spiritual too

Regal had a rebellious streak Little did it matter that his
completeness had been appreciated He had no desire to live
in agreement with this other side whose vibration he didn't
feel The feminine energy The idea seemed odd to him He felt
like a concentrate of masculinity That and that alone pushed
him to other men He'd kept all this to himself to have some
peace Someday he'd leave As soon as he felt ready He knew
this right from the start

Old Country empowered him to accept with no shame his attraction to other men It had taken years It was mainly Sita Toko who spoke to him of these things He could feel passionate about men Have sexual relations with them There was nothing wrong with that It was his way of loving

The fact of being incarnated nevertheless imposed on him the obligation of procreation Of giving life in his turn He should copulate with a woman Make her pregnant Take care of his progeny Become a father Sterility itself didn't deliver him from paternity He must look after children Be called *dad* Protect advise educate Set an example

Sleeping with a woman wasn't impossible for him It was not what he preferred but he was capable of it On the other hand being called *dad* bothered him Regal didn't understand this duty to form a family He'd left Old Country the day he turned twenty-seven He'd gone to Sita Toko's at daybreak Had said *I'll visit you at the shop Thanks for everything* And he'd left That's how he'd landed in Merry Widow

Unlike Old Country this district had a fragrance of sulfur that stung the nostrils of all who adventured into it

Here everyone lived their own way Even after they'd decided to pool certain resources You could be half a man three-quarters or not There was a place for one and all A boozer lived next door to the Pentecostal church Sunday morning the pastor and his flock would leave one and go to the other No questions asked People went to see the spell caster or the nganga What did it matter Their missions were complementary Prostitutes lived in the same courtyard as religious bigots Some were both at the same time The sauciness of exchanges did not leave anyone indifferent

One called out to a neighbor saying *You there* lep mon gars *Go get your own guy There are men all over the place* And the other flung right back *I picked him up on the road There was no label on his body Anyway I didn't see your name* And the girls were at each other And the torn-out weaves of hair went flying And the scarlet false nails vanished in the dust And they threw sand into each other's eyes Bit each other's throats Tore the semblance of a t-shirt sticking to a small piece of the body That was Merry Widow for you

Life had left a touch of filth on the souls A ray of light too at times Old Country's renewal of ancestral morality had no purchase here Merry Widow was a chaos-world A present born of itself valiantly heading to an uncertain future Not chicken at all Merry Widow was this place of urban savagery An anti-futurist state of nature A tangle of contradictory possibilities Roots turned into rhizomes to spawn who knew what

Time would tell

That's life The dance of humans Sparks flying from their friction The inevitable unforeseen

Each had something to hide Beauty to reveal Each knew oneself to be impure Defeated time and again Each had a power deep down inside A form of grace This permanent disorder didn't stop them from contributing to the communal kitty It didn't stop them from tilling the soil in the garden whose crops were equitably divided They could come to blows Make the sharp blade of a shank flash in the night This didn't bother

Regal That violence rubbed shoulders with kindness was reassuring That people were capable of the best and the worst

He felt free The residents of Merry Widow's plank houses did not expect his semen to be productive He could squander it to his liking Evenings at GeeBees made this possible Sometimes he hooked up with people elsewhere Looking for pickups at the dance clubs of the big hotels

This happened only on nights when he felt the shadows of the past tugging at him That was when Regal needed to feel those other skins Get inside those other bodies Hear himself refusing to be paid Invited to diner Everything was fine He was there for the pleasure For pleasure alone He needed nothing They wouldn't see each other again during the guy's stay That wasn't the point He just needed to fuck someone who desired the same

He came straight home afterward As soon as it was over No matter the time Back to his lair His refuge And this taste of defeat left him GeeBees was a blessing There he maintained his dominant posture The role that gave him a sense of security But sex at GeeBees was fun There was nothing at stake besides pleasure The place was not open to foreigners No tourists there out for a bit of slumming No expatriates trying to conduct an ethnological survey at a minimal cost

GeeBees was the realm of Akata He was not alone in seeing this self-acceptance as a victory With others like oneself Nothing to do with reconnecting with practices known to the ancestors No one cared about that The regulars were trying to be themselves Nothing more To live their lives Share breakfast together Go home with a happy heart and a sated body Ready to face adversity Especially when their penchants were known outside the protected circle of GeeBees

Regal didn't open his door to his partners from GeeBees He had more in common with them than a type of sexuality How they'd discovered it How they'd each strayed on the road to finding themselves The shame The wounds The grief flooding in Again It wasn't his thing People unburdening themselves Listening to others telling their stories Crying with them

The place known as Merry Widow was a paradise A dream land A level had been added to the house where Tute lived The woman whose nickname had become the name of the neighborhood That's where he spent his days peacefully His apartment overlooked what was once a cornfield The residents had turned it into a vegetable garden They took turns Everyone had a stake in it Regal had never seen a two-story house built in carabote Old Kambon who owned it had already lent it to Tute back then

The man boasted about the great idea he'd had Ecology was a big thing up North His house was right in the groove By enlarging it he could promote a new way of life The foundations were reinforced to support another floor The boards were made of thicker plywood than usual Solid logs visible here and there reassured the fearful It was an enhanced house in carabote With no chemical treatment A living house

The idea of opening up the ground floor had come to the owner while watching a report on TV A short feature on the evening news On the cable TV stations that deliver the madness of the world right into your home

In every format and color imaginable

This report then It showed Northerners steeped in post-modern well-being Yearning to get back in touch with nature knowing it was irremediably polluted They turned their back on the neoliberal system that suffocated them Ate raw food because nourishment must live It too Including inside the body Eating dead comestibles was harmful You could die from it That was not the fate of the human being Death was heresy

Only nutriments that can reproduce when they're put into the earth should be eaten That was the path to permanent regeneration To eternal life This diet put an end to fat And a good number of diseases if not all It also brought constant joy Depression was defeated Definitively All it took was a handful a day of sprouted seeds sprinkled onto slices of heirloom tomatoes

The man watched stupefied The belated about-face of those who had gone around the world Covering life with concrete Deviating watercourses Making night itself disappear Burying their toxic wastes underground This colossal undertaking accomplished over generations now seemed unworthy to them They were not going to apologize Simply change their tune That's what they called civilization

Treading on everything

To realize some centuries later that they'd destroyed Life Beauty Greatness And that none of this was exterior to them They'd caused their own death With each crime perpetrated

The inventors of progress now wanted to live in carabote houses *Yep son I swear I saw it with my own eyes* Those shacks were the same Exactly the same as the ones in which the poor people of Merry Widow lived Regal would feel good here Kambon was sure of it He shouldn't forget to like the old man's social network page That'd be cool

The man wanted to attract Northerners who were into green tourism Rent them rooms with no amenities Just the wall The bed The mosquitoes The geckos A breakfast guaranteed with no gluten no animal proteins no cereal of any sort Meals with nothing if that's all that was required to satisfy them It was simple here Easy as 1-2-3

His sons would act as guides for these authenticity-seekers The hikes would be so exhausting they'd be babbling their thanks when they were brought back to their rooms Here On the ground floor of what had been the Merry Widow's house The great of this world were willing to repent for the damage they caused to nature which was not about to recover They denied humans healing words So be it They'd pick their pockets They'd take what they wanted without asking It wasn't much in the way of justice but what the hell

They'd keep their thoughts to themselves when the others spoke of safeguarding the environment for future generations They wouldn't tell them that here they were looking forward to the future Come what may They were ready They would survive it like the rest As for the generations to come They'd manage One way or another *That's for sure* Old Kambon was hoping to reach a critical mass of followers on the web To establish his credibility Publicize the existence of what he modestly named the *Merry Living House* The word widow did not go over well One of his children advised him to leave it out *Merry* jazzed it up with a pleasant scent of relaxation

Regal had laughed aloud It wasn't in Old Country that he'd have met anyone like this

Life was as brutal outside the neighborhood as in it Levity had packed its bags with the nineteen-eighties He'd never known what it meant to be carefree But sometimes a certain light-heartedness had floated in the air Not anymore Each new day confirmed this fact Tonight in particular he was over-whelmed with nostalgia He was getting together with an old friend A guy who made him slide back into adolescence They'd met only once in the past It had been so unforgettable that both thought of it often

Life had arranged a reunion for them Almost in the same circumstances Like in the past they were waiting for their turn in an administrative center They recognized each other right away The man had asked about his passion for science No one else was interested He never had the chance to speak about it His solitary passion In his wildest dreams he wouldn't have imagined that anyone would want to support him finan-cially This single thought brightened his life as much as it hurt him

It was easy for this dude born into a wealthy family He'd won the scholarship that he himself would have needed Regal didn't have very friendly feelings toward the man He hadn't resented him at the time It was just the way it was That was life He saw things differently today He'd often recalled their meeting The name of the scholarship awardees had been read aloud to the young people gathered from all over To find out if the country had wagered on their talent If they'd be given a chance to excel

He'd graduated high school with outstanding grades But hadn't been selected The other one had His parents had connections Regal's were farmers who'd received each announcement of a new birth as a fatal gift from God One more famished stomach that would grumble with hunger They'd named him Charles-Bronson Because life would thrash him every time it could He'd have to be thick-skinned like the characters played by his homonym

Amok was now Monsieur Mususedi Son of his forefathers Man of his caste These roots authorized him to flout the rules To go in person to the administrative offices To associate with people who were not from his circles They saw each other several times Regal felt Amok's guilt It hadn't been expressed in words There'd been that offensive thoughtfulness That way of paying for his drinks The invitations to the Prince des Côtes restaurant As if it was everyone's dream As if it could make up for the injustice of the past

He'd spoken of his research out of politeness Maybe also to show off a bit He'd regretted it afterwards That he hadn't been able to own his position as a small-time university professor He'd needed to add luster to it all So he'd mentioned his invention The fellow had found it marvelous Impressive Really *I'm not surprised coming from you* A few days later he'd proposed to finance it He had to apply for a patent That was the first step Make sure that no one could claim credit for his innovation They were to get together very soon to talk it over

Regal had felt like being well dressed for the meeting Not looking like a beggar Not giving the other the chance to make amends He was not about to facilitate this bourgeois redemption Everyone has his own cross to bear That was life The idea of putting a touch of Kid Creole on Luther had delighted him He'd chosen an appropriate hat Then had opted for the contrast of classic shoes Black Stan Smith to go with the t-shirt

He'd stepped back to look at himself in the wardrobe's full-length mirror Perfect He shimmered gracefully Without lapsing into a look He congratulated himself In all modesty He'd seen the sky darken Out the window Abruptly Dark gray masses converging Like huge soiled cotton balls It wasn't the season Yet the storm loomed Hard and heavy

Regal had hurried out He didn't have a car Merry Widow was a good distance from the city center Old Country had come to mind Without knowing why Maybe because he'd been welcomed there that year when he and Amok had met He'd just turned eighteen Had graduated with honors His family had gathered together They'd invested quite enough in his studies They'd said so already at a previous family reunion Now he was a man He'd have to earn a living

Nobody from his family had gone beyond elementary school They hadn't the means to send him to study abroad Or even locally They barely understood what he meant when he talked about scientific studies They'd been okay with waiting for the state scholarship decision Now it was known The young adult had to assume his responsibilities

The uncle who'd put him up in the city while he was in high school had found work for him A good job The family was happy to announce the news to him A hardware dealer was willing to hire him to do the accounting He'd also take care of orders An ideal situation for a *long pencil* like himself

They'd broken out in applause Burst out in song Vibrant and vigorous He was going to be able to support his parents Be their security in old age A rock to which their laminar daily existence could cling That was the meaning of life Human beings came into the world to take care of their forebears Give birth to descendants who would do the same Living meant entering this dance

They had a feast

There'd been meat That one-of-a-kind braised pig that was a regional specialty Goat pepper soup Porcupine with pumpkin seeds Game straight from the countryside An orgy in anticipation of what his income would enable him to provide Soon Often They'd spent an exorbitant amount of money for this festive meal By way of showing confidence in the future In his family this is what giving amounted to An investment This Regal knew long before that day

He'd gone to the hardware dealer That provider of a good job It was a street stall not a store At the end of the day it had to be folded up Then it became a chest serving as storage Wheeled away in the evening It spent the night in its owner's garage It would be his job to go get it Set it up early in the morning Monday through Saturday

The young man had wondered what kind of orders such a stall could accommodate Until the day he was asked to go door to door Push the merchandise Get people to buy They always needed something Nails Bulbs Wire Some couldn't travel Many couldn't afford to pay They'd be encouraged to put down a deposit Even a small one That's what taking orders meant The deposit amounted to an outright purchase They'd see these customers again and again until the last payment They'd be offered something else shortly before the final due date In order to anticipate their needs Or invent them They always owed a little money

A good job Ideal for a *long pencil* Chase the poor Squeeze money out of them Keep records of their debts Claim payments relentlessly With a smile But firmly Regal couldn't see himself doing this He'd sold his own flesh Becoming an agent of consumerism seemed much more degrading Those who were presented to him as potential customers mainly needed assistance

His relationship with the uncle who was putting him up was not great This relative had found him a job to get his money back Then see his nephew clear out as soon as possible He hadn't waited to be driven out The city streets seemed less hostile to him than the family circle where he'd have no one's approval It was the long school break Little by little he'd given up on the possibilities that he would have had abroad Decided to enroll in the local university

Regal had wandered around for several days Determined not to spend any money Not as long as he was homeless Without a lasting solution He had some *dos* from his disreputable work He'd decided to put an end to that Already before leaving his uncle's house To feel entitled to touch other men he wouldn't prostitute himself anymore He'd walked aimlessly Needing to devise a plan Nothing had come A complete blank

In his misfortune luck had smiled on him He'd passed out in the vicinity of the central market The sun hereabouts was pitiless Even during rainy season When he awoke someone was leaning over him He was taken to Old Country To the hut of a dazzling being who introduced himself as Sita Toko He'd been nursed Fed

Sita Toko's wife had made sure he was comfortable The couple had adopted him as a matter of course Without questioning him about anything He was the one who'd felt the need to tell them all Toko had raised his hand *Don't worry about a thing Welcome home Everything will be fine from now on* Regal had smiled thinking about those moments Toko and he still saw each other

He'd rushed out to beat the rain Little Jamaika was playing as usual Too close to the street The gray falling from the sky caressed her albino skin It gave her a lunar hue She was magnificent He'd kissed her forehead Jamaika had stiffened at first Then smiled She'd pressed against him Little gentle-hearted warrior They'd picked her up in the wild grass Not far from what was now the vegetable garden

She'd just been born She wasn't crying Her tiny hands were making circles in the air They'd found her nonetheless There Waiting Without fear Already No one had ever found out who'd left her Swaddled in a blue fabric Scarcely come into the world Near the garden where greens and roots were grown The lemongrass marking the boundary of the domain had protected her from snakes

A prostitute named Ayona had given her a baby bottle and the light of day A churchgoer called Sara had watched over her at night Together they still brought her up They came to know each other thanks to the child The same wounds had led them to different choices Each saw in the other what they could have become And more still What they felt they were unworthy of

Sometimes they sat together Afternoons On the front step of their huts They moved with the light The sun's position in the sky Together they watched their little one play Ayona wore clothes that were open all over Bare strips of clothing Sara's clothes were as indescribable as they were unnamable All you could say was that they covered her up entirely Only her head and her hands remained visible

Jamaika hated being at any distance from Merry Widow She went to the school under the tree Ayona took her there at daybreak While Sara left Merry Widow to go to the hospital where she worked The school was located at the far end of their neighborhood A retired teacher provided some basic education there An association of shopkeepers had wanted to learn to read and write Jamaika was the only child She stayed after the adult class Followed a more complete program Was a little ahead of other children her age Her mothers would have to enroll her in public school someday That would be the only way for her to attend middle school

She'd have to pass the national entrance exam to the sixth grade Regal had told them so They'd nodded in silence Looked at the young girl with a weighty gaze Filled with a love at once cheerful and concerned They were worried about the world affecting her Too early Before she knew how to defend herself Before she had words to speak of it

Prowlers were all around Lurking right here in Merry Widow Ayona knew them They were just waiting for an occasion They were horror and agony They'd see about public school Jamaika didn't need it yet They shook their heads from left to right At the same time Jamaika didn't need to leave Merry Widow Not yet

Regal hadn't seen a single transport vehicle Not a clando Not a bensikin anywhere He'd figured he'd walk a bit But the rain was fast approaching He'd turned back Asked Jamaika to call Eposi A young taxi driver who only worked nights He'd pay her more *Tell her I'll make it up to her* He'd waved to the girl's mothers They had put out two chairs in front of Sara's house

Night was approaching Ayona had stood up to go with the child They'd come back with Eposi who was willing to drop him off at the Prince des Côtes The first bolts of lightning streaked across the sky when they parted Night was falling A dark mass over the city Regal hadn't been able to sit on the terrace as planned He'd waited at the bar instead He'd decided to refuse Amok's offer Politely With compelling arguments His invention required government backing It would be a good idea at least to patent it

He hadn't thought of that

He'd see about it

The truth of the matter was he didn't want to owe anything to the person who had robbed him in the past Neither comfort Nor renown He refused to provide this chic guy with salve for his bad conscience He was always very warm when they got together But that didn't change what he thought He'd noticed a sadness in the man It had intrigued him

Regal recognized people who were like him Those who had to pull themselves up after a trauma He was hoping to learn more Find out what cloud could dim the eyes of a dude who drove wheels like that Wore gear like that Got up in the morning to park his ass in an air-conditioned office He mustn't rush things He gave himself time to reach his goal

His bitterness would dissipate if he managed to get the man in the sack A single night would suffice Then he would trust him The past would be abolished The one wouldn't need to take revenge anymore The other wouldn't have to buy a conscience He didn't want to have an affair To talk of love What interested him was to squeeze something out of him To see it in his eyes every time they'd bump into each other The evening had slipped by The busy movements of the hotel guests had distracted him

The uncle who'd put him up hadn't felt obliged to feed him This had served as a pretext for him Hunger Deprivation What better excuse Regal no longer asked himself what had driven him to rent out his flesh To charge for it in order to see it as valuable Sita Toko had interrupted him when he'd tried to confess Confide everything about his disreputable life Then he'd sat him down One day

The young Regal had listened A story from the depths of ancestral memory He remembered it as if it were yesterday Toko had worn a loose green dress Donned yellow and red bead necklaces Regal had listened to the elder speak Of a land not far from here Farther down on the Continent In the immense Bantu area In bygone days boys loved each other freely Down there In this brother country Formerly Before the arrival of the foreigners who came across the waters from the North

In those times Boys loved each other in the light of day Declared their intentions to their respective parents Presented the chosen of their hearts Offered gifts to the family Laid the animal slain in the hunt at their feet Then they built a hut The lovers lived peacefully For a while Only for a while

One day they'd have to unite with a woman Have children For the community to live They weren't required to give each other up The love nest was not destroyed They'd meet when their obligations as adults permitted The wives would be introduced to these lovers from their youth Lovers for life Sometimes it lasted unto death Beyond death The other side of life The boys having become men continued to love one another

Regal had to know that the forebears had not all condemned love They'd sometimes been receptive to its diverse expressions Had seldom found it useful to reduce beings to their way of loving To name it

The ancestors had only been human Some had distinguished themselves by their stupidity Others had been wise Those of the brother country had codified things in their way Ancestral societies had sought a balance Between the needs of the group and those of the individual At time they'd failed Regal should not feel ill-at-ease He was the child of his forefathers His desires His feelings They had never been alien to them

Here in their country the colonizers had banished customs Drafted laws repressing some forms of love Made the aristocratic practice of the *beau vice* the privileged vice of Northerners A deviancy reserved to superior beings

Colonizers and missionaries had spread a good many myths across the Continent Could we blame them They hadn't come in friendship Had made no bones about it One of them had left behind bitter memories Not so long ago His name was still on the lips of the elders

Léon-Pierre Audeberge

The name was uttered in hushed tones

He was mainly known as *the maker of kings* This Northern politician who liked fresh meat The young boys of the Continent Assembled in an association that he headed Sita Toko had heard of those things The drunks in a bar next to his central market perfume shop talked of it Alcohol loosened their tongues

That was how Toko had heard the story From the mouth of a man who'd witnessed the scene A certain Archibald Kula The whole city knew him He'd been the first one from the country to study in the Grandes Écoles The prestigious institutions of higher education In the North of course Still ranked among the best

Archie had earned several degrees Everyone knew he had a bright future He himself had no doubt about it He'd taken risks Played Lost Beginning his career as a top-level international civil servant Archibald Kula had dug his own grave

The damned fool had a passion for other men's wives Only married women aroused his desire He'd lose his head over them Do all he could to seduce them Succeeded most of the time That's how Archibald Kula had been caught with his supervisor's wife He too a Coastlander from here

Doing a man's wife was like banging the guy himself Such an affront was unpardonable In the old days this act was punishable by death or servitude Adultery was a source of instability It disrupted the harmony of the community Polygamy was preferable to it

Archie had expected a suspension perhaps At worst a brief removal from his post He was too brilliant to be dismissed

He'd played He'd lost This perilous roll in the hay had cost him his job The country had regained its glorious son The valedictorian of many of his classes To no purpose

For several decades Archibald Kula was unemployed He spent his time knocking back beers in bars Occasionally he still managed to get people to offer him a noodle omelet in the city's tournedos This privilege was increasingly rare These eateries served morning workers The labor force of a country oblivious to its people Idle old men like Kula brought bad luck It was not his age It was the void The emptiness of his life as a man

Archibald Kula hadn't built anything back in his village His own family didn't support him His parents had left no heritage His brothers-in-law refused to introduce him into their circles He might misbehave again They'd be left to pick up the pieces To pay the price They'd never heard anyone boasting that they were Archibald Kula's offspring And they knew by heart his past adventures

The man was asked to keep a very low profile around the tournedos Only the bars still allowed him in And not all of them At first the salons of the city had welcomed him with honors The fragrance of disgrace was not yet too heady The former outstanding student spoke well Still had a few decent suits Hats Gloves Yes Leather gloves Moccasins Boots People could still listen to him Look at him Catch a glimpse through him of that inaccessible horizon The North Winter The whiteness of the snow The whiteness of the masters of the universe Archie had entertained the city And even the back-country

He'd been sought after Celebrated Everywhere He was a five-star jobless man A rare species Then they'd noticed His frayed clothing His seldom polished shoes His poorly trimmed sideburns His overly long nails They'd recalled that they would ply him with drinks for free Stuff his face too With the air-conditioning on to boot Suddenly his insolvency became bothersome Very much so It stank to high heaven

His popularity had collapsed High-society married women no longer sought his company His degrees were obsolete These affluent women had read books Traveled to the North and elsewhere Younger and less costly men waited open-armed for them

The honorable Kula could no longer impress anyone outside the poor neighborhoods High-school students majoring in science came to see him under the streetlamps It appeared that he'd known Mr Cessac and Mr Delagrave in person No exercise was too hard for him They brought him a plate of beignets-haricots A portion of braised mackerel Gave him a swig of matango On good days he might have a Beck's or two

Archibald Kula then poured libations to those who were gone Looked lovingly at the bottles Fondly examined their emerald-green color A glass container for a precious substance Yes Archibald Kula had a way with drinks That forced the respect of the most confirmed drunkards And they were gifted Very capable But he That man Was great They admired his mastery He imbibed every cell of his body with beer Sometimes it seemed his fingernails swelled like sponges

Archibald Kula drank But he did not sink And the most distant memories resurfaced Images of the past Edged with foam but positively gleaming Crystal clear Old Kula had retained a vivid memory of his years of study That blessed age when he touched so many peaks Beck's beer took him drifting back to those bygone days That was when the declamation began This psalmody of memory

Archibald's chant streamed out from his throat Flooding a good part of the tumultuous central market Without a megaphone The power of reminiscence alone carried his voice The ardor that took hold of him as he relived those times forever gone

It was not the first time that Sita Toko was subjected to the wild chanting of the boozer The swell threatening to sweep away everything in its path A well-known bayam selam supported him more or less Rode him when she felt the impulse Gave him a few coins once she'd satisfied her urge And so Archibald Kula was often around

That day Toko was supervising the delivery of items ordered ages before Scented oils from the Orient His customers adored them He stood on the threshold of his store An eye on the pallet boxes Another on the young man who was unloading the merchandise Kula's voice had cascaded to him

Carrying incredible revelations Sita Toko didn't pay much attention to idle talk Usually People did a lot of it in this country But this The most jaded person would have listened

Kula had a thing or two to say about an important person He claimed to have seen him Indicated the address Described the layout of the place Archibald had seen the man who was president of the Republic Currently A student at the time In the room of the deputy Audeberge Hiding under the bed so as not to be detected Then ceasing to hide First because he'd been recognized Then because his lover was quite a rake

The president of the Republic who at the time was not even secretary of state But who clearly aimed to climb that ladder The president of the Republic then enrolled in law school A young man with a baby face and a flabby butt A *genu valgum* already gave him that unsteady gait Unreliable This physiological peculiarity made him noticeable from afar He was readily identifiable even in the half-light It would have been best for him to wear a manjua A flared skirt People should take their morphology into consideration when they choose their clothing It was the basis of elegance He Kula knew something about it The country was governed by bushmen The result was impressive

The big shots of the regime resented him Had always been envious of him He Kula who was head and shoulders above them without even opening his mouth Stupid and vulgar as they were They laughed at his misfortune That tight-assed bunch Every time he'd turned up at their office Yes Every time He'd found the door closed With a disdainful air the attendants had ushered him over to the secretaries These assistants had hardly glanced his way He'd had to make an uproar to get them to Consent to announce Him After which they'd refused to see him Without even bothering to make up an excuse

Archibald Kula had a heavy heart His country preferred to do without his talents They mocked his incomparable intelligence What use was it to him It hadn't helped him behave himself Sometimes he would see them Those high-ranking officials Those portly gentlemen with folds in the nape of their neck. They took pride in being called *cous pliés* It meant that they were well fed The others could drop dead They had thighs that touched each other That's how much they stuffed their faces Brainless Hot-air balloons

Those ignoramuses forgot that he knew a thing or two And to begin with their ruler His butt flabbier than ever Kula recalled the time when that guy behaved like a vulgar fishwife *Yes Yes Yes The capo of tutti capi himself* The strong man of the country He went to see his rivals Stood before them A blowtorch in the eyes Hands on his hips His *genu valgum* warping the pants of the beautiful suit paid by Audeberge The one who would preside one day over the destiny of a people rolled his eyes Sucked his teeth Looked scornfully at the smart-ass who'd dared to attract the attention of his lover and protector

Then he shot out with a teeth suck *You think that Léon-Pierre could leave me for you* He accompanied this with a gesture of his hand A gesture everyone here knew well A gesture that removed any doubts as to the nature of the individual The limp wrist Fingers dangling Yes The president of the

Republic The strongman of this country He'd succeeded with his rear end Not only That wouldn't have been enough to rise so high But his flabby butt and his gammy leg that gave him a damsel's gait had helped him That's how old Archie put it

Sita Toko wouldn't have encouraged anyone to give credence to Kula's words Not under normal circumstance The genius's general condition would have dissuaded him from doing so But one thing he knew for sure Archibald Kula was incapable of telling a lie when he'd been drinking That's why they refrained from shutting him up at times like that They opened wide their ears They paid for another Beck's if the gossip was worth it

There wasn't a single person in the country who hadn't heard of Léon-Pierre Audeberge It was known that he'd rewarded his lovers across the Continent This country had been his masterpiece No doubt he'd found fertile ground here A soil conducive to the blossoming of all sort of depravities

Léon-Pierre Audeberge had thrived hereabouts His darlings had received this still embryonic nation as a gift They'd formed a caste of men with weighty secrets to conceal A form of desire that they would only ever experience as a vice And wouldn't hesitate to commit crimes to satisfy it The hatred of people toward *depsos* was their doing Their belief in the mystical character of what should have remained solely a way of expressing love Of giving love

Deputy Audeberge had for a long time been at the head of a brotherhood A sort of secret society After the student organization He'd had to find another structure to bring them together And hold on to them Access to political power in his days had been tied to the sex trade They'd gone from the *beau vice* reserved for Northerners to a magical libidinal practice

The Northern deputy had kicked the bucket like all humans The system he'd set up had prospered Become more savage They'd shown no mercy anymore Hadn't bothered to even pay the boys for services rendered Buy their silence People had seen their sons stripped Raped Sometimes butchered

This was the environment in which Regal was supposed to find fulfillment Sita Toko's words had reassured him somewhat He wasn't a monster No reason though to rejoice The country had no fondness for people of his kind The manufacture of scapegoats here was running full tilt

Regal wasn't waiting for the man of his life He had no taste for martyrdom or for activism Still less for romance He continued to flutter around Go to GeeBees Take a trip to a neighboring country for a change of pace Hunt different game there His life didn't displease him It was a man's life

He and the barman had exhausted their supply of jokes He'd had just enough to pay for one non-alcoholic cocktail Everything was overpriced there The procession of high-society people crowding into the lounges of the Prince des Côtes had begun to weary him He found particularly exasperating this young woman newly arrived from the North The alcohol had disinhibited her She was shouting at the top of her lungs Seeking to be heard by the Northerners Her tirades on racism and integration were aimed at them

The Northern migrants were summoned to enroll their children in local schools To close down those cultural institutions that served to spread their world view They had sown enough confusion in people's minds What were they still doing there Huh What pleasure did they find in the company of apes Why didn't they just buzz off

It was hell in their country They had nothing but hatred for humans And to begin with for their fellow citizens whom they filled with pesticides Pollution was in every aspect of their life Employees had to take drugs to survive the cruel methods of their hierarchy Poor workers had to scavenge for food See the world those people had built for themselves What they were doing in their country Among themselves

The mbenguiste was shouting her head off Not taking the time to swallow To breathe between sentences She was all wound up Regal had noted a trembling in the ranting woman's voice A quivering that indicated that she wouldn't be staying here The country wasn't suited for emotional people like her Here the pesticides and other poisons didn't have a name But they were here Obviously Since they'd been allowed in

He'd watched her closely Her outfit must have cost the equivalent of a year's salary for a professor like him She'd probably inherited a fortune She was at home in the hotel's elegant lounges Her parents had brought her there no doubt as a child She'd returned later with her friends For tea For scones And for a Victoria sandwich She'd always belonged to the *highest of the highest* as people said around here Was ill-prepared to be the target of contempt from this North where her name had No significance And impressed no one Where the color of her skin defined her Where no one Cared about her individuality

Her whole being had melted into outpourings of bitterness The man who was with her blushed with embarrassment You half expected to see him disappear under the table from one moment to the next A tall somewhat spare dark-haired man Not sturdy enough to calm her fury He'd already heard her sounding off More than once Regal had wondered how these couples lived How they protected their privacy How they managed to remain untouched by everything that the woman was revealing How they endured this country's shortcomings The impossibility for them to flourish here

Those two were not made for the zaniness of this place That was as clear as day That night the girl would have liked to gun down the Prince des Côtes's Northern customers Tomorrow she'd be out to dispatch the local charlatans and feymen before fomenting a coup d'état He'd hoped that this couple would not procreate

Regal's phone had rang It was the person he was there to meet Now he was waiting for him to arrive He'd gone over to the bay windows The storm had no intention of quieting down Soon a metallic gray sedan appeared The driver was wearing a white suit visible from afar Turning to the bartender Regal asked if there was an umbrella At no cost did he want to damage the delicate fabric of his pale yellow suit His hat wasn't made for this weather either

A bellhop wearing a uniform was sent over to him The young fellow escorted him to the vehicle Sheltering him under a large umbrella Amok opened the door for him He slipped inside the air-conditioned sedan Thought he heard that old Commodores song *I bet you're singing proud I bet you'll pull a crowd* The schmaltzy chorus He put it down to nostalgia The eighties were not so easily forgotten

He barely had time to buckle his seatbelt Amok roared off He heard him say *I hope you're not in a hurry to get home, we're going to my father's* His eyes were riveted on the road Unspoken suffering thickened the silence Welling up from him A cry Ancient Too weighty for the voice to carry Too trenchant for words An inner burning that would only be expressed in gestures Death blows to the self

Regal was very familiar with this He refrained from speaking It was not up to him to do so And he knew how to keep still It had long been a specialty of his *We're going to my father's* A casual line Like *We'll just stop by I'll drop you off right after It won't take long* It would be exactly the opposite No one paid a short visit at this hour In weather like this The storm made rushing impossible

They were driving toward the city limits The road had been asphalted partway One of the government bigwigs had a second home just past the exit The paved surface led there Original nature all around A small hamlet and its residents Soon the road was but a track Red earth as far as the eye could see Slimy mud on rainy days

Regal wondered where his father's place was He cast a sidelong glance at the man whose hands were clutching the steering wheel His jaw clenched Everything about him was tense He was not paying a warm visit to his father Sinking into his seat Regal focused on his breathing He hadn't imagined this turn of events

At the most he'd thought to spend the night at the hotel Due to the storm Amok and he would have stayed together A lot of things could have happened He wouldn't have made a move right away It wouldn't have been a great idea to declare his feelings It should come from the other Regal knew how to make himself desired Turn on men who hadn't considered sleeping with him and who wouldn't get over it That's what he wanted To be coveted Give him a taste Then reject him saying *I'd rather stay friends*

Tonight they wouldn't talk about financing a science project They'd go to the man's father's It was an excellent start Something would be revealed to him in this father–son confrontation All he'd have to do is observe to put his finger the pain of this rich man's son The family was bound to have something to do with it That's always where things first went awry

That old song again Like a breath An exhalation Somewhere in the car Regal had always believed in invisible forces This was not inconsistent with his scientific mindset or his spiritual ineptitude One thing was not to be confused with the other Matter had its sphere Not everything that existed belonged to it He listened attentively It was definitely inside the vehicle He was positive of it How odd The choice of song There were worse No doubt But there were so many better

He wondered who it could be Was there a code in *Nightshift* Regal mentally unpacked the text Well if you could give it such an ambitious designation Nothing special struck him The song was bound to the circumstances of its creation Hard to take out of its context No negative energy was perceptible

Someone wanted to establish a connection Maybe to transmit a message Without realizing it he began humming A counterpoint Very softly He had the impression that he heard laughter in the engine It didn't last

Regal gave a start Amok had turned to him abruptly With something like fear in his eyes That's when he noticed First the spots Something had splattered on the elegant white jacket The lapel and the right-hand pocket were blotched with it Then he noted the resemblance How had he not seen it before

He could no longer take his eyes off this profile The contours of the face As if chiseled with a knife Regal recognized the plump lips The dimples The nostrils flaring out on either side of a straight bridge The vehicle stopped A gas station The man rushed to the shop The attendant must have been there No one was outside Regal came back to his senses

Yes There'd been that girl He'd met her at the Prince des Côtes The hotel belonged to the family It all fit together She could very well be the sister He'd never asked him if he had one Hadn't wondered about it

That girl She must have been no more than sixteen at the time She was at the cutting edge of fashion Her hair neither curly nor wavy She wore gel in it To give it that famous wet look She sometimes wore big gold hoop earrings And nearly always cowgirl lowboots The kid was on the warpath She had quite a bone to pick In her battle against the male She seemed fearless But she was groaning inside She'd paid him to get rid of her virginity Not to fuck her He'd been nothing but a tool He'd never experienced anything like it since

Sita Toko who liked to instruct him in ancestral customs had taught him that such things were done in the past In certain Bantu communities The girls at marriageable age got rid of their own hymens

Regal had raised a questioning eyebrow The other had laughed There was no militancy in the act on the part of those young women It would be anachronistic to think so People had this nasty habit of reading the past through the sole eyes of the present They did what they did to save face

To arrive at marriage a virgin meant that they had no sexual experience So they wouldn't be able to satisfy their husbands Inserting a tuber or something else into the vagina wasn't as bad The most sought-after women had experience Had even given birth That way the men were sure to reap the utmost of benefits Erotic skill and fertility

Regal had remained a bit dubious after hearing this information The Bantu area was decidedly diverse A three-ring circus Anything and everything could be found there Bantu meant humans The explanation was right there A little bird told him that the teenager of his memories ignored those ancient techniques She hadn't come to him with the intention of preserving her honor Or else she had an utterly different conception of what that was

What she wanted was to maintain control Let no one have the opportunity to appropriate her virginity Her body He relived the scene She hadn't looked at him There was a bitterness in her The memory that he had made him think of a Yoruba aphorism *The weapon that death uses to eliminate the living should be used by the living to escape death* That's what she wanted To gun down death

Regal had thought about that kid a long time One day she'd come back to see him She wasn't looking for sex A sarcastic smile played on her lips She wanted to get to know him This declaration made him suspicious He'd left her with her glass of *sky* No time to monkey around with her And then He was the one who'd gone looking for her Found her Where she'd told him The final exams were approaching He was afraid that he wouldn't get the scholarship he'd applied for What would he do then Who could he talk to There was no one else Because he didn't really know her Because he wouldn't have to see her again

He watched Amok stick the nozzle into the tank Put it back into the dispenser Regal let the door slam shut Before the car started he asked *Bro Your old man Where's he at* The road was not paved the whole way There was no lighting either They might be forced to spend the night in the sedan That would be the best way of making sure they wouldn't be butchered Or robbed They saw nobody but somebody was there Always You were never alone

Amok named their destination Regal exhibited no particular emotion He limited himself to recommending *Beta falla a mapan to nang* The driver kept on going After a while he replied *Mebbe When the road ends we'll see What's for sure is ain't no going back* Regal began humming *Nightshift* again Amok had a unique way of mixing accents and language registers It came to him without thinking He was from here and from there So not really from anywhere

Regal sank into thoughts on the subject The conclusion came quickly to him Everyone in this country was a bit like that Mixed on the inside What was annoying about the members of these old bourgeois families had nothing to do with that It was the extent of the Northern influence It took up more room than all the rest That's what they were first and foremost You couldn't identify with them

His fears were soon borne out The risk of getting stuck in the mud An opaqueness that the sedan's headlights barely penetrated As if several nights had gathered into one Darkness blanketed the landscape

No house was discernable

People here had no electricity

The storm wasn't subsiding Lucky no tree came crashing down on their heads Silhouettes appeared out of the blue Shadows drawn to the orangey glow of the headlights Both men leaned forward without a word The moving shapes were hurrying to what looked like a cave at first

When they saw the doors close they understood It was an opep A people-transporting van The driver and passengers would go no farther before daybreak Too risky The silhouettes climbing back into the vehicle must have gone out to relieve themselves behind the bushes Regal reiterated his recommendations

Amok nodded his head in agreement But he'd rather put some distance between them and the opep He'd no desire to stay in the neighborhood of these strangers There were at least ten of them in the van And only the two of them in the car

Fortunately the road was still passable They had to drive carefully Not to hurry Lean forward Squint Cross their fingers hoping the ruts aren't too deep It wasn't a good time to have to leave the car in a ditch

Progress was slow The sedan wasn't built for roads like this The small bumpy city streets were already a challenge They were driving now on vestiges of a trail Regal knew what happened when vehicles passed through during the day The people living nearby made sure they were compensated They provided the needed assistance To push the car out of the mud To throw shovelfuls of gravel under the wheels Sometimes the locals blocked the route A wooden slat would do the trick Or the trunk of a tree Then a kid came running Sent by the community Watching from afar No one would come at this time of night

The two men fixed their eyes as well as they could on what was unfolding before them The shrubs growing on either side of the road seemed to meet They formed a dense arc of foliage There were white flowers The size of a fist Visible in the darkness The storm whipped them with no effect Not a single one came loose Something shone in the distance The vegetation encircled this unexpected shimmering

They began to think that the passengers of the van might not have been the worst possible company Amok murmured *So this is where the sun's lair is* The allusion to Craô's son's quest did not make them laugh They weren't looking for that mythical place They'd have been satisfied with a quiet spot where they could wait for the dawn The car hurled headlong toward the light that suffused the space of night

There was a noise Thunderous The clatter of crumpled metal As if the sedan had been a small can crushed with one hand by a supernatural creature Regal didn't understand right away It was too dark to see Amok's head resting on the steering wheel Something had flattened part of the roof of the car Possibly a big tree They had to get out of there

The rain continued to thrash the world The door on his side was blocked Amok's was out of reach and he wasn't stirring Regal moved his head closer The man was breathing He didn't hear his cries But he was breathing The only people they'd seen on the way were the opep passengers They'd left them behind There'd be no one to come to their aide before morning And only if they happened to pass that way

Amok had taken a slight fork in the road before this dazzlement First the light had been bright but distant It turned into a huge ball when the car had plunged toward it This fire had enveloped them Lifted them from the ground Then they'd fallen back down It had lasted only a fraction of a second but that's what he saw Felt Experienced What he'd say if he had to testify

The light had softened but was still there All around them He couldn't discern its source His reaction was to squint in an attempt to pierce it To see through it A path A dwelling A shrub Anything Regal stayed like that for a while His eyes fixed on the light before him He thought he caught sight of a silhouette A woman whose naked body hugged a curve of the halo She was dancing in the rain Her body was at once water and fire Rain and sun joined in the heart of the night In a place without a name

The man pulled himself together Shut his eyes Shook his head He believed in the invisible This scene was unrelated to that An optical illusion caused by the shock Digging into his jacket pocket he took out his telephone Pointless reflex No signal In any case he couldn't have called emergency assistance People did that on TV shows from the North His gaze wandered to the man who'd lost consciousness Amok seemed to be asleep Not worrying about a thing And this was the guy who'd recklessly set off after nightfall In the storm Pitched his sedan into the flames

Regal hoped he'd live He asked the forces that had embarked him into this mess not to stop midway To give his hands the strength to mold this child overly spoiled by life To make him his thing So he took off his hat Put it on the dashboard Began to talk to the sleeping man To catch hold of a piece of his slumbering consciousness Maintain it in reality First he said that people called him Regal not Charles Yes that indeed meant royal He'd put a crown on his head A fantasy of the unprivileged A name with a bang So Regal He told his life story

He didn't notice that the rain had stopped Gusts sent leaves and branches flying through the air Amok's steady breathing suggested nothing more than exhaustion Only Regal's attempts to wake him up had convinced him that he'd endured an injury He'd touched his cheek His forehead Something sticky had stayed on his fingertips A little blood

No doubt He accepted this without too much emotion Regal knew the underside of life That more than the rest He'd managed to arrange his life so that only the best of him would show At least what seemed acceptable to him

The other aspects of his personality didn't embarrass him He just didn't want to have to explain himself He never kept his nights after GeeBees going in his apartment in Merry Widow It was his separate planet A few of his students lived in the neighborhood where cheap accommodation was available Those who'd recognized him at GeeBees kept it to themselves

No one would risk mentioning GeeBees which remained what it was supposed to be A commonplace take-away where you could buy everyday supplies You'd have to be invited by a regular to be let into the basement Near the shed The name GeeBees was written nowhere on the outside It was whispered here and there Those who frequented the place cherished their marginality They hadn't chosen what brought them together Yet they found a beauty there that social conformism would spoil

Others saw things differently They didn't go to GeeBees They went to nightclubs Campaigned during the day to be granted a place in a deleterious society whose customs they'd have the honor of perpetuating The couple The family Regal felt he had nothing to declare Nothing to hide He didn't put himself on display His life wasn't a spectacle

He didn't have an ideal Nothing but this body straddling irreconcilable universes The somewhat stiff man that professors and students knew gave no hint of his troubled twin The wild beast The boy-catcher who hated romance Regal didn't like men He desired them sexually What he knew of love was different It was Toko's attention Little Jamaika's rigid and silent embrace And that was a good thing

The man whose head was resting on the steering wheel of the sedan heard nothing of his confession It didn't matter He spoke in hushed tones Whatever crossed his mind And that was it His way of living in the world The comfort of solitude The fury of his appetites The need he had to arouse affections that would not be returned To dominate Perhaps because he was submissive Perhaps because he'd been ashamed and thought of ending his life Perhaps because he'd hoped that his former clients would grow attached to him That they'd become lovers and friends And save him

It never happened Some had taken pity on him They'd paid him a little more And gone back to their normal lives To wives and children who had no idea what they were doing on the Continent To presentable lovers He'd suffered from it for a long time All that was over now He didn't like the weak either He had no use for the love-hungry He was content with taking what was offered to him The only restriction that he imposed on himself concerned students He didn't touch them Even after seeing them at GeeBees

Regal pressed on the button to roll down the window With no specific intention or expectation He did so It slid down with a hiss The surprise immobilized him for a moment Then he thought it was worth a try To slip outside Find help He leaned his head out Surveyed the surroundings Saw nothing The light was gone Nothing had replaced it In the darkness his eyes could make out only shadows Pitch-black vegetation danced and howled in the wind

He looked at the ground Couldn't get a clear sense of it He wasn't going to make a hasty decision A violent storm had pummeled the region The earth hadn't absorbed the water yet Plunging headfirst into the mud didn't seem like a brilliant idea It would be harder for him to get back into the car His legs could also hit Amok That was not the way he'd imagined contact between their bodies Maybe he could go about it another way Get his torso out Pull himself up by gripping the roof Lift up his lower limbs Bend them No This too wouldn't work He had good abs But not enough room Not to get a decent hold on the wet roof

The man kept his cool Then he had this reflex Did what people hereabouts do in many situations When cars couldn't be opened from inside He put his hand out the window Reached the handle Pulled it up Opened the door

A vehicle more suited to the roads of this country would have protected him better A muddy wave gushed into the sedan His haste to shut the door did not spare him He felt his Stan Smiths and his pants becoming drenched with this muck Amok began to cough This shook his upper body He remained nonetheless glued to the steering wheel Peaceful in his unconsciousness

Regal who only ever exercised violence in the sexual arena felt a furious desire to hit him to wake him up He did nothing of the sort Told himself simply that the night would be long That he wouldn't sleep a wink That no one would see him at the university the next day He no longer felt like talking Not to this Amok who only brought him trouble He'd stolen his scholarship from him And now this Past possibilities would never be restored But he'd thought he'd have an opportunity to amuse himself To help himself to something in return

Refuse Monsieur Mususedi's generosity Lure him into his bed Make him come Then hold himself back from him Offer him friendship with a smile An outstretched hand Open As if to say *We're even* Make sure they're not Ever Cast a shadow onto this man's life Share a guilty secret with him He nodded to himself In the silence

The night blew cool air through the lowered window of the car This night was not the end He'd seen others and he'd hold firm When Amok would open his eyes In six months In a year He'd find him at his bedside

Regal would not let go of his prey this way It was to himself this time that he told the story of his life Considering only its most painful aspects This was easy for him This rumination filled with bitterness reinforced him He had nothing but reasons to live For himself alone In his sole interests and for his sole pleasure

The wan dawn light dispelled the night Regal's eyes were red from lack of sleep From worry too Amok had moaned then cried without opening his eyes for a moment Without a single word escaping his lips as happens in the middle of a nightmare Regal reassured himself figuring that a coma would have been quieter At bottom he didn't really know The man clung to the gnawing anger that had possessed him It was through this that he scanned the landscape He leaned his head out the window

Reddened by the clayey soil the water seemed at rest The tumult of the storm had ravaged the surroundings Shrubs with twisted trunks were not willing to fall More imposing trees had been knocked down Uprooted Perhaps before their arrival

in these parts The road had vanished under torrents of laterite
No way could the sedan be driven out of there Impossible to
climb out Nothing to do Not a hut Not a living soul He
turned to see if the opep was approaching He'd signal the passengers So they'd call someone Not leave them here like this

The fatigue was getting to him His body was stiff and
hurting He hadn't thought of reclining his seat until daybreak
His night would have been more comfortable Too late for that
now He had to remain visible Someone could pass Regal knew
this road He had the impression that he was discovering it
That he was nowhere in this world

The events of the night came back to him The whole trip
from the Prince des Côtes His mind kept coming up against
that ball of light first seen from afar Beyond a path Behind an
arcade over which grew a climbing plant strewn with white
flowers

The sedan had leaped forward toward it And everything
had stopped in that plunge There was no trace of the road
None of the plants growing there had immaculate blossoms
He decided to keep what he thought he'd seen to himself He'd
say nothing of the halo that had surrounded the car Of the
vision he had had of a woman He drove these thoughts away
The desire to drink took hold of him Nothing else existed but
this sensation of thirst The impossibility of satisfying this need

Regal thought with little consolation of the cohorts of
young people that this country drove out Having to cross on
foot the deserts where smugglers had abandoned them Their
thirst was much worse Maybe they collected their own urine
to drink He wouldn't hesitate Getting back at Amok was now

the least of his concerns He wanted to scream To howl For the world to wake up and come to his rescue *Somebody Please*

The last time he'd felt like pleading was a distant recollection Erased from his conscious memory He'd managed to wrest from this world what he wouldn't have been given without his rage He'd escaped a life as an untrained accountant employed by a hardware dealer with a street stand He'd cut off relations with his blood relatives to create a world where he could feel free Apologize for nothing Not hear himself say that he was a demon An abomination That he'd have to be exorcised

He wasn't rich His apartment in Merry Widow suited him fine The firm futon was to his liking It was the ideal bed for him His uncle had made him sleep on the floor for years He'd throw an old fabric on the ground Lay his body down on it Do so only when his exhaustion was such that a mattress of thorns would have seemed welcoming

Regal had himself financed his university enrolment His books His photocopies His daily commute First with savings from his last few tricks Then with money from odd jobs Often for merchants Craftsmen He'd spent years handling material Unloading pallets Pushing carts During this period he had the impression that he hadn't broken free from his family's low expectations That he was living below these at times

He'd put all his strength into his project To live his life Ask nothing of nobody Not have a living soul to care for Not be the graduate who'd feed the toothless mouths of the newborn and the old He'd studied Defended his thesis Continued his research for the sheer pleasure of discovery It couldn't end like this *Somebody Please*

His heart was lurching in his chest He could no longer bear waiting for the dilly-dallying day to put an end to this interminable night The silence oppressed him It was morning Not a bird call had been heard Not a cry from an animal lurking in the thickets Regal had made a friend of solitude He liked to be a world unto himself Live among others Interact with them And never be with anyone but himself The void on the other hand terrified him It was the absence of life The window was still open Yet he was gasping for air He felt like he was suffocating *Somebody Something*

He turned around again Stayed like that As if his gaze riveted on this nothing Could create something Make a life appear He'd have given anything to catch a glimpse of a dog a monkey a turtle Any sort of creature with which no conversation would have been possible He stared unblinking Forcing his eyelids not to move To see even a fly would have reassured him

The rear windshield was smeared with spots Marks of ochre mud that looked like fingerprints There was not a thing Only him Only Amok's long sleep Only this interstice between night and day A duration whose course had been disrupted That was all there was to grasp The compactness of time

Regal soon felt a tingling at the inner corner of his eyes Tears welling up Never had he heard that they could quench the thirst of a water-deprived human He refused to cry To surrender to despair

There came something A movement in the distance As he struggled to hold back the flow A sound of an engine Of wheels carefully cleaving through the reddened water A tarp-covered van was advancing at snail's speed The body was yellow Big green letters of an inscription traced a half-moon on the hood *Black no de crack*

The local take of this saying made him laugh Regal laughed Wept tears of laughter of joy of relief of unfamiliar emotions Instinctively he understood the meaning given here to the expression *Black don't crack* It was no longer about the resistance of black skin to aging It was about one's very being One's resilience One's ability to face the worst conditions You had to have faith in that To consider driving on that road after last night's deluge The driver of the van hadn't waited for the sun to start doing its work

Regal began twisting and turning in his seat He couldn't get out Stand by the sedan Wave his arms in the air to attract the driver who might be the only one to pass by there for hours The palms of his hands hit the ceiling His elbow bumped against the interior rear-view mirror which came unhinged He wanted to call out Make himself heard Loudly signal the presence of a human being The life of a man who'd journeyed through the night tunnel Make his triumph over darkness and emptiness known A croak escaped his lips

His parched throat denied him any help His tears were no longer of joy The van continued its slow progress The driver leaned his head out of the window from time to time Looked down Tried to assess the depth of invisible cracks Looked behind You could get stuck in the mud without knowing it At that time of day no one would come to his aid Throw shovel-fuls of sand Or gravel

He who'd ventured out on this road knew he was man enough to face the challenge

Black no de crack

Yes

No taking chances though You couldn't run up the moun-tain You had to take your time Set out before daybreak to grab life by the throat Prove your patience The balance of forces in the match were unequal

Man had only his ingenuity his intelligence his intuition Nature had anteriority and power The unpredictability of its reactions It could start raining at any time The inundated cracks could turn out to be ditches Ravines Open graves wait-ing to be occupied Regal understood He had nevertheless an urge to urinate Coupled with the need to drink it made the situation unbearable

Presently the van arrived close by He heard voices The first notes of a track by Tout Puissant OK Jazz The driver leaned his head out the window On the left side Regal and the sedan were on the right He reached his hand toward the yellow vehicle Let out a soundless cry The man must have seen Amok's car Maybe he thought it was abandoned

He had to call out Signal their presence Do something Long planks protruded from under the brick-red tarp Held by firmly attached chains The load was reeling somewhat The circumstances justified the driver's extreme caution The state of the terrain The need no doubt to deliver these items first thing in the morning

Losing his composure wasn't an option Regal told himself it wasn't for him either The man turned his head toward him just as he was about to try to cry out again Do what he could vocally Even if it meant tearing his cords Their eyes met Time came to a standstill The man turned off the radio Stopped the engine Not a word was exchanged The driver of the van leaned back for a moment Stared at the road ahead A river of mud He'd only get out once he'd reached his destination

He leaned to the right Discovered Amok's head on the wheel His eyes moved back to Regal who shook his head *He's not dead We need help* The sound of his voice was inaudible to him He had to improvise a gestural speech

The driver maneuvered the van around the front of the sedan Came as close as possible The door on the passenger side opened for Regal to climb in No way of extending one of the planks in the rear to him He'd have to muster the last bit of strength to hoist himself into the vehicle He opened the door to get out The muck from the day before had thickened It didn't attack him this time He stretched a leg out toward the van No It didn't work The distance between the vehicles was too great It couldn't be reduced without closing the van door

Regal reclined his seat Got on his knees Threw his body toward this unhoped-for raft that the universe had sent him This plunge got him halfway into the van He lifted his legs so they wouldn't disappear into the mud The driver didn't congratulate him Regal's effort to save his life seemed to make little impression on him He sucked his teeth and shot a *Balock* at him Those *children of the barrier* again who'd thought they were stronger than nature

Normal people had hunkered down in their homes last night All had seen that this rain was not simple All had prayed not to be swept away by it To be graced with another day There were so many things one could do in a day Make amends for a wrong Express one's love Ask for forgiveness Smile at someone They all wanted one more day But these people apparently didn't

Everyone dreaded this road on rainy nights Especially during dry season There were dazzlements that caused accidents Not everyone survived They'd been lucky Well Maybe not Regal had his eyes fixed on his Stan Smiths His feet had steeped all night in water Everything was surely decomposing

He looked up at the man who was talking to him *My friend had to see his father It was urgent* If that had been the case he wouldn't have gone out in a storm in dry season Wouldn't have taken this road *My friend comes from Mbeng He no savvy the country anymore* Then he should have dissuaded him from undertaking the journey With a toy car The man spoke while maneuvering around the sedan Back to his initial position Facing the liquid path that led to where his planks and himself were awaited He asked about the other guy's condition

Regal replied that he'd lost consciousness but was still alive. His rescuer opened the glove compartment Took out a bottle of whiskey that had been filled with water *Drink* Regal would have deserved to be left to die of thirst But the sound of his voice was unbearable *It's for me that I give you a drink Not for you* Regal and his friend didn't even have youth as an excuse They were at least as old as he was

The man said his name was Misipo He indicated his destination A village not far away But given the state of the roads Anyway All they could do was report the other fellow's presence once they got there Who knew who'd take the risk of coming all this way before the water had been soaked up There was only a small country clinic there They'd see It was the only solution There was a small village before the place where he was headed A few farmers who had only their legs for transportation and the opep that drove from place to place throughout the region

Regal thanked him for the water Took a sip Thanked him again Really He added that the village in question was precisely the place where the father lived Misipo wanted to know who he was He knew the residents there well Regal pronounced Amok's surname The driver of the van fell silent Cast a furtive glance at his passenger Clapped in astonishment And very visible disapproval

It was going to be a dismal day The man whose name had just been mentioned was his customer He was waiting for the planks at a construction site It would be out of the question to leave his son injured in the middle of the road of dazzlements Misipo would not be able to help out He had to return to the city for personal reasons An important visit to make after last night's storm He'd drop off his load and drive straight back Misipo wanted to be home that very afternoon Last night's rain had affected many people He had to find out whether any of his family or friends had suffered He wouldn't be persuaded to do otherwise

They arrived mid-morning The last few miles had been easier to negotiate The young people from the nearby village had poured sand and gravel on the road They'd slipped thick branches under the tires when they spun without moving forward The ground was very slippery in spots Misipo had held out some bills They'd refused them There'd been a dazzlement the night before They'd perceived its radiance from afar A circle of light Serious events may have occurred No They'd take no money in such circumstances

Regal and Misipo had kept silent Continued on their way Amos Mususedi's house had appeared in the middle of a park planted with flamboyant and ebony trees There was no fence No direct access for a four-wheeled vehicle You had to park outside and walk down a lane to the front door It was visible from a distance You had an immediate sense of the thickness of the wood from which the two panels had been carved There was something antique and novel about the look of it

The ochre walls covered over a good stretch of the terrain Turrets resembling upraised arms reached for the sky Regal doubted that the structure was built of clay No one did that anymore Least of all for such an imposing edifice A construction site would necessarily be disrupted by bad weather Rainy season lasted several months The work had to be suspended as a result for an unpredictable period of time And this architectural folly had not been built in two or three days He wondered if it had been inspired by a well-known Sahelian mosque A more fanciful vision had been tacked onto it

The result was utter blasphemy It was not a tribute to the divine It was the kingdom of a man An offering to himself His dream Misipo told him that the house wasn't finished This wasn't apparent from the outside Only the ground floor was partially inhabitable Sundry building materials piled up in a many of the rooms The master of the house had an original project His idea was to invent the future architecture of the Continent The experimental nature of the enterprise was obvious It was unlike anything else

Regal didn't see it that way It looked like itself He wasn't convinced that the whole Continent would want to adopt this particular aesthetic Yet it contained an idea Not everything in this creative boldness was to be discarded It could no doubt be pared down He thought of his landlord Kambon The promoter of the living house

He liked the fact that there was no fence Everyone could walk right up Knock on the door That was what he understood The intention had not been to arouse envy To force it on commoners The scale of the building was offered to them Like a new destiny A foundational chaos

Suddenly Regal looked forward to meeting the elder Mususedi He'd have liked to do so under different circumstances Not have to tell him that his son had fallen into a suspicious sleep at the wheel of his car After an accident on the so-called road of dazzlements This thought dampened his enthusiasm

No one was in front of the house The planted areas in front of the building were carefully tended They hadn't suffered much from the storm A few broken branches were strewn on the ground A small quantity of fruits and leaves had fallen A little water had accumulated in one or two lanes The estate was plunged into silence Misipo parked his van where the road bordered the plantings He honked and shattered the tranquility of the place A man came running He'd appeared from behind the house the front door of which opened after a while

Regal didn't see who'd pulled door panels open from inside The man who'd joined them greeted Misipo He was right on time despite the rain They didn't think they'd see him Most of the workers would be absent today They'd unload the van anyway Put away the planks They could install the parquet floor the following day if he could come back with his apprentices Misipo said that all of that could wait a moment He pointed to Regal *This man needs to talk to the boss*

The employee answered that the gentleman was up They were about to serve his meal in the garden The man sized up Regal *Good morning Follow me* Regal got out of the van The state of his Stan Smiths and his pants drew attention *No You can't go into the garden* They'd wash his feet Get him a clean pair of pants Some slippers The man pointed to the back of the house from where he'd emerged

Regal must have looked confused Misipo explained that the garden was inside the building They headed to the staff compound The employee walked briskly ahead of them He found it difficult to keep up He'd spent the night in his mud-soaked shoes Now they were caked dry It was like having laterite sarcophagi on his feet It wasn't the most pleasant of feelings He didn't complain The walk seemed to last as long as several rotations of the Earth The pointlessness of a fence was obvious Anyone wanting to enter the house would have to arm themselves with patience Regal could better assess the distance that had separated them from the entrance a few minutes before This too that had kept him from seeing who opened the door They'd been too far away

The staff's quarters were actually individual huts Three of them were large enough to house a family of four each They seemed comfortable Many people living off the city's poor districts would have loved to live in such homes

The construction material wasn't the usual mudbrick of village shacks Nor the second-rate cement bricks of ordinary houses in the city A straw roof had been harmoniously set atop these circular buildings The rain had not caused no particular damage Containers had been placed on either side of the buildings As reservoirs To collect rainwater

Feminine voices could be heard Laughter Children protesting There'd be no school this morning But they still had to get up The fritters and porridge would cool off Regal felt his stomach growl His last meal had been lunch the day before The employee stopped in front of the most imposing house A smell of coffee wafted from it They'd added cardamom to it Not a common spice in this country

The man hailed someone A window opened and a teenage girl smiled at him A figure from a time and place when the Continent had been called Alkebulan It was Makeda as one might imagine her at fifteen or sixteen Her beauty did not originate in this part of the Continent Her hair was only partially braided From the nape toward the front Thick bangs fell on her forehead Her eyes twinkled mischievously

The employee relaxed at the sight of his daughter Basic questions assailed Regal This apparition was not commonplace

Women from the eastern part of the Continent were rare here-abouts Yet the man whose family lived in this house had found one He hadn't confined himself to admiring her from afar Perhaps she was a Haal Pulaar A Baggara There were some in the northern part of the country But those women married within their communities His eyes turned to the employee His features seemed Bantu And not particularly graceful at that

Misipo stood at some distance He nodded at the girl who brought a bowl of water so that Regal could wash his feet He'd then be taken inside to change his pants Regal was grateful that the employee and Misipo had stepped away to talk The teenager had gone back into the house He'd bought his Stan Smiths second hand They'd cost him an arm and a leg

They were the sharpest footwear he owned Along with two or three other pairs perhaps They weren't designed for walking in cassava peels But here he was Regal was afraid to see pieces of his beloved sneakers fall off The sole of his foot was stuck to the sole of the shoe No doubt for good He examined for a moment the muddy sarcophagus that clung to his feet Then he set about untying the laces

An unfriendly thought toward Amok came to him There was nothing to lose by waiting The condition of his sneakers strengthened his desire for revenge He admitted to himself that that was what he sought Since the day they'd met again in an administrative office The other stood in line as if he was forced to do so Disdain for the privileges you enjoyed was the paroxysmal expression of social superiority

Regal let out a fierce teeth-sucking noise That his shoes were nearly intact didn't make him feel any better He wouldn't wear them again His pants too were done for That was not as serious His tailor would fix the problem But the Stan Smiths He didn't see Misipo approaching The sound of his voice startled him He was going to unload the planks with the help of the workmen who lived there Then he'd go say hello to the boss and hit the road again

Regal was given a pair of pale purple sirwals and flip-flops made from used tires He'd left his hat on the dashboard of the sedan Luther Vandross and Kid Creole had forsaken him He hadn't a clue what he looked like to others He walked head down behind the employee who'd requested unceremoniously that he follow him to the garden to meet the owner of the estate

The building had been constructed on a steep slope You couldn't see it from the other side From where the road was This wasn't visible from the staff compound either A stepped valley unfolded a hundred yards from the rear façade It was part of the estate Another cultivated area was there And fields As far as the eye could see

He was ushered into a corridor with an impressively high ceiling The vault was at least twenty-five feet above the ground A fresco had been painted on it He felt at once dizzy and nauseous He concentrated on the heels of the man walking in front of him And on what he would say He hadn't given any thought to how he'd break the news What words he'd use It was up to him to inform a man that his son had been unconscious for many hours In a car On an impassable road

He'd hardly touched Amok Hadn't thought of reclining his seat Ensuring that he could breathe properly His anger had been overpowering Maybe they'd find a lifeless body Regal's throat was dry as his eyes met those of the man who got up to greet him The table was set A feast for raw foodies The Mususedi father was wearing a velvet sanja tied at the shoulder He was bare-chested Nobody did that in this country

Furthermore this type of wrapper was a formal garment Coastlanders wore it for ceremonies But the gentlemen of the Coast didn't stand up when their servants entered the room with a stranger Regal was old enough to be the son of the man who smiled at him quizzically Maybe the stranger needed help A lot of people must have been affected by the unexpected storm *Na titi jembu nu sangu I don't recognize this gentleman* The employee shook his head *The carpenter says this man needs to talk to you He is the one who brought him here*

Regal felt his bones decomposing when the elder Mususedi's turned his gaze back to him He'd be turned to dust without having spoken a word Images of the night flashed through his mind Superimposed on the things he could have done to check Amok's condition The sun would soon be at its zenith The body of the sedan would smolder Regal felt his legs give way beneath him He was on his knees when words came to him *In the car It's your son Back there On the road of dazzlements*

Resurrection Blues

I

Amok thought he'd lost his mind. Nothing around him seemed real, even if it were true. He was living through all this, somewhere. Where? He didn't know. The question didn't really interest him anymore, he needed to see Ixora, to talk to her. Nothing else mattered. By listening to his pain, Ixora had made it possible for him to live again. Even more than Kabral, her presence by his side was what opened the possibility for him of reinventing his life. He wanted to walk this path with her, discover it and make it more and more beautiful every day. Maybe they wouldn't make love, in the sense that people use the expression, but they could give each other more than many couples in love. The thought of her refusing to forgive him paralyzed him. Amok tried to project himself into the life they'd have after that night of violence, after he'd deserted her. First, they'd have to leave the great house, to free themselves as much as possible from his family history. He'd thought he had worked toward this in past years, but it was just the opposite. Leaving the great house could also mean giving up his activities, the income he earned from them. It wouldn't be easy to find such a lucrative job, and no one would understand why he needed to look for one. His studies in finance wouldn't do him much good either, he'd never worked in the field, and the few positions that existed were taken.

The man couldn't make any decision alone. It would all depend on Ixora and he had no news of her. He felt such a sense of helplessness just then that he yearned to flee once more, postpone the moment of confrontation. He had to talk to someone. A thousand questions flitted around in his mind like fish packed into a small jar. He understood why people do crazy things in certain situations, why they resort to lies, corruption, and witchcraft. But he had no gift for any of that, and he wanted Ixora free. Wanted her to choose him. They'd moved in together at Kabral's request, without ever telling each other, in their long conversations, how good it had been for them. They hadn't put their feelings about the quality of the bond that united them into words. The man refused to speak of all this in the past.

Amok stood up again, felt his knees creak, as a sharp pain shot through his shoulders and upper back. He stayed there motionless for a moment, eyes lowered, inhaled and exhaled for a long time. He didn't trust that he could walk, was afraid of falling, losing consciousness, opening his eyes in a different place. Turning to the interior of the hut, he saw his jacket, smudged with stains. He didn't want to call for help, wanted to reach for it himself, look through the pockets for his phone, see if he could use it. He started to walk, doing his best to listen only to his mind, not his body, which was reluctant to obey him. He leaned against one of the side walls in the room, advanced with slow steps. Concentrating on his goal, not letting the contents of the hut distract him. There was only this jacket, it hadn't been cleaned, it was hanging on a nail. When he was close enough to grab it, he tripped over something, a utensil that had been left there, saw himself falling, regained his footing. With feverish fingers he tugged at the garment, took it in his hands, avoiding the sight of the marks left by the mud.

Doing so wasn't enough to drive away the image of Ixora lying in the rain. Amok's eyes filled with tears as he found his phone. He sat down on the floor of the hut, leaning against the plank wall, the metallic gray case of the device looking ridiculous to him. It wasn't him, the white suit, the sedan, this ever so superficial plaything which he saw as a lifeline right now. Sharing his grief, confronting it by spelling it out would be a whole different thing, a change from this inner lament, this serpent biting its own tail. It would restore reality, bring him back to it. There'd be no escaping then. There was only one person in the world who could hear his words, someone he rarely called, someone who often exasperated him. He waited for the phone to reboot, didn't bother checking if it was possible to make a call from this remote hut. He hadn't saved the number the last time they'd spoken, so Amok had to scroll through the incoming calls, scrutinizing the screen to make sure he recognized the country code, immediately laid his finger on it. He didn't put the phone to his ear, though it wouldn't have been an unreasonable thing to do.

When he realized that someone had answered the call since he could see it, he wondered how to formulate things. What could he say? Staring at the phone, he put it on speaker. It helped him to converse in a natural position, as if he wasn't on the phone but in a room talking to his sister. The sound of his own voice surprised him. He'd heard it earlier in the morning, but its sepulchral tone had not struck him then, neither had its authoritative dimension, which could hardly be justified in the circumstances. This didn't impress Ajar. When she shot back, *What the hell? Ya want to sissia me or what?*, he was sure he'd made the right decision, was glad she couldn't see him, trembling like a leaf, sitting in this unlikely place. When he thought about the people whose presence in his life was a gift, his sister's name didn't come to mind. She'd always been there, even when he refused all contact. Ajar would cross town to visit him, grumble, berate him, say she didn't understand, and come back. No one had been more faithful, no one knew him as profoundly. She carried her name, Tiki, the precious one, that their mother had chosen for her, well. The name Ajar, which came from their father, suited her perfectly too. It spoke of mystery, of character, sounded like it belonged to some ancient figure. They'd given each other nicknames, she called him Double Bee or Big Bro, he called her Sissy.

He hadn't the heart to laugh, his words were drowned in a sob when he tried to speak. How could he tell her? He saw them as children, two tiny bodies in the belly of the great house, doing their best not to be crushed, clinging to each other for protection. They'd breathed in a single breath so many times. He heard himself in that past that he'd never really left behind, expressing the deepest contempt for those who physically abused their partners. At the time, he didn't question the behavior of these men, didn't look for the source or meaning of their acts. Ajar's soothing voice interrupted him, *Double Bee, calm down, I already know. She's been taken to the hospital, her life's not in danger*, most of all they needed to know where he was. Everyone was looking for him. Madame hadn't wanted to alarm the husband until she'd learned more about what happened to her son. She hadn't expected to be contacted by their father, to hear him tell her that an accident had occurred, that the sedan had been found with no one inside.

The storm had made the area where the search was taking place difficult to cover, but the police had been notified. Ajar wanted to know where he was calling from, so she could reassure their parents. Madame would probably cut him into thin slices before throwing him, one piece at a time, into the grave she'd have dug especially for him, but that was merely the expression of her boundless love. Amok couldn't figure out what he was feeling. He'd have liked to talk about Ixora, to talk to Ixora, to understand how their father had learned about him, but he was speechless. As usual, he pushed the problem aside, to get a better view of it. When his sister asked him once again how to get to where he was, Amok replied that, given where things stood, there was no need to hurry, and firstly she hadn't told him how their father found out about it. Ajar told him that a man had shown up, someone named Regal, who'd related the events and the location of the car. The vehicle was indeed where he'd left it, but there was no trace of the driver. They'd imagined the wildest scenarios, none of which left her expecting this phone call from her brother.

Amok knew that Charles was also called Regal, he'd had him tailed for several days before proposing to finance his invention. Having come back after such a long absence, he'd taken care to be informed about the people he met for business. He didn't like doing so, prying into other people's lives, but his status left him no choice in a society where hyenas could disguise themselves as hummingbirds. The ancestral masks had been kidnapped, replaced by inert replicas with no power of speech. They'd come up with other masks, of a new kind, ones that no longer transmitted messages from the invisible, no longer gave body to the unbeholdable. They were fashioned to conceal, to deceive. And they were everywhere, having become more powerful than the people who put them on. Unlike the merchandise made for tourists looking for souvenirs to bring home, social camouflage was alive, and it devoured its wearer. Charles wasn't really hiding, he was simply discreet about certain aspects of his life. Amok understood why. He asked for news of Ixora, which gave his sister the chance to assure him that everything would be alright.

He felt a crushing sense of horror to discover that it was Amandla who recognized him, and contacted Madame. So their mother had gone over to her son's former lover. *To make a long story short, Ixora was driven to the clinic,* she was receiving the best care, and her first words were for him, she wanted to know if he was okay. His son had asked the same thing. They were waiting, losing sleep, it would be a kindness to let everyone know that he was alive, after two days of being on tenterhooks, she wanted to believe that his selfishness, although long affirmed, could not go so far as to dismiss their perfectly undeserved solicitude. And she'd appreciate it if he'd stop crying, for he had beaten this woman, he, not some supernatural creature, and he'd gone away, leaving her for dead in the mud, and here he was calling two days later, and having to be pleaded with before answering questions with information that he should have given from the start.

Amok agreed with her, this didn't make things any less painful, he wasn't so sure anymore that he wanted a second chance with Ixora, he wasn't worthy of it. How could he look her and Kabral in the eye? He kept himself from moaning aloud to his sister, who was receiving his asinine ramblings without threatening to hang up. When the man was able to speak again, he muttered that he'd have liked to reply, but he hadn't the faintest idea where he was. He'd been told the name of a place, but he had every reason to doubt the very existence of the village in question, anyway it wasn't what mattered most. If the road he'd taken last night actually existed, if the sedan had been found there, the search party would eventually lay their hands on him. If he and Ajar were having this conversation right now, there was a good chance these people would not come upon a corpse. The problem was not the physical place where he was but the inner swamp in which he'd been mired for so many years. The stagnant waters had overflowed, pouring out onto Ixora without him being able to do anything about it. He hadn't thought to beat her, he'd had no thought whatever at the time. There'd been nothing but this maceration in which he'd been sunk, and which had overwhelmed him. That didn't seem a valid excuse to him. On the contrary, to insist on it would be to manipulate those around him, Ixora to begin with, who'd find it hard to leave an emotionally handicapped person, a sick man. Abandoning someone who is unwell is wrong, not helping them puts your own humanity in jeopardy. He wanted to be loved, not pitied. It was in telling his sister this, in all simplicity, that he himself admitted the nature of these needs.

Ajar listened in silence, she always did that when people came to her, giving them more than a shoulder to cry on. This he'd seen in his sister's relationship with their parents, the way she had of receiving the weight that others unloaded, never complaining about it, bringing an element of calm. *Sissy, you're not going to solve my problems. Tell me about yourself.* Ajar laughed, he couldn't be serious, had somebody switched brothers on her, where was the one who was persuaded that bourgeois girls of her kind had nothing on their hands but time to waste, and no lives of their own to live. Well, she'd become an artist's agent, she'd seized an opportunity without thinking, the desire to do something she liked. Her most important client, the one who provided her with the most substantial income, was a jazz singer adored by the public and feared by professionals. She enjoyed subjecting them to the power of her fame. She was not satisfied with having unreasonable clauses included in her contracts, demanding another room in the hotel after the accommodations had fitted specifically to please her, or ordering a cup of blue tea at a specific temperature at any hour day or night.

Aside from these and her many other whims, it was formally forbidden for anyone who crossed her path in the corridor leading from the dressing rooms to the stage, to lift their eyes and look at her. Everyone had to lower their heads, stand still, and wait for her to pass before breathing again. They didn't want it getting around, but concert organizers were under the obligation to ensure that this clause was respected, otherwise the performance would be cancelled, and three-quarters of the fee would have to be paid anyway. Amok knew the singer well, of course, even though he didn't listen to her music, all her songs seemed to revisit Billy Strayhorn's *Lush Life*. He found her as boring as can be. Plus, she seemed like a difficult person. *No, you're mistaken. She's a sweet, affectionate woman. She just likes it when white people suck up to her, that's all.* She named her production company Field Negress's Rule, not only to evoke the history of her community but also to embarrass anyone she could. She laughed about it. *I'm doing them a favor, my little Ajar, you see how much they need to atone.* She wasn't wrong about that, and the fact that she wasn't from one of their former colonies gave her an advantage. That of not being in any way their thing, their product. They were white folks nevertheless, having accepted this legacy and intending to make it bear fruit on the same bases as those established by their predecessors. She did her utmost to fight them, using the weapons at her disposal.

Ajar discovered sufferings through this woman that she'd only grasped in an abstract way until then. She still asserted her right not to be interested in the political aspect of things, to seek only her personal well-being. It was, to her mind, as unsubmissive an attitude as that of confronting the force that her client called the *white supremacist capitalist imperialist patriarchy*, citing all these epithets whenever a thought on the subject occurred to her, which was several times a day. Ajar only sought to enjoy life, it was of this that history had thought to deprive the people of the Continent, and that was her sole political stance. In a word, Amok concurred, specifying that it was her other life that he wanted to talk about. *Are you seeing anyone?* His question was met with a long silence, then a sort of affirmative grunt which nearly made him laugh. *Sissie, I'm not asking for details, it's just that we don't talk to each other much.* She was willing to answer, she didn't mind, but it might disturb him. He didn't think so, but maybe it wasn't the ideal moment. The time would come.

After all, together they'd lived through things that were difficult to share with others. They'd been two wisps of straw tossed about by violent currents. To be honest, there was no good reason why they should still be alive, and reasonably sane, even if the latter descriptor could not exactly be applied to him. Not after what happened. He hadn't meant it to happen and now he didn't know how to live with it. Ajar had no answer for him, she hoped he understood the reasons for his act, so he could avoid repeating it. Amok thought it was too late to start therapy. What's more, their environment made it impossible, he didn't believe in professional confidentiality for people with a name in this society. Talking about himself would mean divulging their family's private life. What was happening in the great house had often made its way outside, doctors and nurses had seen Madame's body covered in bruises, her face battered by blows. People knew every time the husband had changed careers, every time he'd invested in a lame project, and everyone knew that the Mususedi couple's fortune was the wife's. This didn't make things easier. And there was something else. Each of the discordant elements of the quartet that they formed in the great house had gone through his or her own experiences, and solitary battles. Because these had nevertheless been experienced in the intimacy of family, it was difficult to perceive them as distant and personal. In any case, he was skeptical of the virtues of therapy, didn't see himself doing that kind of thing. Perhaps he'd agree to it if Ixora would insist. When he expressed his desire to do his utmost so that Ixora and he could have a new start on a healthy basis, his words were met with silence, then his sister suggested that he see Ixora without delay. He thought he detected a warning in her voice, refrained from asking her about it. The revelation would take place in good time, he felt it approaching. *Sissy, I love you. You don't have to say that you do too, I've had plenty of proof. I love you.* Ajar was a tough cookie. So she didn't cry, which would have only embarrassed her brother. It was difficult for her to hide her emotion, but she didn't let it get the better of her, *It's just like you to do this. The day you come home, it's with dirty hands, and we have to accept you as you are. You know we will.*

Amok got off the phone to avoid draining the battery, and also because he was no longer alone. The conversation with Ajar had not delivered him from his deed, nothing could, yet he felt calmer. Not peaceful, but a little less feverish, less lost. He looked into the eyes of the woman without a name whose face was Ayezan's, wondering who she really was, why this face was pursuing him with such insistent tenderness. She was holding a bowl that others would have taken the precaution of putting on a tray, steam rose from it, a familiar smell of vegetables. He signaled to her to leave it on the mat, over there under the window. He wasn't hungry, but would force himself for her sake. His first impulse was to crawl there on all fours, he was afraid of hurting himself if he stood, his head was still spinning somewhat, his neck and shoulders seemed blocked. He leaned forward, but when he saw his hands approach the floor, he sat back up, thinking it would be better to accept the pain. Everything he'd tried to escape had come back to hit him in the face, unceremoniously, and laden with consequences. The effort took his breath away, made sweat bead on his forehead, increased tenfold the burning sensation running across his upper back. Once he was on his legs, he leaned against the wall, almost hitting his head against the nail on which his jacket had been hung. The woman rushed to his aid, offering him her roundness and her strength, the kindness in her eyes. He clutched her arm, pressed his forehead against hers in a gesture of affection which the old one responded to, accentuating the movement, moving her head to one side, then to the other. Amok would have liked to have exchanges with her of a different nature. The silence forced him to acute attentiveness, a quality of listening that he could barely explore given his state. He yielded as best he could, trying to establish a dialogue, beyond sight and touch. The woman sat opposite him, on the mat with the strident colors and synthetic fabric that had attracted his attention.

Lowering his head toward the broth she'd brought for him, a regional vegetable soup accompanied by roots, he closed his eyes. The woman's presence enveloped him, he soon felt transported to another place, a space where the unknown woman was leading him because she was there, the rhythm of her breathing supporting the silence. He found her inside, not only in the vision that unfolded behind his closed eyelids, but in his very being. The woman was no longer distinct from him, she was an element of what constituted his inmost being, attached to the part of him that had crossed the ages, adopted different forms, beyond what he was capable of envisaging on the rational level. At first, he rebelled against the idea, but it overcame his resistance. It was not a hypothesis, nor a possibility that his mind trained in criticism and contradiction, could place at a distance and analyze. Neither was it an intuition taking hold of him before turning into a sensation, and then an emotion. Amok listened to the voice inside him, whose inflections were clearly those he'd heard from the nameless woman, without being able to dissociate it from his own thoughts. Having become his, the voice of the unknown woman expressed itself in a language that he understood perfectly, that he had always mastered, although it was not spoken by any population he knew of. *You'd promised yourself that you would not lose me. Before being born among the living, before leaving for this journey whose stages you'd chosen, you'd promised yourself you would not lose me. I don't blame you . . . Soon they will come looking for you. I can see them from here.* Amok's inner voice asked him not to follow those who were on their way, those who'd be coming soon. He must spend one more night in TaMery, it was indispensable. Before returning to the world to carry the weight of his deeds, for there was no way around this obligation, he had to descend into himself, to lay the foundations of his new existence. This he had to do before seeing his loved ones again. On the night of the dazzlement, he'd put up too much resistance to Ayezan's work. She had to follow him into the day, into the tangible world, where her forces were reduced. The man's agreement was now needed to complete the journey through his night.

Nothing would be as before the storm, this he knew. Night had been the usual time of course for the living to slumber, hoping to see the coming of the next day, the rooster's lament and his recommendations. This night, born of others, had sunk him into his inner darkness, into the chaos of his soul. What had he learned from it? The voice said he had to be careful not to hasten daybreak, he hadn't defeated the monster. Not the force of which he thought he was the plaything, but the beast chained in a region of his being, and that he hadn't been able to hold back. That beast had existed and acted because he'd given it life, because he'd nurtured and strengthened it before letting it loose. Upon himself, upon the life whose course and span he accepted without ever having elaborated a real project, finding no significance in it. As brutal as this news seemed to him, Ixora and Kabral were not the goal of his life, they had no way of giving it meaning.

Afflicted by his deed, he'd had the presence of mind to seek the path of TaMery, but he'd recoiled before the immensity of the task, and the contours of the beloved land had been no more than those of other people's dream. These wanderers of Negrohood, as he saw them, lost in a torment from which he thought he'd escaped. Maybe he was right about this, if it were possible to remove yourself completely from the pain of those among whom it had been given to you to come into the world. That wasn't the point, anyway. What they were trying to make him understand was that there was a land to love in each of us, a soil in which the being could sow its offerings to life. If solitude and sorrow were all that had grown there, it was because they were what Amok had cultivated. This was not what he was being advised to examine further, these elements were not bereft of value. *You'd promised yourself not to lose me. Before being born among the living, you'd chosen the stages of the journey. You knew we were strong enough and spoke of sublimation. But when faced with the challenge, you turned away . . .*

The room was bathed in a bluish light, similar to the hue that had mingled with the mauve of dawn. It streamed through the window and the door, both of which had been left open. Facing him, distinct once more, the woman smiled with the kindness that never left her. Yet he perceived a gravity in her attitude, which made him think that he hadn't imagined this exchange. When she nodded, Amok knew that it was not only in approval of his emptying his bowl of broth. The woman was staring at him, waiting for an answer. Nodding in his turn, he said, *I'll stay.* She got up, helped him to do the same, and supported him to the bed where he stretched out. The wood didn't seem as uncomfortable as it had in the morning. The unknown woman walked to the door, and Continent Noir appeared. Amok recognized him from afar, saw him enter the room, take away the empty bowl. When he reached the threshold, the man turned to him, stayed like that for a moment. He was no longer the screwball who'd raced over to him earlier, driven by spirits who'd dictated a message that he clamored to cover Bobby Hebb's voice with his own. The radiance that repeated the morning twilight, folding the day back onto itself, imparted a painterly quality to his coppery skin, to the whole of his body. He walked out without a word, his back slightly bent, the weight of a defeat on his muscular shoulders.

Amok couldn't put his finger on whom this man reminded him of. The name hovered on the edge of his mind but slipped away before his memory could embrace it. It would come back to him. When the time was ripe, it would come back. The woman took her place at his side, on the stool left there, sat in silence. Continent Noir reappeared, without entering the hut. He stood outside, with his back to them, arms crossed, ready to meet those who might come before twilight. Amok had no need for these things to be said, to be warned that when night fell, this place and the path leading to it would no longer be accessible to ordinary sight. Those who were coming for him would arrive when they were permitted to do so, in the remains of the day, and would go back almost immediately. They wouldn't be told of his presence, they'd find him in due course. Then Amok would know why and how to live. Voices came to him soon, an animated conversation, whose content he didn't grasp. He didn't see whom Continent Noir was speaking to, using his body as a barrier to guard what would have been only a semblance of sleep.

The rooster didn't sound its morning wail. Amok knew he wouldn't see the entity again whose faces and names had been revealed to him. He would lose her no longer, wondered how he could have wandered that far away. He rose, swept the hut, tidied up, thought he'd have liked to leave flowers. A bucket of water had been left for him on the doorstep. A bar of plant soap had been placed on a folded bath towel. The man first thought of taking all this inside the hut, then changed his mind. It would have been a pity to spatter the floor he'd just cleaned. The day was slowly breaking, still holding back its light, letting the night withdraw at its own pace. Already you no longer knew what the night had been, you still ignored what the day would bring. This then was not a moment of blooming or of wilting. Yet neither was it life as it flowed between the two. This struck him suddenly. The idea that the morning twilight that opened an interstice between night and day did so only to better escape both. Borrowing from one as from the other, it belonged to itself alone.

Humans had tried to reassure themselves by inventing an hourly system that subdivides duration, including in it what could never be part of it. Amok had no words to define what was not strictly speaking a moment. It was a passage, the path that day and night took to come to meet the world, and then leave it. The man took the bucket into the garden, set it down by one of the royal palms that grew there, a vicariant species from the other shore. There, he undressed, began to wash himself as he'd so often seen people doing in the poor districts of the city. First, his face, the inside of his mouth. Then, his whole body, from head to toe. The cool water invigorated him. He hadn't felt life course through him so powerfully in a very long time. A feeling close to joy welled up in him, which he tempered without brutality. It was premature to yield to it. He had things to do first, he would not be remiss.

The ground beneath his feet was tepid. He realized that the moon did not every night have the coldness that was associated with it. As he finished rinsing the soap off his body, emptying the bucket on his head, Amok saw the face of the woman who'd called herself Ayezan, when she'd visited him two nights in a row. To come to meet him in this dimension, she'd given herself a name evoking that of a spirit known as the guardian of passages, places and times intended for choosing. This spirit also presided over healing, over the transmission of the power to do so. The royal palm tree represented this in the plant world. The ones in the garden grew tall, their foliage looked like a cluster of huge feathers that nature had shaped into a headdress. A crown. The towel with which he dried himself was sparkling white. He'd placed the bar of plant soap he'd used on a guava leaf blown off the tree by the wind. Amok thought he'd take the soap with him. He had its scent on his skin, a perfume of smoked wood, earth, and fresh fruit. It had the yellow color of a ripe kasimangolo. Having wound the towel around his hips he picked up his wrapper, hung it over his left forearm, put the makeshift soap dish at the bottom of the empty bucket, checked that the soap was clean, and put it there too. In the hut, he noticed that his jacket had been washed, his pants and shirt too. But it had become impossible for him to wear these clothes, it would be a step backward, when he felt the strength and desire to move forward. Amok no longer asked himself the questions that, whirling around in his mind, heightened his anxiety.

He scanned the room, hoping to find a change of clothes. A simple wrapper would do. Continent Noir was not a dandy. He owned very little and needed everything he had. Amok shrugged his shoulders. He didn't see anything that would do, that he could borrow for a time. He was about to rummage through a trunk on which a few paltry pieces of crockery had been carefully piled, when he heard a cough. Continent Noir was there, tall and coppery, looking as fresh as if he'd just come out of a luxury hotel spa. His broad smile, added to the slant of his eyes, which made him look mischievous. *The ancient one left this for you.* He handed him a short bogolan tunic, the baggy pants that went with it, canvas sneakers. Amok smiled back at Continent Noir. The man didn't step outside to let him get dressed. He stood there, happily, a look of childish innocence on his face. Asking him to turn away would have been rude, an offense to the purity of his gaze. Amok unwound the towel, put on the pants, and then the tunic, sat down on the bed to put on his shoes. Continent Noir nodded. *You're ready.* He didn't eat in the morning, so he had nothing to offer him but he'd made some coffee. It would be an honor if Amok would share this with him before leaving. Having received his guest's consent, Continent Noir signaled to him to get the rolled-up mat from the corner of the hut. *Take a seat in front of the house, I'm coming.* With these words, he withdrew.

The rooster wailed, and his cry blew the clouds away, as if he were opening the curtain to make the stage appear. The men drank together, in silence, while the sun took its place in the sky. The mix of coffee beans with peppery berries gave the drink a flavor first of cubeb then of nutmeg. The first time Amok had drunk coffee like this, it was Shrapnel who had served it to him. In the course of his journey of several years that took him to the North, his brother-friend had traveled through many countries, he'd brought with him many customs and flavors, including café Touba. He thought of him with heartfelt fondness, Shrapnel would always be in his life, he'd left him a son. Continent Noir had added only a touch of sugar to the thick, brown molasses mixture. Amok would have liked to talk, ask who'd come by the night before, he'd heard voices. It wasn't important. He had to stay here, to be in that moment, in the presence of the unloved child who'd become a man on his own. Continent Noir asked nothing more of life than life itself, as it came, one day after another. He did not experience solitude because he was inhabited, because he'd walked in search of others, bringing them back in his footsteps every time he returned to his piece of land. He too had stories to tell. The one about his ghetto blaster. The one about this coffee that wasn't seasoned like this hereabouts. And many other things still, which did not bind him to the injustices of his youth. Maybe he didn't see things this way, but Amok found him beautiful, powerful, enough to become, for the time of a song on the radio, the messenger of a living god. This was one of the things he wouldn't tell anyone, his certainty that Shrapnel had visited him. His brother-friend had been there throughout the ordeal, whispering lyrics, the melodies of old songs. The farewell to brothers by the Commodores and Bobby Hebb, and Greg Perry's manly lament. He rose to take his leave, Continent Noir followed suit, reached out his hand. *I saw that your car was taken away.* Amok had no intention of driving the sedan. He wanted to walk. He shook Continent Noir's hand, hugged him, and headed for the road.

Amok didn't look back. His hand in his pants pocket, he clutched the cell phone that he'd feared he'd forget, and the wallet containing his ID. Sure that Continent Noir wouldn't accept money from him, he'd left some inside the hut. He relaxed, letting his arms fall to his sides. The red laterite had dried, he was not alone on the road. He passed a farmer from whom he asked directions, schoolchildren in uniform, food vendors hoping for an opep or a clando cab, a goat tied to a tree. When the sun reached its zenith, he left the roadway, took to the shade of the trees growing on either side, walked less quickly. Amok tried not to let his mind attach to any of the thoughts that came to him. Feeling tired, he sat at the foot of a tree, leaned back, was about to close his eyes, when he saw them. No doubt it was lunchtime, he hadn't looked, but nothing else could have driven them out of their quarters in this weather. An abruptly enraged sun threatened to finish off the living. You had to have a good reason to get behind the wheel of a jeep. Yet everything was quiet, just an ordinary day in the country. Nevertheless there they were, actually in no great hurry, for hungry gendarmes. One of them was scrutinizing the surroundings more intently than his colleagues. There were three of them, quite young, and he was surprised that their superiors had authorized them to travel in this practically new khaki-colored Wrangler. Amok had no intention of moving. His eyes met those of the observer, who immediately tapped the driver's shoulder.

Two men leaped out of the vehicle, took a step in his direction, stopped to exchange a few words. Turning toward him again, they shouted for him to come over to them. His dress attracted attention, it was not the fashion in this country, the bogolan was a foreign textile. He obeyed, it was the most reasonable thing to do. *Is this your land?* Otherwise, he had no right to make himself at home like that. They asked him the question out of politeness, for they knew the owner. On the other hand, they didn't know him, he'd never been seen in these parts, he'd have to show them his ID. As he reached into the pocket of his pants, glad that he'd kept his wallet, the questioning continued. *Where are you going?* He indicated the name of the place, added that it shouldn't be too far away, he was resting for a moment before hitting the road again. *On foot?* Amok nodded, holding out his identification card. Yes, he was walking. A silence followed his reply. The gendarme who'd taken the document passed it to his colleague, who looked at it in turn. They didn't tell him that his father had notified them, that they'd towed the sedan to a garage. They didn't tell him that they'd been looking for him for more than two days now, that nothing obliged them to traipse around the countryside looking for a grown man, but that they'd done so, everyone in the region had respect for Monsieur Mususedi. Only a great mystic—no one dared say a sorcerer—could lead the life he led, living alone in such a place.

The night before, they'd shown up at a man's home, a somewhat deranged guy. His hut was the only house they hadn't yet visited. They didn't insist. This mental retard expressed himself like a child, and surely didn't know how to lie. When he'd put together the few words in his vocabulary, stammering that he hadn't seen anyone, they'd left him in peace, decided to continue their search today, with little hope, to be perfectly honest. Many people had witnessed a light in the sky, the sudden appearance of a night sun, during the recent storm. It wasn't the first time that this had occurred, and it had sometimes happened that the victims of car accidents had not been found in such circumstances. They didn't say this, nor that some of them had never recovered from having been dazzled. Those who stayed in a coma or lost their minds. Most of all, they kept to themselves that, sharing the beliefs of the locals as they did, they had serious questions about him and were wary. The strangeness of his clothing added to their unformulated fears, and the fact that he stood there before them without a scratch, in full possession of his faculties, only confirmed their misgivings. According to regulations, he should be taken to the police station, questioned, they should write up a report, decide whether or not to bring him to his father. They didn't have to confer before agreeing on what to do.

The young gendarmes gave him back his identity card, bid him to follow them, Amok didn't demur. He noticed that the jeep was heading for the locality where his father resided, the police station must be there too, which worked just fine for him. Neither he nor his fellow travelers had uttered a word, when the vehicle stopped in front of a huge building that looked like it was made of unfired clay. One of them climbed out of the car. They watched him follow a lane, too narrow for the Jeep, that led to the entrance of the building. Amok had a vague presentiment, he didn't let it solidify, sediment into an emotion. Maybe he didn't know what he was feeling, what he should be feeling. The trees planted in front of the house were not unfamiliar to him. They were the ones his father would have liked to see growing in their family home's garden, and that Madame thought were too imposing to surround an urban villa. He hadn't expected such excess, but that wasn't surprising either. This megalomania, this eccentricity, this poetry too, were the marks of his father. The man who spun tales about the rooster's lament, the morning twilight, bygone days when words were important, when evildoers were driven out of the community and entrusted to fate, to divine mercy or anger. The man whose kindness and humor would brutally give way to destructive fury. He hadn't seen him for some fifteen years, hadn't been in touch, hadn't thought of calling him to announce his return. At the sight of Ixora's body in the mud, it was toward this man that he had run, this father who had passed his poisoned genes down to him. What did he have to say to him now? What was to be done with the unbreakable bond that united them, all this beauty steeped in pain? He didn't know. At the sight of his father's house, the feeling of peace that descended upon him at dawn wavered.

Amok wanted to hold on to the tranquility he'd found, resist the whirlwind of questions with no comfortable answers. The door of the huge house opened, the gendarme took off his hat, wiped his feet on the mat, in a movement that seemed to last for hours. A gong resounded in Amok's chest, a slow and deafening beat that he didn't try to escape. It was there. Despite the distance, despite the long silence. It was there. The most profound love, the most acute anger. Both, with the same intensity as on the day of his departure for the North. But he was no longer the young adult who, draped in bitterness, had decided to cut himself off from his parents, no longer return to this country that he didn't see as his own. It had been nothing to him but the land of his progenitors, of poorly kept secrets, of unhealable wounds. Then, his life had changed. In unexpected ways. There'd been a child, a woman. To protect them, he'd found nothing better than his native land, his family home. Maybe he'd made a mistake, but it was laden with meaning. He'd returned to the place where he'd almost been destroyed, the place where he'd been loved, expected, desired, long before all this. Amok wiped his sweaty hands on his tunic. The gendarmes in the car were impassive, mute. One of them opened the glove compartment, took out a packet of kilichi and began to chew, chew, chew, without swallowing, without losing his composure. His colleague reached into the newspaper cone, began chewing in turn, because that was the whole interest of kilichi. Amok didn't realize he was opening the door until he heard a voice say, *Wait in the car*, without knowing which of the two men had spoken.

The gendarme who'd entered the building came back out. He took a few steps up the lane, stopped, turned back. Charles was the first to come out after him. Amok recognized his tall stature from afar, his catlike way of putting his feet on the ground, the mahogany color of his skin. Then came this man, dressed in a velvet wrapper like his father would sometimes wear in the morning for breakfast. As children, he and Ajar laughed about it, it was actually an old bedspread, because it was too long, it dragged on the floor and with each step their father had to lift it up and tie it around him again. By the time he reached the dining room, he had a lifebuoy of fabric wrapped around his waist, which didn't bother him. It made him feel good, like a child having decided to spend the day in pajamas. The man who now stood between Charles and the

gendarme had tied his sanja differently, in the manner of dignitaries in the western part of the Continent. He was bare-
chested under the crimson garment, his feet were nowhere to
be seen. With a single word, Amok was given permission to
get out. The door didn't slam shut behind him, he'd only had
the strength to open it. His progress was slow, he didn't have
the feeling he was responsible for it, but the distance between
him and those awaiting him was shrinking. He could not yet
distinguish the expression on their faces, yet certain details
stood out, the white hair of the middle-aged man, the tips of
his shoes, which he immediately knew were boots. Without
having ever learned horseback riding, Madame's husband had
always dreamed of wearing such shoes. She'd mocked him,
this man had a storehouse of whims, each more ridiculous
than the other, all equally unproductive.

Madame's sharp tongue had the futile impulse to voice
lengthy commentaries divided into chapters on each of the
whims, large or small, which had sprouted in her husband's
mind. What amused the children was insufferable to Madame,
horrified her most of the time. Amok couldn't recall having
laughed or played with his mother. He'd only ever heard her
advice, her demands, her suffering, her refusal to be pitied.
Scenes from his childhood assailed him, filed past at high
speed in his memory. Everything had been spoiled by the violence of the husband, the father. He stopped in the middle of
the lane. Some flamboyant flowers, red, delicate, hung from
the branches. Some fell on the crushed rock that covered the
path. His eyes saw nothing but this, these still-fresh flowers,
already dead. The man who came to meet him could not be

hated. That was the problem, what he felt riling him, more acutely since he himself had struck his fiancée. His father hugged him, caressed his head, his face. He'd always been like that, affectionate, reassuring. His voice said what it had always said, that he was ready to listen, that no subject was taboo, no question forbidden, that he'd do his best to help. *Junior, come.* His mother was worried sick. They must call her right away.

II

They'd settled into seats in the garden, after visiting the house. The early-morning arrival of the first workers had roused him from his bed. Amok almost felt bad that he'd slept so well. He'd opened the window, watched the housekeeper leave the outbuildings and enter the house. He'd gone out. The singing of the workmen came to him from the upper floor, from the still unfinished section of the building. They were working spiritedly in the new day, you could hear them joking and laughing. Amok had found his father in the interior garden. Daylight flowed in through the lightwell. That was where flowers were grown, where meals were taken. The two men had only exchanged commonplaces, the son hadn't been ready for a conversation. He'd preferred to rest, put it off to the next day, something he wouldn't have done in the past. Charles had to leave in the morning. Amok and his father would take to the road in the afternoon. His return to the city couldn't be postponed any longer. Seeing his son, the man had stood up, opened his arms. This time, he didn't move forward, he let

Amok come to him, accept or refuse the embrace. He'd thought about it part of the night, until he couldn't fight sleep off anymore, his reflections had bled into his dreams.

There'd been no images, just voices, hers especially, cartloads of reproaches poured out, and his father's who'd only been able to say, *Forgive me*. That had made him even angrier, it was not what he wanted, to hear him apologize, though he didn't know what he wanted. That part of the story was written, no one had the power to erase it. In the dream, he hadn't dared ask the question that tormented him, the reply to which could have indicated that there was a difference of nature between his deed and his father's repeated acts. Some people took pleasure in inflicting violence, this was alien to him, but was it to his father? Amok refused to believe that one can regularly lose control because words were gone, and only blows were left. That was what had happened to him, what, he wanted to believe, would never happen again. When he woke up, the turbulence had subsided. There'd be no questions to ask. He'd have to listen.

Amok had embraced his father. They'd sat down to an unusual meal for Monsieur Mususedi, who used to start his day devouring a ham omelet served with sweet potato fries or leftovers from dinner, such as miele ma sese and peanut sauce with chicken, dishes that tasted even better the following day. The abundance of green covering the table was quite surprising. Amok had raised an eyebrow. That was how the conversation had started. The input of the son had been limited to nods and looks indicating his presence. His father had begun at the end, announcing that he wasn't in good shape. He was taking medicine, a lot of it, but he couldn't complain. He had the means to pay, and his doctor, a long-time friend, wouldn't go around town gossiping about him. His lifestyle had changed radically, he thought this was good for him. The day Madame had pressed a handgun to his belly, asking him to leave, he was going to stop. Knowing he was already sick, the sight of blood on his wife's forehead had frightened him, he recoiled when she'd spoken. He didn't know why, it was only at that point that he'd come to his senses.

Of course, it would have been easy for him to claim, with few if any scruples, that they were both to blame for their bad relationship. That it was hard to share life with a woman who believed less in the equality of the sexes than in the inferiority of men. Only her father, Conroy Mandone, found grace in her eyes. The first time he'd raised his hand against her, Madame had scoffed at the failure of a project that he cared about, drowning it in waves of contempt, before concluding: *It was a foregone conclusion. You think you're smarter than others, but you really don't have a knack for business. Anyway, don't worry, I'm here. I'll fix it, but next time, talk to me about it, huh? Tonight I'm sleeping in the guest room. You can have the maid in your bed.* Those last words were what had triggered his fury.

The next day, mortified, ashamed, he asked for forgiveness, swore. He'd gone as low as one could go, he wouldn't lift a finger against her again, he'd do what she wanted. The mark of his fingers on her neck, the black and blues on her face had been the most horrifying sight. He'd left the house for a few days, not knowing how to make amends, calling himself every name in the book. That had been his second mistake, second because there had been so many. He'd found her furious, circling the house like a caged beast. The rest was not worth dwelling on. All four of them had lived through it, each in a different place, each suffering in their own way.

His father didn't seem to be making excuses. If he thought he was suffering from a psychological disorder, he hadn't said so. What he said had gone beyond what a father could share with his son in the society from which he came. AIDS was not a word that could be uttered, the topic was off limits, but Amok had understood. Cases were frequent but remained unspoken, particularly in their circles. People could die from lightning meningitis, from long, unspecified diseases, from cancer at times. Never from this, never from this ailment that sanctioned sinful ways, a life of vice. His father had no illegitimate children, news thereof would have made its way back to the children he'd recognized. It wasn't Madame's severity that had caused his violence, it had simply provided a support for it. There was something else, but it didn't concern Amok, who was carrying his own burdens.

They hadn't eaten much, a few bites of raw vegetables, some slices of solo papaya. His father had stood up, suggested that he take him on a tour of the house, his creation. *Did you know that the young people in the area call it the Palace of Shabazz?* Amok had smiled, his father had probably never heard the legend. Pronouncing the name of his wife tenderly, the man had confessed his hope that she'd come one day, he'd extend a formal invitation to her, when the work was completed. The result would impress her, no doubt about it. And when she would see the plantings. For the moment, the yield was not as good as he'd expected, he could not yet export crops to neighboring countries. That would come. Parasites had infested the pineapples, some orange trees had been lost, just like that, for no obvious reason, but everything would be sorted out soon. Amok found himself faced with a man who was racked with guilt. Someone who, having failed to ask himself the right questions at the right time, lived on dreams alone. He made broad gestures to explain where he drew his inspiration, related how he had sometimes had to destroy what had been built, because the result wasn't what he'd imagined. It was a matter of inventing the future architecture of the Continent, such was his project. The house was to be a model, concrete evidence of the possibility of drawing inspiration from Katiopa's architectural gems, inscribing in matter the trace of the past, the promises of the future. The result was this building that evoked the huge Nzi we mabwe, the legendary Timbuktu, ancient Ityopya. It was just like his father: it was unachievable, you'd have to live several lifetimes to complete it, the man would be dead before he could invite the one whose forgiveness he would never get. He'd only ever asked her for it between two thrashings.

Amok recalled, he would never forget, the day when his father had grabbed Madame by the hair, dragged her out of the villa, onto the road that had not yet been paved. To marry her, he'd given a dowry of cattle, alcohol, cloth, and hard cash to the Mandones. So she was his property, like the trinkets he'd purchased, like his car or his ties. She could call the police, they wouldn't do a thing to him. Something was amiss, something was amiss with him. Objectively speaking, Amok didn't think he was suffering from this. He admitted this to himself, without feeling that he was abandoning his father to his affliction. One of them at least had to pull through, only that would reconcile them. Amok would be able to love him without suffering from it, if he didn't let himself fall into the same pitfalls. Until then, thinking he was a replica of his father, he'd bolted the doors on all sides to keep the monster from running loose. It had devoured him from inside.

They'd walked the corridors, whose ceilings were so high one couldn't look up without feeling faint, unless you were Monsieur Mususedi, this man with his head in the clouds, his feet off the ground. He spoke of what had been accomplished, what remained to be done, rhapsodizing about the future, his eyes sparkling with visions of it. Then, the visit was left aside, the man brought his wife up again, their meeting. He hadn't noticed her right away, but after they'd spoken, he'd thought of her only. He'd wanted them to settle in the North, where they'd met and married. He'd been promised a job when he finished his studies. They wouldn't have been rich, but there they could be anonymous, freed from the burdens of coastal society, from the weight of their two names. Nothing swayed her. She'd preferred living here, at home. From the start, their aspirations had diverged. This he said. Then, *You know, my parents stayed married for forty years*, and Amok wondered what he was getting at. Madame hadn't asked for a divorce. She was the one paying for this Nzi we mabwe, for the plantations that would supply food to the people of this part of the Continent.

The library, with its massive proportions and shelves three-quarters empty, invited silence. There Amok had discovered an entire wall dedicated to his paternal grandfather's memory. He was familiar with most of the pictures. Black-and-white photos, all they revealed of the forefather was his career, he hadn't had any other life. A few more photographs, taken at his funeral, showed that he had been mourned, that people had come in their best clothes to have the honor of escorting him to his final resting place. Amok hadn't wanted to see more. Ajar had taken great interest in the man whose name they bore, not he. He didn't want to know, didn't want to hear when they told him, *He'd have loved you, you resemble him a lot*. His reluctance, he sensed it, went beyond Angus Mususedi's involvement in colonial history, the fact that he hadn't chosen the side of the independence movement. He didn't like the man, the severity of his gaze, the haughtiness written all over his face. Looking at the pictures, you saw not him but his armor, he hoped that the resemblance between them was limited to physical features. Unlike the other rooms he'd visited, the library was Northern in style, not one object, not one shape, called the Continent to mind. This added to the coldness of the setting. He'd motioned to his father to leave the room, turned to the door without waiting, when a display case caught his eye. Set vertically on barely visible supports were two rifles. They'd appeared as imposing as in his childhood, when he and Ajar had come upon them under their parents' bed.

He should have seen them as soon as they walked into the library. They stood there, close to the door, rigid and silent, like totems. His father had approached the case, without opening it. His admiration was undeniable, as was his fear. After a lengthy moment of contemplation, he let out a sigh: *You know, son, you can't criticize your parents.* Amok had kept silent. His father had never said a thing against Angus Mususedi, that peerless giant. Yet these few words, the first that had come to him since they had been there, suggested that there was cause for criticism. Amok had imagined his father alone in this place, no doubt he came here sometimes. What conversations did he have with the hero, the decorated soldier? His father had seemed very small to him, a boy at the foot of a stone colossus, a sensitive being who needed someone to listen to him. Silently he'd thanked him for having been different. Very imperfect, guilty of serious acts, but open to the words of his children whom he'd coddled and had wanted to be free. He'd offered them what he hadn't been given, what he'd no longer receive, the strength, not so much to kill the father, which didn't make much sense, but to leave him in his place, not to be burdened with him.

He'd wrapped his arm around his father's shoulders, *Come, Papa, let's get some air*, and had led him out of the mausoleum. It felt as if he were moving a statue, a monument of silence. His father spoke easily, this he'd demonstrated again at breakfast. His words, however, never went beyond a certain threshold. When it came to Angus, the affable man that Amok had always known was struck with muteness. The whole city knew of his alacrity, it had been a precious asset in his business. The whole city had also got wind of his fits of rage, the waves that swept everything in their path. But no one knew who he was, nobody wanted to know. Amok himself had been reluctant to approach this ground, didn't think he could. All he could perceive were its shadows and pale glimmers, nothing that would enable him to have a handle on it. The man who was by his side, it was clear to him, had no need to know that his relative had raped his son, nor that his children had had a terrified love of him.

They'd gone out to the park, behind the right side of the house, the outbuildings occupied the left. From there, they could see a part of the farmland that stretched out below, a cascade of red rock leading to it. Amok didn't see any other way to get there, but hoped there was. His father hesitated: *Junior* . . . The name made him smile, he was going on thirty-four. His father had wanted to give him his own first name and had done so. The registry employee had mistakenly written *k* at the end instead of *s*. With his characteristic humor and fantasy, Amos had thought it was wonderful in the end that his son was called Amok. He liked the sound of it. It had more character than Amos, whose biblical origin made it sound antiquated. Yet he had only ever called him *Junior*. Madame had found out she was pregnant with Ajar while the couple was visiting a region in the west of the Continent that bore that name. The husband had seen it as an obvious sign. In both cases, Madame had let him have his way. She'd chosen their mina ma mundi, their village names, and would not call them by anything else. Her children were Dio and Tiki. Like many young people of his generation, he'd seen the film adaptation of *Cry, the Beloved Country*, a novel that students in his day read in their junior year of high school. Like the television series *Roots*, this movie depicting the violence of apartheid had been a shock, and a catalyst for revolts and political activism.

Those were the days when rap music was born. Finding in his turn that his first name had character, Amok had worn it with pride, and never departed from it. His belated reading of Stefan Zweig had not led him to reject it. That had come at a time when Amok was convinced he was harboring a monster, so his father's extravagance had seemed premonitory. Analyzing the question more deeply, he'd seen Amos's apparent frivolity as a way of passing the burden on to him, a reinvention of the ritual consisting, for fathers, of spitting into the mouths of their sons in order to transfer a power, whatever its nature, to them. The man he'd seen in the library had no prepotency to transmit. He hadn't received it, but was still subjected to it, in a way. *Junior . . . This woman, your Northern companion . . . If you love her, leave her . . . You know, your grandfather, he too had this.* Amok took his father's hand. His trembling fingers, prickled with gray hairs. There were tears in the knuckles, pain in the tips of the nails. Impotence. The dream, frantically kept alive, of a second chance that would never be granted.

The two didn't cry for the same reasons, but they cried together, without a sound. At no point had his father reproached him for his long absence. He'd awaited him without hoping to see him again, without finding the strength to reach out, having stopped writing after a while. They hugged, their head buried in each other's neck. *I didn't say anything to your friend*. Amok nodded. When they separated, he held his father's hand in his. There were now workers in the fields, men and women busy weeding. The singing of the masons barely reached them from afar, but they could be heard laughing. Charles's presence surprised them. A car was driving him back to town, he'd come to say goodbye. Amok rose to shake his hand and walk him to the road. They hadn't spoken much, but they'd soon make up for lost time. His father and Charles exchanged warm words of farewell, Amok noticed that the younger man gave the older one a long, somewhat seductive look. This made him smile, he was sure that Charles was interested in him. When they reached the edge of the property, a car without license plates was there. Cords had been attached to the trunk, bundles of plantains kept it from closing. The vehicle seemed, in spite of all, to be in good-enough condition. Amok patted Charles on the back: *Hey man, je te call dès que je back*, I'll call you when I'm back.

III

His father took the wheel to drive him back to the villa. They'd send Enoch, the family chauffeur, to pick up the sedan once it was fixed. He'd catch an opep to get there. They said goodbye in front of the house, the husband figuring he wouldn't be welcome. Besides, it wasn't the right time to be introduced to Kabral and Ixora. If he left now, he'd be back before nightfall, spending time away from the countryside was becoming more and more difficult for him. Amok didn't expect to see Kabral rush out to him, hear him shouting *Pops, I'm so happy*. When the child ran back to announce his return, he knew that he wouldn't speak to him. That day would come, but first he'd do everything he could to make amends. Ixora and Madame were sitting in the parlor, he sensed they were somewhat tense. They rose in a single movement. He approached to embrace them, first Ixora, thinking that even worse than hitting his companion, was having to look her in the eye afterwards. Her upper lip was still swollen, there was a gash on her right cheekbone, a dark mark under her eye on the same side. The three of them sat down. Amok didn't look down, but his gaze was not fixed on anything in particular. They spoke little, hardly at all. All excited, Kabral bounced back and forth between the living room and the kitchen, where Makalando had apparently cooked up a feast. Amok recognized Madame's manner. She wouldn't vent her anger until much later. First she'd feed him, make sure he rested. Then she would chop him to pieces, no need for funeral preparations, there'd be nothing left. Kabral was having fun naming the dishes that would be served, they were those that Amok had loved most as a child. Madame was out to remind him that they'd always known how to please him, that he'd been dead set on spoiling everything for a long time. Only a few days before, he wouldn't have hesitated to throw cruel words in her face: *If you'd divorced him, your son wouldn't have felt entitled to beat his wife*. He'd come a long way since then. Taking advantage of Kabral's absence, Amok stood up: *Mama, excuse us*. It was up to him to initiate the conversation. He didn't know what he'd say. Though he'd thought about it a lot, nothing specific had come to him, he had no plan. Ixora followed him, he stepped aside to let her pass in front. When they entered the bedroom, Amok wondered whether she was still sleeping there, realized she wasn't. What had Kabral been told? The child's life had begun to change, he was too smart not to have noticed. Ixora had a foot outside the great house, which she would leave once she'd recovered. He'd thought of begging her to stay, that was all he wanted. Yet Amok felt he had no right to force things, to implore her to change her mind, to try to buy time.

Ixora had sat down on the bed, at the head, her back against the wall, her legs folded underneath. She was wearing a short skirt, as she often did, with a hemline at the upper thigh. The man remained standing, took a few steps to the window, drew the curtain, feeling ill at ease in this bogolan outfit that he didn't usually wear. He turned around: *You first*. Amok didn't receive the barrage of insults he might have expected. Ixora's tone was not aggressive when she told him that she'd met someone, that she was looking for a house where she could live with this person. Amok felt the need to sit, which he did immediately, letting himself drop down to the carpet. *Because this man is homeless?* He was not trying to be sarcastic. His question, asked in a childish way, was sincere. Ixora smiled, which disarmed him completely. *She's a woman. I don't think Kabral would be at ease where she lives now.* Amok didn't ask her where they'd met, the stages in the development of the relationship. His work had absorbed him utterly, Ixora had had plenty of time to see people, he was surprised that Madame hadn't rushed to tell him that she was going out alone. He remembered that he'd bumped into her one late afternoon as she was walking on the street. It had pleased him that she was finding her bearings, getting adjusted. He'd driven her home without giving it a second thought, they'd slept head to toe as usual. Of course, he'd seen her change, without knowing what to attribute this to, he'd found her less and less indulgent toward him.

So there was someone. Obviously, getting off on kamut was no longer on her mind. It was not that Ixora was falling in love, someone had touched her. Amok knew this gives people wings. The feeling, but also the pleasure. He nodded, remembering his sister's unspoken warning. She knew. And Kabral? *The little one. What did you tell him?* She and Madame had talked about it for two days, until they had news of Amok. Then, when the call came from Ajar, saying she'd spoken to her brother, that he was doing well, the two women had risked making up a story, hoping he'd return very soon. Madame had taken on the task of talking to the boy, both had decided it was better not to tell him what had happened before Amok's disappearance. So Kabral thought his parents had been assaulted, his father had been kidnapped by the criminals, but they hadn't gone into details. He knew that she was looking for a house, the real estate agent had come by the day before, Kabral figured it was because of Ixora's bad relationship with the mistress of the great house. *He thinks we're getting along better since I decided to leave. I thought you should tell him. That you won't be living with us.* Would it also be up to him to say that she'd have a partner? She didn't reply.

Ixora had proven that she could surprise him, but he knew her. She wouldn't confide in her son, not yet. Two women together could still pass for friends, without arousing suspicion. Kabral's mother, in her son's eyes, had no sex life. *Listen, Ixora, I ask you to forgive me for what happened. And . . . I have no excuse. I intended to plead with you to stay. With me. But okay. There's no point anymore.* It would be from her mouth that Kabral would learn that she loved a woman. She'd let him know when she was able to. And who was the woman anyway? When she told him, he nodded again. *I see.* She was heading for disaster, it wouldn't last. Madame's hairdresser was certainly a sensual woman, with many precious qualities, but he didn't think she knew how to read. Their love was mainly physical now, Ixora was discovering the needs of her body, was exploring its possibilities. She had years to catch up on, he would readily grant her that.

The day would come when her intellect would demand its due. Masasi wouldn't be able to satisfy that need. Unless she discovers that she has talents as a hunter, Ixora would go through a period of uncertainty. He'd be there. Very much so. She had no idea how much. He would provide her with the most secure existence she could have in this country: to be in a marriage with a man who had no desire to have sex with her, to continue to see all the women she wanted. He, too, would find a place to live. All she'd have to do is move in, when the time came. *Ixora . . . Okay, understood. I hope you'll be happy . . . I'd like Kabral to come spend time with me often. Can we work something out?* Amok was wagering on the future, and was prepared to lose. He'd be there when what he saw as an adventure came to an end. Maybe Ixora would want to go back up North. That possibility didn't escape him.

Nothing had happened as he'd imagined. The intrusion of another person into the emotional equation had never for a moment crossed his mind. He had seen nothing, heard nothing. What he'd perceived at the time seemed superficial to him, he thought Ixora was irritable because she was idle, and that would change quickly, in a matter of weeks . . . The separation was to begin without delay. If he'd listened to himself, Amok would have left the great house first, taken a room at the Prince des Côtes, while he figured out what he wanted to do. Questions surfaced, which he immediately tried to push away. It was no use wondering whether he'd suddenly slipped into the costume of an ordinary male. That was not how he saw himself, he wasn't a primate. He'd had an outburst, just one, it had made him sick. That was his problem now. Ixora was no longer the intimate friend to whom he could confide his most painful secrets. When the time came that she would break up with Masasi, their lives would not be the same. Ixora would have sexual appetites to satisfy, she'd go out at night after work, wouldn't necessarily come home, would become attached to these women or to one of them, it would be complicated. The thirty-six-year-old who'd never squatted over a mirror to look at her sex was gone. He had no idea what had become of her. Something inside him clung to her in spite of all, it was too soon to give up.

So he forced himself to focus on one aspect of the person before him, to see Ixora as Kabral's mother first and foremost. It was in these terms alone that he could imagine a future with her. It wasn't insignificant, but it wasn't enough for him. Amok admitted to himself that their initial situation suited him better, that that was what he'd have liked to maintain, that he was making a feeble effort to patch things up. It bothered him much less to be the one in their couple who, having known the transports of sexual pleasure, had given it up. The abstinence through ignorance that Ixora had practiced didn't disturb her all that much. She didn't miss what she hadn't experienced, why would she go looking for it at her age? Now all that was shattered. Without realizing it, he took his head in his hands, sinking little by little into the thoughts from which he'd wanted to escape. Ixora's voice startled him: *Maybe you could look after Kabral at first? He likes it here a lot. I'd see him weekends and during holidays.* Not a word came to him in response. Amok was discovering the heartbreak of being abandoned, the strange sensation of being left by a woman he didn't even know he was in love with. What howled inside him, this desire to chain her so that she wouldn't take another step away from him, must have something to do with love. This inclination from which he'd thought he was exempt, because he didn't desire her.

Nothing pleaded in his favor, he had no argument to put forward. The idea crossed his mind that they wouldn't be in this situation if he'd been willing to come out of his shell, and not only in conversation. If he'd seen her, not as an image, but as a woman. If he'd realized how preoccupying the abstinence she'd imposed on herself was, she'd done so because she hadn't liked making love to Shrapnel, because she hadn't imagined herself in the arms of a woman. It was his presence by their side that had separated Ixora's body from Kabral's. Without ever touching her, he'd put distance between her and her son, had given her back her flesh. Should he have gone farther? Amok hadn't changed in this respect. He didn't take the initiative unless he was invited. It simply didn't occur to him. Like Ixora, it hadn't dawned on him that her lack of desire for him was because she was attracted to women. He'd never told her about Mabel, the borderline adventure that had led him to wonder about his sexuality. He hadn't mentioned his role-switching fantasy, the somewhat mad idea he had of penetrating a woman who could do the same to him.

Amok had not said how shaken he'd been to see his aunt's face appear, at the very moment that he ejaculated in Mabel's firm posterior. Nor how he'd had to discipline his will to keep from going back and knocking on the door of that divine, that complete creature. Had the recurrent, disturbing memory of Mabel pushed him toward Amandla, a woman without ambiguity, just like Katie, and like all those who'd preceded the shemale? A woman with broad hips, a slender waist, generous breasts, well-rounded thighs. To flee the oddity that the macabre initiation had lodged in him. If he'd spoken about Mabel, maybe Ixora would have revealed her own desires. Maybe she'd have confessed an attraction to women that she'd repressed, fearing rejection. One didn't discover one's sexual inclinations at the age of thirty-six. One didn't restrain them for so long just to backtrack at that age. The man nodded silently, absorbed in his thoughts, oblivious to the question he'd been asked. Ixora took that for an answer: *Good. I'm going to join the family. We have time to tell them. Are you changing for dinner?* The woman left him alone, careful not to slam the door. Ixora was all delicacy, she didn't make any noise.

Amok plodded through the following days rather than really living. For the first time since his return to the country, he didn't go to the office. He didn't give Madame the opportunity to say anything, took the lead in making sure that Ixora would find a house as quickly as possible, paid the required eight months' rent, had Enoch take her on her errands. At no time did he interfere with her choices, limiting himself to sharing his opinion with her on the location of the villa she found. He didn't frown, didn't smile either, he acted with the elegance of a trained mime. He'd collapse soon enough, would make sure no one saw him, as usual, as always. Kabral didn't seem troubled in the least to see his mother leave. With all-too-mature kindness in his eyes, he helped her pack her bags, folding her dresses, finding mislaid shoes, the bottle of perfume forgotten on a shelf in the dressing room. The presence of the hairdresser the day of the house-warming didn't disturb him. Having seen her often in the great house, then at his mother's bedside at the clinic, he didn't ask himself any questions.

At the dinner table, Ixora and Masasi didn't betray their feelings, exchange knowing looks or complicit smiles. Amok was unnerved to see how readily Ixora had adopted local mannerisms, the kind of equivocations that women were compelled to use to shield their well-being and freedom from the what-will-people-say. Nothing transpired as they passed around the dishes of misole and braised ñomo, the matété of scampi then the breadfruit chaudeau. Anyone who knew Ixora for some time was aware that she didn't usually wear jewelry in her hair, or dresses as loose as the one in ndop that she had on. A strength emanated from her that Amok noticed, a little surprised. Ixora was serene. He had the feeling that he'd never existed, that he'd only brought her to this country because she had to come here. She was the one who suggested they have dessert on the veranda, they each took their cup of chaudeau with them, hardly spoke in the quiet of the evening. They watched the fireflies flickering in the grass, as the gathering shadows covered the sky.

Kabral started school, the great house was once again what it had been in Amok's memory, a fortress of solitude. Madame and he avoided each other without trying, there was room enough to do so, hours enough in the day too. The man felt the need to express his distress, the desire to confide in somebody. Who would want to listen to the litany of questions that, once again, occupied his whole being? Of the dreams he'd had after the accident, the inner comfort he'd felt before leaving Continent Noir, he was left with nothing but a sensation of meaningless ramblings. He'd thought he was a better person, that he'd come to know his true personality. Just another illusion, a trick of the mind to make the pain of living seem more acceptable. Amok found life interminable, he didn't see how to fill it, where to find a semblance of joy. Only Kabral lightened his heart a little, but the shared moments were becoming rare. Now very busy, more than ever surrounded by friends, who'd invite him over as he would them, the boy, like a boat hitting its cruising speed, was moving ahead without him. He was a dispensable tutor, his disappearance wouldn't be an insurmountable loss. Two days after the housewarming party, Kabral asked permission to spend the weekend at Kumar's, his new best friend.

After driving him over, tasting the delicious palak paneer served at Kumar's parents' table, and an equally tasty aloo matar ka pulao, Amok returned to the emptiness of the great house. He had nothing to occupy his time, unwilling as he was to take care of the Prince des Côtes or the real estate properties of the Mandones, over which his mother kept a watchful eye. He flopped down on the sofa in the living room, with its bay windows that looked out onto the garden, and watched, like a zombie, five or six episodes of *Law and Order* on a Northern cable channel. No sooner did he see an image than it was instantly forgotten, he hadn't a clue what the episodes were about, wondered what he was really feeling. In the worst moment, watching TV was not really an option, he and Ajar had spent too much time viewing videos over and over again. As children, they didn't go out much, they never spent two days in a row at a friend's, didn't receive visitors outside the family. School was their only form of social life until they were teenagers. Amok thought of calling his sister, less to unburden himself than to hear a voice, to escape the silence. He decided against it, it didn't seem right to be so intrusive all of a sudden. Evening was about to fall when he took the station wagon, he no longer drove the sedan.

The car followed a road that led him to the only person capable of listening to him. He'd thought of going to her place, but had given up on the idea, not knowing what to say. When he climbed out of the car, children were still playing outside, pushing flat tires with a stick, rolling cars made of tin cans in the dust. They paused for a moment, then resumed their games, with enough spirit to outrace the night. Amok directed his steps to the small house from which a woman had emerged in the storm, to come to Ixora's rescue. A lantern lit the front, the door was closed. He went around the back, knowing that such houses often had a courtyard, which was not fenced in. There too he saw no one. Amandla had a vegetable garden, he wasn't surprised. It was a dream of hers, a red-earth hut, vegetables from the garden, oil bought from a street vendor. It was a plank house whose plain appearance was in keeping with her desire for simplicity. He walked along one of the side walls, approached a window he'd notice was ajar, hoping to see her, that would give him an idea. The first words to say to start up a conversation.

And see her, he did, it took his breath away. Of course, she had someone with her. He hadn't come courting, far from it. What's more, he wasn't displeased for her, but that didn't make him go away. He saw her from behind, the hands of the man she was riding kneading her and spreading the cheeks of her buttocks a little. She'd tied her locks up on the top of her head so they wouldn't fall over her face. Amok was familiar with this way she had of styling her hair for lovemaking, the brisk toss of her head forward, her hands drawing together the strands on the sides, coiling them into a knot to form a high ponytail, right in the middle of the skull. The lover who looked her in the eyes seemed quite vigorous, worthy of her voracity. They didn't speak to each other, at least Amok didn't hear any words. No cries either, that would have been like showing one's underwear to the world, it was still a busy time of day, children were out playing nearby. Amandla moaned and gasped faintly in the orange glow of a bedside lamp, rising and falling on her partner who was feeling her breasts with one hand, while keeping the other on one cheek of her backside. With a single thrust of his pelvis, he swung her over, she let out a laugh. Amok's eyes furtively met the man's as he stood up to go behind the woman. He closed the window without a word, thinking there was no point in remarking on the presence of a voyeur. The one who was spying on other people's lovemaking didn't have the build of a rival. The man was sure of what he shared with this woman, he knew the foundations that underpinned it. He exuded a kind of tranquility that had the shape of authority, simply because you could count on it. It was not the seeming calm that was Amok's specialty, that bogus composure cloaking the inner trembling or stomach cramps that convulsed him. There was nothing left for him to do but leave. He lingered at the front door, thought of writing a note, slipping it underneath, so she'd know he came. He began to do so in his notebook, tore out the page, crumpled it up. No point. Their relationship was dead, he'd put an end to it without looking back. She'd retain the memory of his violence, he'd have to live with that.

Calls, responses, the laughter of children, the chatter of street vendors all rose in a choral harmony, amid the changing colors of the setting sun. A breeze coming from the river offered its caress to the living who received it as a due, the day had been hot, it was not too early. A beignet seller, already seated behind her hearth, was serving her first customers, others were arriving, enamel plates in hand, taking their place in line, they would all have their share, no one tried to push their way up to the front. He climbed back into the car, drove slowly at first to capture this moment of simple life, hold it inside him, become a receiver of beauty. His terrible deed had not damaged this, the drama would live only in him, and that was the way it should be. The car radio was playing *In the Mood* by the Whispers. Schmaltzy music for a Friday night. Who listened to those songs anymore? He thought of the video clip, and found himself laughing, he whom life hadn't endowed with much of a sense of humor. The Whispers looked too old for the girl who was shown getting herself in the mood all by herself as the foursome walked down a street, telling her from afar, point by point, what they planned to do. In their already outdatedly elegant overcoats, a boy band of middle-aged men, smooth in the extreme, on their way to do things to the lady. One of them, with a bushy beard, looked like a cross between an oversized teddy bear and an ogre, and had a sex appeal all his own. Amok let the song's soft sappiness envelop him, the lyrics came back effortlessly, the memory of swinging moments too, of happy times snatched here and there, for there had been some.

The sight of Amandla hadn't aroused his senses. It had merely sent him back to his present solitude. There was no one there for him, maybe that wasn't such a bad thing. It would be if he decided it was, he had done so before. Amok stepped on the gas. The city center was busy as usual in the evening, especially on weekends. A languorous impatience was in the gestures, you had to be in the know to be able to discern the eagerness and enthusiasm in the nonchalance of the attitudes. Everything would be more alive and unrestrained in a short while, they'd soon be wolfing down what they were only picking and pecking at now. The rhythms of the city would turn electrifying, verge on cacophony, the devil would invite himself to dinner, and under the skin. Some wouldn't survive, that's the way it was, nighttime did its housecleaning, implacably. The big bang was reenacted every night in the city, with human bodies and souls as explosive elements. Amok dashed into a stationery store, smiled at the saleswoman who didn't do so in return, her sales had not been terrific that day but the time had come, she was closing up. He paid for his purchase, took the wheel again, stopped once more to get what he needed for dinner, something he could immediately share. He wasn't expected but he'd be welcomed. Night had fallen by the time he reached the garden planted with fruit trees and royal palms.

Continent Noir's hut was right where he'd left it, he was glad it hadn't been a figment of his imagination. A hurricane lamp had been set in front by the door, near the chair on which he'd sat convalescing. Another had been hung on the wall above the top crossbar. Continent Noir was inside, wearing the white suit Amok had left, without a shirt or shoes, but the clothing had been cleaned. The room was plunged in darkness, the only light came from the entrance, conforming to a logic that he didn't question. Sitting cross-legged on his synthetic fiber mat, the man was turning the pages of a book, too fast to really read them. When he reached the end, he started all over, again and again, the meaning of the words would ultimately sink in, he didn't seem to doubt it. Amok coughed. Continent Noir turned around, a smile on his lips, motioned him to draw near, as if he'd been there waiting for

him, and whispered: *My name is Continent Noir. I'm crazy.*
Amok noticed that the book whose pages he kept turning was
upside down. It was a collection of poems, written in a language that Continent Noir couldn't have known. Amok nodded. It was okay to be crazy. He thought he was too, wouldn't
bother him, their troubles were compatible. He had things on
his mind, wanted to bring some order to them, write them
down in a notebook. Maybe it would yield a story. He was
going to project himself into the characters, figures who'd
marked his life, discover them from the inside but also repair
them. He would erase nothing, on the contrary, it would all
be looked at in full light, put in its proper place

To his host, he held out the meal he'd bought on the street,
miele cooked in embers sprinkled with njabi, and a few
skewers of beef. No, he himself wasn't hungry. He'd spend
two days here; the place seemed right for his undertaking.
Before eating, Continent Noir had put the book down, opened
to the last page on which his index finger rested. Amok took
a look, read the famous lines by William Ernest Henley,
smiled. Continent Noir's madness provided him with what he
needed. He didn't read the poet's language, he didn't need to.
What was beyond language came to him, inside him, it didn't
matter how he held the book. Amok went to sit on the door-
sill. Placing his notebook on his knees, he wrote, in somewhat
schoolboyish fashion, his pen name and, underneath, the title:

Amok

Return to TaMery

Then, turning the page, he jotted down two quotes that would serve as his compass. One summed up the reasons for his return, the other had to do with his vision for the people whose destiny he'd decided to embrace, since here he was, since here he would live, since he was giving this country to his son, since it was with this land as a base that he intended to offer his child the world:

> *Il est possible de se réconcilier avec le fait que sa propre vie soit ruinée, mais lorsque c'est la vie de ses propres enfants qui est ruinée, il n'est plus question de réconciliation, mais de désespoir.*
> James Baldwin

> *Nous devons chercher une nouvelle manière d'être au monde . . .*
> Jean-Marc Ela

The words of his elders would light his way and fortify him, he needed to know they were there where he put them, to return to them again and again, even if they never made it into the final work. Rereading Jimmy in the French translation, he thought that his translator could have taken the trouble to find synonyms, and avoid the repetitions that weighed the sentence down. It sounded heavier in the target than in the source language. He refrained from correcting it. The words of Jean-Marc Ela meant a lot to him. They were from an essay in which the priest-cum-sociologist had unleashed his fiercest critique of the return of the peoples of the Continent to identity-based mythologies. For Amok, what Ela had to say about Negritude applied equally well to Negrohood as he conceived it. His project was not to write an essay. This form, he felt, wouldn't be conducive to examining himself in depth, to gaining a good understanding of the person he was, how he'd been constituted. He also needed to know what he'd transmit to Kabral. The time had come to open himself to other ways of thinking, beyond the speculative practice that places the subjects of analysis outside the self. If there were indeed a dark force within him, if this came to him from his ancestors, it was up to him to get a hold on it and govern it. He had failed at this task, putting what was in his power into other people's hands. Transforming his heritage was impossible without accepting and owning it totally. The dark material from which he'd wanted to dissociate himself was not evil in itself, it was a force whose effects he alone could master. Otherwise, it would dominate him, would turn against him, he'd had proof of this.

Ixora was gone, and with her the secrets he'd confided in her, the affection they'd given each other. If a bond subsisted between them, it would no longer unite them in the same way, Amok had had to admit it, face his nakedness. Kabral, who had stayed with him in the great house, couldn't be a bulwark against this, it wasn't his role, his son would be entitled to his childhood. Here he was alone, at a starting point, a crossroads. The work he was about to undertake was not, to his mind, a simple therapy, an act destined to cure him. More than that, he wanted it to be something generous, an offering to those who'd be receptive to it of what he'd perceived through his meditation. For it was a matter of that, of discovering and probing the spaces opened by thinking turned inward, and the possibilities of action that would emanate from it. The spiritual journey to which he'd been invited by the woman who'd first introduced herself as Ayezan, would find its culmination there. If, as he'd understood, she was one of the figures of his soul, its loving and creative part, she'd help him bridge the distance still separating night and day.

The shadow would surely descend again, but never would it be quite as thick, and he'd make his way through it with greater ease. Without averting his eyes, he'd go back in time to his childhood, the text would begin and end in the garden of the great house. He'd write to forgive himself, to give back to his parents their failings, which were not his. To be heard by Paula, to embrace her, to ask her for directions. To know at last all the girls he hadn't even taken, waiting as he had to be invited to satisfy his longings. To talk once again to Shrapnel, the brother-friend, the living god with his Olmec head, whose fictional character would be called Shabaka. Pronouncing the name of the deceased's tutelary tree, Amok had a fleeting impression that he felt him nearby, he welcomed this, smiled at the invisible. There was so much to write about. The stories of his past would not unfold on the pages as they had in life, he didn't see the interest. Reinvented, they'd be stripped of their venomous power. What would remain were the possibilities yet to be explored, a world to create. He felt alive, didn't recall ever having experienced this with such intensity.

The man wanted to reconnect with his body too, inhabit it without reproaching himself for having one, derive pleasure without subsequently seeing it as debasing. No longer suffer from enjoying as he did what he'd been forced to do as a child.

Accept that it had left him with uncommon desires, and wrest his flesh from his aunt's bony hands. Be free at last from her appetites. So that the silhouettes of his male ancestors would no longer flow into each ejaculation, stop imagining their heads at the tip of his spermatozoids. He'd have himself sterilized. Reproducing in that way didn't interest him, he didn't think he'd change his mind, one life wasn't enough to elevate himself as high as that. Having a soul was undoubtedly an excellent thing, he'd see how it felt over time, but it wasn't the be-all and end-all. Right now, conscious of having durably repressed his sexual impulses, having almost extinguished them, he meant to reconnect with them through his imagination to begin. The memory of Mabel would be precious to him. Her literary double would carry a goddess's name, he'd call her Oshun. And on these pages, he'd crown her with his love.

Negro Spirit

Coda

At the moment, Shrapnel was in the sedan engine, savoring his condition, for once. Being rid of his body protected him from the smell, the heat, he felt nothing. All the same, he'd have liked to control his crossing from one dimension to another better, to do it with more precision. His intention had been to slip into Amok's mind, his brother-friend, to talk to him from inside, to act as his conscience. It wasn't as he'd imagined it would be, but his presence among the living was already a miracle. The authorities had given him only a short time, he couldn't appear to mortals, couldn't touch them or speak to them, except by way of an intermediary. These restrictions would complicate his task, but he was glad to have obtained this favor, the opportunity to act in the life of a loved one. He'd pleaded his case vigorously, a case of force majeure, he argued, contending that it would have been inhumane of him not to turn back upon hearing the voices of those who called out to him from the world. Yes, yes, the instructions had been clear, however he'd just extricated himself from his body, was but a mass of emotions deprived of the physical envelope that had contained them in the past. When Gabrielle had started to scream that he'd made a fool of her, that all he'd wanted was to fuck her, he'd turned back to proclaim his love, to say that he'd never loved a woman so much, to explain that he'd died, just like that, foolishly, one ordinary night.

This instinctive movement had disrupted his progress along the path to the Spirit, the entity that many called God. Ras, the guardian of passages, who'd welcomed him at the threshold of the realm of the departed, had warned him that if he wished to ascend to the Spirit to receive answers to his questions, he had to turn a deaf ear, never look back in the direction of the land to which he no longer belonged. This was the condition to attain the rank of ancestor, to have the power to walk in the dreams of those he held dear, to converse with them. It was also an imperative if one wanted to be reincarnated, which didn't appeal to him, to be honest. Shrapnel loved the guy he'd been, the one whose life had ended after a day of work like every other. To be reborn in a different body didn't interest him, especially since it could mean changing sex, which was out of the question. Buddha himself had declared that a woman could only attain enlightenment by reincarnating as a man. Now, his virility was minimal, he didn't come off as a phallocrat, didn't revere virgins, had no fear of a woman's head of hair, this Buddha was a decent guy. So Gabrielle had screamed, her words had pierced his heart, he'd wanted to speak to her, look her in the eye, that was when he'd been ejected from the path leading to the Source, swept away like a pile of goat droppings.

Shrapnel had slid down to the wayside, into the immaterial brush, alongside the other men who could do no more than try to signal the countless people who mourned their passing. They were held for eternity in what was neither purgatory nor hell, and certainly not heaven. None of them had the power to walk the dreams of the living, none had the ability to convey recommendations, none would return to the physical world, none would be called to the Spirit. Little did it matter that they had led honorable lives, that they could be credited with positive transformations, that they were the object of noisily expressed profane worship. Little did it matter that people were clamoring to them from the depths of their despair: they hadn't become ancestors, entities endowed with the faculty of intervening in the world after they'd departed. These men had not reached Sodibenga, the home of the deserving forefathers that was promised to them, or *Sisi*, where the ordinary dead dwelt. The memory of their struggles did not irrigate Wase, the land of the living. All that remained of them were posters, t-shirts with their effigy, online videos, vain incantations. The man who had a dream. The man who replaced his slave name with the antepenultimate letter of the alphabet. The man who'd wanted to turn his country into a nation of men of integrity. Those and others still, icons of the Continent or its diasporas, drowning in torrents of tears. To escape boredom, they played cards or dominoes, but nothing calmed their sobs. Knowing what had happened to their message, they no longer turned their gaze to the world, sunk as they were in never-ending grief. This assembly of souls in sorrow was not the best company, no matter how much you admired them, you had your fill after a while.

Having failed to pull them out of the lachrymal inunda-
tion, Shrapnel had moved away from his former idols, followed by some who, like him, had not respected the passage
keeper's instructions. With them, although they were surely
not without their faults, things began to change. Backed by
one Tupac Amaru Shakur, he managed to persuade them to
protest against the injustice. Could love be punished? For that
was the force that prevented them from complying with the
rules: this sentiment, this attachment to beings, beyond death.
The order of things that imposed indifference on souls barely
dissociated from their bodies was wrong. It was the opposite
that should have been cause for concern, that people who'd
just died have not the least regard for their loved ones left in
the other dimension. The authorities could have ignored the
protesters' appeals, but this commotion added to the sobbing
of the great men was disturbing the newcomers on their path.

Two guardians of passages had been dispatched to them.
Ras, who welcomed the departed, and Kalunga, who guided
candidates for incarnation. To mark the solemnity of the
moment, Ras had abandoned his manjua for a pharaoh's costume. Kalunga, for her part, had put on a dress reminiscent of
those worn by battle-ready Kandakes. Having been elected by
the group as their spokesperson, Shrapnel intervened on their
behalf. He summarized what they had to say in a word: injustice. He had the impression that Ras and Kalunga had heard
all this before, so unyielding did they prove to be. The trial that
deceased humans had to undergo had nothing to do with being
impassive, they were allowed to cry, and most of them did so
on the path to the Spirit. They were asked nonetheless to agree

to go to the end without turning their backs on the light as they had so often done during their earthly sojourn, not that they were now being reproached for those failures. Many succeeded, and that was how Shrapnel had the good fortune, during his incarnation, to be accompanied by his grandmother's soul. He was only a child when she had been snatched from him.

The cries with which he'd filled the universe had tormented the old woman, but she'd understood the risks of yielding to them. She'd endured the trial for his sake, so she could remain present in his life. Ras remembered her passage, the weight of her every step, she'd stopped several times, trembling from head to toe, her eyes blurred. She had only a short distance to go when she'd knelt on the path, overwhelmed with grief, calling for support from Inyi, the female figure of the Spirit. Old Heka had remained in this attitude for weeks, the equivalent of months in the world of the living. Then, she'd stood up straight, walked without looking back, reaching Sodibenga, the home of the valiant forefathers. This was the requirement, the immutable law, they weren't about to revise the order of things for a bunch of softies who'd been unable to pull themselves up to higher planes, after all that was what this painful progression was about. These procedures had been established since the beginning of time, suffering was necessary for the souls of the dead. The transition, the return to the Source, was a serious matter, not a circus act, proximity to the Spirit had to be earned.

Unimpressed, Shrapnel had interrupted the mingled voices of the passage keepers: *It makes no sense to impose the same* trial on everyone, we were not equal before death. Heka was already a great spirit when she lived on earth. You've described the difficult path that was hers. How can you expect ordinary souls to measure up to her? The messengers of the divinity had kept silent for a moment. Ras was about to continue, but Kalunga spoke first: *We can't tell you more, but you should know that the universe is in turmoil. The situation is both serious and unprecedented. It is unthinkable to revise laws as ancient as these in such circumstances, and for as big a group as yours.* Calling him Shabaka, she'd opened a space between them. *Look,* she said. Moved as he was that the guardian of the passage had given him the name of his childhood *moabi*, that plant double in the shelter of which he'd grown up, all he could do was stare at her. *Look,* she'd repeated. Then he saw him. Amok, his longtime friend, his son Kabral and Ixora, the child's mother, with whom he'd had an awful relationship. The three were in the departure lounge of an airport, ready to board a flight from the North to the Continent. Being deceased had its advantages, swallowing the wrong way or hiccupping with surprise were henceforth impossible for him.

Spared these discomforts, Shrapnel was able to concentrate on the scenes, listen carefully, try to understand. The situation didn't bother him, he was touched that his brother-friend had adopted Kabral who seemed to be attached to him. He was about to ask Kalunga what she was so intent on showing him, when he'd heard the argument, seen the metallic gray sedan screech to a sudden stop. He shouted, *Man, don't be an ass, damnit, stop,* to no avail. Ixora lay on the ground, in the thrashing rain, while his longtime friend got back into the car.

He'd have liked to swallow the wrong way or hiccup with surprise, rather than feel this pain welling up inside. The passage keeper had said: *She'll be alright, her time has not come. You do not want to be stuck here, you would like to manifest yourself in the lives of those who were dear to you. We're allowing you to visit your brother.* His mission was to help free Amok from his death wish, for he was more dangerous to himself than to others. His friend had always kept himself on the periphery of life, thinking this was the way not so much to free himself from an atavistic evil, but at least to contain it. Now the dam had burst, he'd fled, frightened by his own deed. What would he do now? Would he end his life? If he decided to live, would he manage to wrest his mission from the darkness in order to accomplish it? Amok's destiny seemed to be a series of questions without answers.

The living were masters of their own fate, the Almighty Creator did not intervene in the affairs of the world, people had to exercise their liberty. On the other hand, the ancestors could lend assistance. Kalunga would support the group's grievances more readily if Shrapnel proved that he could be useful to the living, so he was given a few days on earth to demonstrate his talents. Given that his case had yet to be decided, he wasn't authorized to touch anyone or be seen, except by those who communicated with the higher planes. Only through the three other senses could he reach others, and this would necessitate a support, it was up to him to find the means to establish contact, to make himself understood, they warned him, it wouldn't be easy. The situation would be reexamined upon his return. Other entities surrounded the living, each playing a role, he'd have to respect them, persuade them to join him, if they shared his aims. Once again, the Spirit could not be called upon, a plethora of emissaries had been sent into the world to let everyone know this, but nothing doing, the living preferred to be deluded by masters of genuflection, teachers of prostration. The prayers whose plaintive buzzing filled the universe were irritating in the end, what could be done with them, where could all this accumulated despair be put, very often, the only solution was to return it to its senders, they'd been talked to so much, had listened so little. Kalunga didn't think he could do anything about it, but you never know, maybe he could bring at least one person to probe the depths of his being for answers that could be found nowhere else.

He hadn't had time to ask his fellow protesters their opinion, a gust had blown him back into the world of the living. So here he was, curled up in the engine of the metallic-gray sedan that Amok was driving. The vehicle hurtled through the rain, eating up the miles. Both the driver and the passenger kept silent, while he wondered when would be the best moment to manifest his presence, how he should do so. He wished that something other than that Commodores song had come to mind. Then images from the video clip flashed through his head, the band applying powder and foundation to their faces to look clean, to make it clear that they were human beings, civilized guys. They did so in good spirits, erasing the stigma of Black men, with the help of their puffs. Only recently, at the time, had Black become beautiful, something persisted from the old days, an uncertainty, the weight of this other humanity that race had fabricated. The guys looked so casual, beyond cool, as they put the finishing touches on their eye makeup, combed their mustaches and beards, and added a drop earring. Then they smiled, performed their well-mannered, somewhat stiff dance steps, nope, letting loose was not their style. Their diligence in dissimulating any hint of the untamed made it all the more obvious. The smoother they were, the more you imagined all the hours of hard work needed to escape the fate of Blacks in their country as everywhere else.

The smoother the song sounded, the rougher the battles fought to get there. He'd never looked into the subject, knew nothing about the musicians' lives, his approach to music had always been more sensual than scholarly. The images and sounds that came back to him touched him because he perceived what they were trying to hide, what they rebelled against. He also liked the fact that the men had come together, dressed in their finest to salute two of their own, two talented brothers, two stars in what was much more than the firmament of music. Whatever the realm, success was a victory over death, this funeral song evoked not sadness but gratitude, the importance of having seen these shining lights illuminate the world. *Jackie, you set the world on fire . . .* This simplicity, this seeming naivety, these rose petals in every note were worth thousands of raised fists. Not a cry, not a tear, let alone a plea, only heads held high, clear voices, colorful duds, for this tribute to the immortals.

He'd probably be able to hum a more invigorating number once he'd reached the back seat. But at bottom he liked *Nightshift*, it was a testimony of love, a farewell filled with admiration, like the one Mingus addressed to Prez with his *Goodbye Pork Pie Hat*. The song's gentle sway made it easier for him to think: he needed a plan, he had none. Unlike Kalunga, he had no idea what was coming, how to prepare for whatever it was. The car was now on unpaved roads. The vehicle would take a beating in this insane storm, the water would cover up cracks, even ravines. He figured they wouldn't have sent him if the worst-case scenario were about to happen this very night, without him having had time to intervene. The guardian of passages had granted him several days on earth, more than one in any case, which reassured him. Once they'd reached their destination, he'd see what concrete steps he could take.

In the meantime, his intention was to get into the rear seat since no one would see him, the guy in the passenger seat couldn't possibly be a medium, decked out like he was. Sure, he too had worn black Stan Smiths, never out of style, but the rest of his outfit was a fashion assault, no one wore jackets with shoulder pads anymore. If there was one thing he didn't miss, it was eighties clothing. Shrapnel could have done it, move there now, matter was no obstacle to him, he'd felt this when, after his death had appeared to him as an established fact, definitive, all that was left for him to do was to head to the realm of the departed. He'd traveled through the city, passed through walls, visited apartments whose occupants didn't perceive his presence. This experience had shown him that he could get into the back seat right now if he so desired, yet he couldn't shake off the feeling that there was peril in moving when the car was in motion. His body had been taken from him, but the memory that he had of it was vivid, he still perceived himself as a body with a soul that he had yet to discover, rather than a soul that had previously been obliged to be embodied. Ultimately, he belonged more to this world than to the other, which wouldn't make accomplishing his mission any easier.

Through the hood he could see the torrents thrashing the city, it had been ages since he'd been back here. Shrapnel had not been present at the burial of his body, he couldn't have faced it, his sudden death had seemed like a bad joke. It was raining cats and dogs on the streets that he and Amok had walked as teenagers. This presented no risk for him, but he'd have preferred calmer weather for his reunion with his country, if that expression still had any meaning. From where he was, he could only perceive the foot of the buildings, the bottom of the houses, the beat-up roads, the piles of garbage crushed or scattered by the storm. He had no need to see more, the city had been on the verge of disintegration, nothing from before had survived, from those years when the world was discovering hip-hop, the time when he'd have given his soul for Air Jordans. Nothing was left but scraps of the past, nothing truly recognizable, it was now a foreign city. Emptied of its inhabitants by the deluge, it seemed even more sinister. His gaze fastened on this cityscape, it looked like early signs of the desolated world in *Mad Max Beyond Thunderdome*, with the downpour to boot, which didn't help matters.

As they drove on, he said to himself that at least they'd made sure to get him back into the swing of things, plunge him into the reality of the country. This was a thunderdome, no doubt about it; even when the sun was out, life these days was surely a fight to the death, and the very young probably knew this long before they'd learned their own name by heart, before they'd grasped its vibration. A shudder of sorts ran through him, there was no other way of expressing it. Things had gotten worse and worse, since the days when the people of his village had been dispossessed of their land, displaced so that foreign developers could do what they pleased with the forest, having paid hard cash to the government for the right to do so. His eyes—he still thought in those terms—sought landmarks, tried to identify neighborhoods, trees, the bottom of street stalls, something. He found nothing, nothing but his memories. Soon, the city outskirts became in his eyes what they'd been before, he saw the *carabote* houses scattered in the thicket when you left the city, the cemetery whose graves were regularly gutted by body snatchers, the cornfields into which bold girls ventured to pluck the ears and use the leaves and silk to make dolls. It couldn't have changed that much, the girls must still be there, repeating the same gestures as their forebears, in these districts invaded by hordes without residence permits, legions bent on approaching the thunderdome where you eked out a living at the risk of your life.

Shrugging off the gloominess, he turned his attention back to the vehicle, examined the passengers again, wondering who the guy was who his friend had stopped by the Prince des Côtes to pick up, a character who still wore those jackets with thick shoulder pads, pants with darts, as if he'd been cryogenically preserved in the eighties. Putting on a pale-yellow suit, especially for going out at night, was like a declaration of war on masculinity as well as on good taste. At bottom, there was something likeable about anyone who dared to go that far, to the point of wearing a Kid Creole–style hat. Shrapnel had nothing against whimsy. When he was alive, he had sometimes missed the sartorial antics of Larry Blackmon or Rick James, but such extravagance had their place on stage, at a show. The rest of the time, Black men, he felt, ought to be intent on elegance, on style, but tomfoolery was off limits, there was too much at stake. He had the impression that the stranger was also humming *Nightshift*, and wondered about this coincidence, was it possible that they'd heard him? The idea amused him, he laughed heartily. The car stopped at a gas station, Amok rushed into the store where the pump attendant must have been.

If he was going to get out from under the hood, it was now or never, his thought propelled him outside, it wasn't where he wanted to be, but it would do for the time being. He hovered over the sedan, let himself be moved by curiosity toward the store where his friend was, stuck his tongue out at the attendant, a plump woman dressed in a uniform that was too tight for her abundant curves. Kalunga had told him that only those connected to the higher planes would see him and this woman couldn't be one of them, he lost interest in her. He watched Amok, wondered if now was the time to try something. His friend was also not one to associate with the powers of the spirit, he ought to know. Shrapnel sighed, approached the candy bars, the jars of forest honey, recognizable by its dark brown color. The urge to taste it gripped him, it had been so long ago, he recalled the woody aromas, the slightly smoky flavor, the sweet notes that only came out at the end, the liquid was nearly black at times. Frustration moved him to go back outside, he let Amok fill the tank, slid into the backseat, he didn't know this place, it wasn't the picture etched in his memory of the periphery of the city.

The storm intensified, you could hear it drumming on the roof of the car, even with the air conditioning on. Yet it seemed to him that it wasn't the season for this. He wasn't sure, but such a violent rain in the middle of dry season was a cause for concern. The scene he'd seen earlier came back to him, Amok throttling Ixora with his fists, he must have crushed her face, she'd fallen on her back, inert. When his brother-friend had gone back after fleeing, two women were carrying the wounded woman to a hut. One of them was Amandla, Amok had fallen in love with her, after many years spent ignoring women. He was the one who'd dragged his friend to the meeting of the Aton Fraternity, the militant movement for which she was then the spokeswoman. Without adhering wholesale to their philosophy, some aspects of which seemed questionable, to say the least—in particular the prohibition against frequenting leucoderms outside professional or administrative contexts—he understood what had prompted them to come together. These young advocates of a cross-border Black nation, rooted in its Kemitic-Nubian matrix, mentally inhabited a parallel universe, abiding by an ancient calendar that said they were in the year 6247. Too bad for those who, latecomers to the world, thought they were in 2010. The members of the Aton Fraternity had been born in a country that wanted nothing to do with them, pushed into a society where their parents had lived with backs bent, when they had not been broken. Determined not to suffer these humiliations in turn, they were groping to find avenues for fulfillment. Sensitive to their distress, to its provocative expression, Shrapnel thought he might be useful to them.

He'd been privileged to be born in a village in the equatorial forest, to have lived there without anything standing between him and the world, and without the presence of his body in the space appearing as an anomaly. This joy had been stolen from him when the government had sold his community's land to Northern developers. They'd been displaced, an uncle in the city had taken him in. But he'd been left many jewels, the memory of Shabaka, the moabi at whose foot he'd grown up, the wise words of Heka, his beloved grandmother. Teaching him about the land, the plants or beasts, instructing him about what existed even though it couldn't be seen, she'd made a man of him. In the eyes of all, he was still but a child when the old woman departed for Sodibenga. Yet, life hadn't brought him essential lessons, giving him only the opportunity to put into practice his grandmother's. Having grown close to Narmer, a member of the Aton Fraternity, Shrapnel had measured the scope of the abyss in which young Blacks were struggling in the North. Since he'd never call himself a Kemite, cherishing as he did his equatorial forest where no pyramid had been built, an idea had come to him, an ambitious project. He'd taken two jobs, had started saving money to achieve it. It was to be called the Shabaka Complex, in memory of the giant plant whose foliage had sheltered his early childhood.

That dream was now long gone. He'd created a significant obstacle to earning the trust of the brothers engaged in the struggle for Black nationalism. Gabrielle, the woman he loved at the time, was white, like the woman he'd loved before her. A leucoderm, as Narmer and his companions called her. These relations, which were frowned upon within the movement, made him lose all credibility, they saw him as a traitor to the cause, a white sheep.

When they spoke of history, all the militants of a return to the self shared the same view and reached the same conclusion, regardless of their obedience to one of the scores of schools. They diverged on solutions, but they all agreed that their ancestors had proved to be overly hospitable, that the nobility of their cultures had been their undoing. Since nothing could alter this, since the *Maafa* had taken place, they needed to implement a policy in the Motherland on the lines of Article 12 of the imperial constitution promulgated by the great Dessalines. This was an imperative measure, a question of spiritual, cultural, intellectual, political, economic, and even ecological health, everyone could see how critical it was, they'd torture their tongues in an effort to enunciate all these points. Alienation was at once the hammer and the anvil, they had to save the Continent, without it the severed body of its children will never be reconstituted, and Yurugu's victory will be definitive. The sharpest tools were sought to fight the battle: knowledge being a weapon, it was essential to refer to the texts, people read a lot, more than they'd ever done in school. Rock engravings, bas-reliefs, parchments, ancient manuscripts were all studiously examined.

Shrapnel had learned many things from the evening classes Narmer had dragged him to. Before that he'd never heard of the Manden Charter or the famous Imperial Constitution of Ayiti before. Reducing the text to this provision only, the brothers had little to say about the following article, stipulating the admission of white women and the children they would bear to the Empire. For his part, Shrapnel fully approved of Article 13, that the liberated nation recognized certain white men as its own did not strike him as offensive. They'd fought for justice, they were brothers in blood. It seemed fair to him. Shrapnel read Article 13 as a bold act to make the racial nonsense collapse. Whites were made Black, constitutionally, because they'd been worthy of being ennobled in this way. Confined to its political value, race was then stripped of its biological stain, something that was confirmed by Article 14. Thereafter, Shrapnel, who'd learned to argue based on documented references, be they oral or written sources, knew the proclamation of Dessalines well. What he saw as revolutionary in it didn't matter much to the militants of the day, they knew nothing of humanity as old Heka had presented it to him. To his mind, the spirit made the being, he stood by this, that was how his people understood things. Of course, he knew. The wounds of history, the degraded image, the powerlessness, the racism. From all that, he too suffered. Yet this did not alter his conceptions, it was the wisdom of his people that he was eager to spread. This was the source of his self-confidence, of that natural authority which prompted people make sure not to get in his way. If he liked white women, it was not only because the sisters looked down on him, finding his features too pronounced, too crude, and his wallet not thick enough. It was not only because blondes or redheads, on the other hand, swooned with desire at his baobab stature, his Olmec colossal head, nor because seeing him as one of the wretched, they wrapped him in solicitude. No. Like the rest of humanity, Northern women were victims of their men, who were by nature as aggressive as they were venal. You had to be clear on who the adversary was, not confuse the sheep and the wolf, the argument that the white man had only enslaved the living to lay him at the feet of his queen, was obviously specious, to say the least. Dessalines understood this when he opened the doors of the Black house to white women. It was simple, but the mountain of examples that he provided was not enough to convince them, he had to give up discussing the issue, lest he arouse suspicion.

Narmer and his fellow travelers saw melanin as a sacred pigment, the mark of the chosen, the biological materialization of the light that found its mineral expression in certain telluric elements. The human custodians of this light had been placed on earth to guide others on the spiritual plane. It was their responsibility to manifest greatness in all things. They had gone astray, the great catastrophe had taken place, suffering had spread in their midst, a crime against their humanity, which they called melanocide, had been going on for centuries. For this reason, love between Blacks was recommended, according to a tactful formula. It took on a metaphysical character, the environment and circumstances made it an obligation. So things had gone badly the night Narmer had seen him with Gabrielle. There were no words to describe the anger of an injured brother. Feeling betrayed, Narmer had insulted him, before closing his heart to him. Shrapnel sometimes thought that the grief caused by the end of this relationship along with the doubts he had about his ability to convince the young radicals had hastened his death. His desire was to move them to self-love without hatred, the *Shabaka Complex* was to serve this purpose. Gabrielle was in no way an obstacle. Before meeting her, he'd never been so in love with a woman. She was different. Unlike the women before her, she knew nothing of the Continent, she didn't have a thing about being with Black men, she didn't wear wraps, didn't boast about cooking mafé or yassa, didn't think of herself as a *sista*. She saw him as a man. The first time they'd eaten together, at her place, Shrapnel found himself listening to music to which he was unaccustomed, some French guy singing about lying at night and taking trains across the plain. This new world appealed to him, Gabrielle had stayed true to herself, she hadn't been introduced to twerking, hadn't treated him as if he were disadvantaged by nature, hadn't taken it into her head to save him. With her, he'd been able to drop the sword and the shield, life hadn't been an ongoing battle anymore, he'd found a peaceful space, a deliverance.

When he'd taken her dancing, Gabrielle had moved all over the place, in her own way, listening only to her own rhythm, soaring high in the immensity of her skies, while Greg Perry invited her to come on down, back on the ground. Shrapnel had stopped to admire her, anyway it was impossible to get into her cadence. That's when he felt it: this woman set his heart racing, wildly. It was delicious, they'd be happy: a man, a woman, like on the first day of the world. But he died, one evening, in the Métro. At first, when the train came into the depot, they'd thought he was asleep. Gabrielle never learned about his demise. Nobody in Shrapnel circles knew her, so no one told her about it. He'd visited her, in that apartment of hers that had no masks, calabashes, batik hangings, or bed throws made of Baule fabric. Having become invisible, deprived of his sense of touch, incapable of speaking to her, Shrapnel had felt frustrated. To communicate with his loved ones, he'd decided to leave the world of the living. His love for Gabrielle had upset his progress. Hearing her call him all sorts of names as he advanced toward higher planes, he'd turned back, shouted *Gaby oh Gaby*, to no avail. At the very moment that this painful memory came back to him, Amok's sedan hurled headlong toward a ball of light. Propelled toward this nocturnal sun, Shrapnel took a while before realizing that he'd gone through the windshield at lightning speed, to dissolve into the atmosphere.

The sedan was at a standstill when he saw it again and Amok's chest was resting on the steering wheel. By his side, the distraught passenger seemed unharmed. The roof of the car had been dented on one side, though what had caused the impact wasn't clear. Rushing back into the vehicle, Shrapnel, now determined to assume his condition, slipped into his brother-friend's body. He intended to wake him from inside, bring him back to consciousness. He didn't find him there. His body was warm, his vital functions hadn't been impaired, everything was alright, but Amok's spirit had escaped. At first, Shrapnel thought he was dead. The situation seemed to have more than a passing resemblance to what he'd experienced. After his death, he'd seen his own lifeless body lying on a hospital bed, as his brother-friend, whose phone number had been found on him, walked into the room. But there was a difference. In his own body, everything had stopped. His rigid flesh was getting cold. Amok's spirit was there, somewhere, as yet unable to reach higher planes. He had to find it, urge him to take his place again. His time hadn't come. Shrapnel sighed with relief. If his friend was wandering around in his ethereal form, it would probably be easier to communicate with him. He'd have liked to take a closer look at the guy in the yellow suit, but there were more pressing concerns, so he pulled himself out of the vehicle.

Shrapnel needed no more than a few seconds to explore the entire area, which he did without worrying about the rain, shouting, between two rolls of thunder, his missing brother's name. He came back to where he started without having found him. The body hadn't stirred, the passenger was there, he was talking, talking, talking, to keep the night from engulfing him. The sedan was surrounded by water, a dense darkness had gripped the environs, there was nowhere for the stranger to go. Shrapnel was flabbergasted to hear what he said about himself to Amok's silent body, and wondered how they'd met. Busy leading a rebellion so that souls which were unjustly condemned to oblivion be authorized to manifest themselves in the lives of their loved ones, among the living, he'd taken little interest in events after his death. All the same, the idea that Amok, while living with Ixora, was having troubled relations with a man was beyond him. The man in yellow was expressing, in no uncertain terms, his desire to dominate Amok sexually, as a way to get revenge for the past. Shrapnel lent an ear, so to speak. What he understood reassured him: the affair, if it existed, had not been consummated.

He felt some embarrassment at the idea of leaving his brother-friend's body with this predator who could do what he wanted with it. Blocking the image from his mind, he decided it wouldn't matter so much, given that Amok's consciousness had taken flight. That should be his one and only focus, he set off again to search for him. This time, Shrapnel kept close to the ground, calling as he'd done before, but without shouting, attuned to the slightest rustling. He thought the passage keepers were watching him, the group of protesting spirits too, since their fate depended on his success. This stopped him for a moment above a crack brimming over with rainwater, he was glad there was no risk of sinking into it, or inhaling its stench. He'd lived in this country long enough to know the effects of hot air on stagnant water, even in a landscape of such compelling beauty. The laterite soil, when waterlogged, gave off the smell of rancid sweat that continued to waft through the air after the sun had done its work. He pursued his exploration, lingered over a ditch that intrigued him around which the water accumulated but did not penetrate. Heeding his intuition alone Shrapnel entered this gaping mouth only to discover a most unexpected sight at the bottom. He beheld a land, an apparent replica of the one he'd just left. It hadn't rained there, that's the first thing he noticed. There was an arcade along which ran plants studded with white flowers that seemed to mark the entrance to a property.

Shrapnel paused at his spot, wondering about what he was seeing.

The flowers' lush corolla protected the yellow stamens, which looked like gold, as did the sepals, buried under the dark green leaves. A lane led to a conical house, of a type common in the northern regions of the country. On either side was a garden planted with tall royal palms. Shrapnel noted that a car had driven by there, there were tire tracks on the ground. On the veranda, a woman sat on a chair with a reclining backrest. She smiled at him: *Welcome to your brother's home, Shabaka. The one you're looking for is here. Take a seat.* Shrapnel didn't ask the questions that assailed him, this woman knew him, saw him. His condition as a dead person authorized to visit the living might help him understand the situation, know what this place was, who this stranger was. He didn't want to make a fool of himself, but he lacked valuable information, that he tried hard to get by circumventing the problem: *Can I see him?* At no time was Amok's name pronounced. The woman replied that he could do anything, according to the laws governing his condition, he was a spirit, that was why he'd found the house. Shrapnel said to himself that she was right, that he had so many powers, but he still had no idea how they worked. What's more, it seemed to him that searching the house without being invited into it could be perceived as an unfriendly gesture. He made up his mind to do so nonetheless, but the walls stopped him. Shrapnel turned to the woman. *The one you're looking for is here, you'll have to trust me. He's undertaking the journey through his night. It's from this abyss that he'll be reborn to the day, we shall assist him.*

Shrapnel railed against Kalunga, suspecting that she'd set a trap for him. Having paired all the swear words he knew with the passage keeper's name, he began to call Amok again, but his voice came back to him. No one but he was moved by it. He collected his thoughts, put some order in them, reviewing the evening's events, from the moment Amok had left Ixora lying in the mud. This was the only place his friend could be, here behind the walls of this house. He didn't pretend to understand everything, that wasn't the goal of his presence. The impulse to pay a visit to Kabral or Gabrielle coursed through him, he could be back before sunrise, but that would serve no purpose. The ability to enter into communication with his close relations had not yet been granted him. He decided to wait until morning, to see what would happen, time would go by quickly. The stranger's cordial authority made him desist from speaking to her, he kept silent, on the lookout, immune to sleep. The woman did not bat an eye, perhaps she knew no other pose. Shrapnel didn't fall asleep, but he lost his patience, without thinking about it, he moved away, instinctively. Dead or alive, he'd never been the type to hold his horses, at the bottom of a pit to boot. He did what any sensible person would have done in his place, he went to get some fresh air.

The city of his youth was not far off, given that he could get around at whatever speed he chose. The torrential downpours had spoiled the plans that any party animals may have had, but he hoped to find, in some underground bar, a few rager addicts with whom he could unwind, a few priestesses of flamboyance who'd shine come what may. The rain had not spared the housing projects, but he was confident. He saw it better now, though he had to admit that he barely recognized it. It was not the ghost of its former self, it was its decomposed corpse, delivered to forces that held no promise of forgiveness for sins. Shrapnel clung nonetheless to his certainties. Those who populated this area, this entire country, were made of the same clay as he was. Their life force drove them, some of its manifestations were independent of their will, there'd be someone, somewhere to celebrate, before dawn, the privilege of having survived the deluge. Those who'd been carried off by the rain wouldn't see any wrong in this, they'd have done the same. Those that the rainstorm had plunged into mourning would also see no harm, they too would sing and dance, to chase the grief away, and to open the way for the deceased to the other world. Some of the streetlamps on Boulevard de la Souveraineté had withstood the storm, Shrapnel noticed that the ones that were still working were those on which a portrait of president of the Republic was hanging, probably welded. Posters announced an international congress held several weeks before. The strongman of the country must have been the only participant, no other face appeared alongside his.

On the corner of a small street in the city center, a women's clothing store caught his eye. It was named after an idol from the eighties, a certain Alexis Carrington-Colby, whom the women in the country had seen as an inspiration, in a society that pressed them to seduce, to cheat, to face all troubles without shrinking, to take the blows, then get up again with style, not to bow their heads until they'd been decapitated. On this bumpy road, the casualties could be picked up by the shovelful, but Alexis's impersonators had made a global reputation for themselves. They were said to be queens of intrigues, of vice, champions of sexual depravity. It was a bit reductionist, it was wise to beware of generalizations: very early on, these women had embarked on a struggle against domination, they'd acquired a certain mastery of the subject. A little farther on what was left of the sidewalk were the offices of an insurance company, that what he was led to suppose at the sight of the small, rundown building that invited the passerby to continue on his way. Between these two buildings, Shrapnel thought he'd found what he was looking for. Muffled sounds came his way, as if from a cellar. This was unusual, few buildings had basements, he saw nothing that indicated the presence of a discotheque, a club, a night bar. There was only a rather ordinary take-away, whose plain sign indicated: *O sapi,* At the shop. Too discreet to be honest: the people around here drank ego-tripping with their mother's milk, so something was fishy. Shrapnel went through the storefront, found himself inside. That was where the heavy bass chords were coming from. He didn't pussyfoot around, the night was going by, he had things to do. The shop was closed, of course, at this time of night, but the music became clearer, they were dancing to "Stomp!" by the Brothers Johnson, which was a good sign. Shrapnel wouldn't have had anything against a more local atmosphere, but funk had become very well acclimated in this country where bass players were revered. He didn't waste any time looking for the way down to the basement, slipped through the cement slab, discovered the party of dancers, men that the storm had not dissuaded from gathering in celebration of the groove.

The room had low ceilings, he shrunk into a corner to enjoy the carousing as much as he could. There had to be a reason that they'd hidden this place under a take-away, he expected to see naked women, waitresses capable of balancing beer or wine glasses on their buttocks. They'd have that pronounced curvature, that muscular behind, those legs planted firmly on the ground. It must be hot, so the women would be sweating, their skin would glisten, seeing them would be like touching them, smelling them. His gaze was drawn to the decor, which he found a bit kitschy, in keeping with the old tunes that the deejay was playing, a man who seemed to take himself for Prince Vultan, given his attire. Not to be outdone, others were donning shimmering costumes, glittering dresses. Vying for the best lookalike contender was a Precious Wilson double being twirled around by a man, and a laughing Maizie Williams clone, coming on to three gentlemen whose tongues were hanging down to the floor. Shrapnel sucked his teeth, a real man didn't express his desire that way, didn't wiggle his hips, in the company of others, waiting to be chosen: a real man pushed his rivals out of the way and pounced on his prey. These people were pathetic, he continued his examination of the surroundings. A huge mirror covered one of the walls, the three others, painted in bright yellow, displayed, in an arc, the midnight-blue letters of the inscription GeeBees that left him wondering. Silver stars adorned the graffiti, another enormous one hung from the ceiling, diffusing a white light through its branches.

He noticed an open door, headed over to it to find another smaller, dimly lit room. He heard the first notes of *Skin Tight* by the Ohio Players, and wondered, with dread, what exactly he was seeing. He went back to the first room, took a closer look at the dancers, saw that there were only men there, whether they were pressed against each other or not, sometimes dressed with no regard for their sex. Precious and Mazie were visibly guys, it was obvious now by the legs of one, the size ten shoes of the other, their affected gesture, that exaggerated way of moving their long-beaded braids. The rager was at its peak, the world could have come crumbling down, these geezers couldn't give a hoot, they let out their impropriety to the rhythm of funk. Shrapnel had no need for confirmation as to the goings-on on the sofas or right on the floor, in the nightclub's smaller room. He refused to put words to these ignominious acts, hoping that they would be erased from his memory. At the heart of the hive, the gay bees of GeeBees were busy destroying a population shaken by history, that needed to engender vital forces, brains, and arms for the future. Shrapnel recalled Amok's passenger, the guy in the pale-yellow suit, whose possible assault on his brother-friend's body he thought wouldn't matter so much. He called himself a fool for having thought he was an isolated, marginal creature, a misfit on his planet. He needed partners, perhaps he found them in this place. Stripped of his body, Shrapnel still retained the imaginary sensation that came to him at the thought of men copulating, this impression of perforation. That was all it took to make him leave GeeBees. Without passing through the take-out, he found himself in front of the Alexis Carrington-Colby vitrine, with its mannequins dressed in satin nighties, silk cocktail dresses, and wide-brimmed hats.

His desire to have a good time was gone, a sadness mingled with disgust overtook him, the spectacle that he'd witnessed at GeeBees raised questions. In the community where he grew up, he was ready to swear such activities never took place. But as he made his way back to Amok, whom he shouldn't have left, Shrapnel was forced to admit that he didn't know the sexuality of his forebears. He was too young when his grandmother died, hadn't reached the age of thirteen at which time a man from his community would have had the responsibility of educating him about such matters. His circumcision had taken place in the city, a travelling circumciser had come to his uncle's house, no doubt summoned by him. The idea of sending him back to the village to have this ritual performed had not been entertained. Having been driven from their lands, the community was struggling to put down roots in a new place, his uncle had thought it would be hard for him to see his family in this situation. This relative, who had converted to Northern practices, had not passed on to him the masculine education that he himself had received in the equatorial forest. When he'd reached puberty, the man had taken him to a woman, saying, *This isn't a brothel, my son, she's a very good mother, she helps people out.* The two had gone to Merry Widow, a neighborhood with a scandalous reputation, where Shrapnel had been introduced into the home of an adipose mass named Maggie, while his uncle went out for a beer. Alone with the woman, he hadn't lowered his eyes, she'd put lipstick on her cheekbones as blush, he'd wondered why a person with such dark skin thought it necessary to have rosy cheeks.

Maggie had watched him at length before asking his age, to which he'd cheekily replied, *Fourteen*, the bountiful lady had sucked her teeth, nodded, shot out: *Wait here, little one*. She'd returned, holding a younger woman by the hand, one of her daughters perhaps, Shrapnel hadn't asked any questions. He'd joined his relative outside, in front of a nearby bar, sitting on an empty beer case. The man had smiled at him, *You're a big boy now, soon you'll go out alone, with the girl you choose, but you mustn't knock her up*. If the girl was pregnant, he'd be forced to take care of the child, at the very least, but they must have explained to him how to avoid this, that was another reason that they'd come here. Shrapnel would have rather had a different kind of initiation, but this was the one he'd had, and he wasn't going to let himself be sick over it, for a boy it wasn't too early, it had helped him approach these matters in a natural way. Much later he'd heard talk of men going with other men, always on a reproachful tone: the existence of this phenomenon in their country was attributed to a settler named Audeberge. The influence of this figure from the past, as far as he knew, had only been felt in political circles, decades ago. Not having known this individual, the copulating dancers of GeeBees were responsible for their own deeds. To be sure, they didn't exhibit themselves in public, they had enough decency, Shrapnel acknowledged, to hide their perversion underground in a basement. But the very existence of such a place indicated that they were gaining confidence, that they were assuming their deviance, that someday soon they'd no longer be satisfied with a basement, they'd want to be seen, approved, and that, well that would be a terrible thing.

Now that he was a spirit, Shrapnel would have liked to rise above his anxiety, have a broader perspective, see souls as requiring all kinds of experiences to evolve, his own could have gone that way, but didn't. These men that history had stripped of power couldn't knowingly throw their manhood into the flames, it was all they had left. Aware of this, some of them expressed it in a flashy way, tilting at stereotypes, which bothered him less, he preferred the caricature to the toxic reality. What bothered him most was that he'd seen only Black bodies in that dive, widespread incest in short, brothers shouldn't fuck each other, that was the first problem. With others, maybe . . . But then again, not even with them, you'd leave an essential part of yourself in this act, there could be no more than one truth when it came to certain things, rarely was it otherwise, no matter how intense such a desire was, it should be restrained, men came to Earth to love women. Hoping the phenomenon would remain marginal, that people would not boast of doing such things in the future, he headed back, his soul defeated. His energy had been sapped, he dawdled on his way, thinking that everything was going to hell, the battered remains of the city bore witness to this, despair had triumphed. Shrapnel had set out in search of life, but had found only its nihilistic face, he sucked his teeth at himself, drove the Brothers Johnsons' groove from his mind.

He'd considered himself more useful in the North, where young brothers had embarked on a frantic quest to find themselves that he feared would lead them astray. In the meantime, what was happening on the Continent? His life had been useless, he'd done nothing but gesticulate, dreaming of grandiose projects without implementing them. His son had been a burden to him, he'd struggled so hard to assume his role as father, to feel that he was one. The uncle who'd taken him to that woman to initiate him had never been a real tutor or a confidant. First he'd had him circumcised, then facilitated the loss of his virginity, but they'd seldom spoken to each other. So with his little Kabral, Shrapnel had often been at a loss for words. He'd read stories to him at night, without ever being able to relax, knowing that Ixora was in the next room, brimming over with bitterness toward him. They'd separated shortly after their son's birth, she'd accused him of using her to acquire a legal status, to get his residence permit.

The deserted streets were streaming with water. Swimming on the surface of gray waves, the detritus seemed to be racing to a constantly receding finish line. Shrapnel passed the neighborhood *Poteau*, the term designated a stall where second-hand books were on offer, usually laid out on a tarp directly on the asphalt. Though there were several of these in the city, they were always referred to as *le Poteau*, as if it were the same place, the same mobile shop or, more likely, a boutique endowed with ubiquity. The bookseller had had to pack up in a hurry, he'd left a few volumes behind, the pages had fallen apart in the rain, some had disintegrated, others were drifting gently on the water, like the wrecks of paper boats. A lone surviving book had found a home under the awning of a nearby bakery, probably blown there by the wind. It was an anthology of poetry. *Invictus* was included in it, he reread the now famous poem, the words brought him back to Amok, they expressed more or less what he'd have liked to say to him. Reproaching himself for getting carried away by futile desires which had ended in disappointment, Shrapnel picked up the book, made it dance around in the air, remembered that he could do that. The ability to touch humans had been taken away from him, but everything else was within reach, he was happy to have the book, smiled at the thought of someone seeing it flying in the night. It was said that witches used tin cans as night vessels, traveling from one hemisphere to another to do their unspeakable acts. They could be found, disheveled, on the top of a tree, when they had to make an emergency landing. A flying book wouldn't be a source of great concern, someone might even film the scene and post it on social media.

It was very worthy company, he could read as he traveled, it gave him a unique experience of his condition, until then he'd made little use of his sense of touch. His sensations were different, now manipulating was more a matter of blowing than handling, being insensitive to temperature or weight, he could have done the same with a moped, or a pousse-pousse. Leaving the city, he recognized the gas station from earlier. It should have remained open, the pump attendant was protected indoors, but there was no one there, no lighting, the place looked deserted, as if it had been closed for years. Shrapnel recalled the pump attendant, saw himself sticking his tongue out at her, thought she looked like the unknown woman from the ditch, and hurried on without really knowing why. According to Kalunga, the living were surrounded by various entities, each playing a distinct role. The guardian of passages had recommended that he associate with these powers when they shared his goals. He'd forgotten her advice. The unknown woman knew everything about him, this had not escaped his attention. Yet, he hadn't tried to find out who she was, his fear of ridicule overriding common sense. Shrapnel realized that his performance so far as a spirit dispatched to the living had not been a resounding success, more like a series of mistakes. An intuition took hold of him, that the walls of the conical house were the ramparts of Amok's mind, the borders of his soul. No one could pass through them without being invited. Shrapnel was beginning to understand, if somewhat obscurely, the abyss from which his brother-friend would have to be reborn to the day. He had to hurry.

Shrapnel was about to quicken his pace, when the book slipped from his grasp. Someone had caught it in mid-air, without batting an eye at the uncanny sight of a flying object. Any reasonable person would have taken to his heels, he stopped, astounded, and looked at the man who was there flipping through the volume snatched from the wind. The guy was as tall as he'd been, though not as burly. Bare-chested and barefoot, wearing black sweatpants, he held a ghetto blaster to his ear the likes of which Shrapnel hadn't seen in decades. He was alone on the street in the middle of the night, bobbing his head to the muted sound of the music. A beggar. A poor homeless man. A simpleton. Shrapnel looked at him as the other would have looked at Shrapnel had he seen him, wondering what was going on. *What now?* But the guy didn't care, he didn't see him. They were going in the same direction, he followed him for a moment, tried unsuccessfully to get the book back. The idea came to him to slip into the cassette player, it wouldn't be more uncomfortable than the car engine. Fitting his words to the slow rhythm of a song titled *The Dark End of the Street*, over Lee

Moses's husky voice, Shrapnel addressed the guy. If he heard him, the surprise and fright would make him drop his book.

—*Hey, what are you doing here?*

—*Walking.*

—*You can hear me?*

—*Continent Noir listens to the messages of spirits.*

—*Continent Noir, that's your name?*

—*My name is Continent Noir, I'm crazy.*

—*I don't know if you're nuts, I just saw guys sticking it to other guys who were all too happy to get it stuffed in them like women, so . . .*

The one who'd said he was called Continent Noir shrugged his shoulders, there was a lot of fucking in the city, much more than in in his native village, but he'd never seen what the spirit was describing to him. *You're lucky, old man, you've been spared this sight. But what do you think about it?* Continent Noir, whose every stride seemed at least a foot and a half long, told him that he wasn't used to thinking much, it was tiring, he was already crazy, or so they'd said. So he only obeyed his heart, that hadn't worked out too badly for him. *The heart tells me that you can screw if the other person agrees, that's love.* There were times he would have liked to do so himself, but no one was interested in madmen, not even other men, they thought he had a strange look in his eyes, that they were too light, a bit slanted, he had never . . . *Okay, man, doesn't matter, you can't understand.* On the contrary, he understood love very well, he felt it deep inside him, that was all there was, that was why he didn't get angry at the spirit who was lacking in respect toward him.

Continent Noir's long strides were impressive, but he was just a human, a living being. Only too happy to have someone to talk to, Shrapnel had kept by his side. They were going in the same direction, the man could be useful to him, losing track of him would have been stupid. In answer to his question, Continent Noir said he'd left his hut at the first roll of thunder, running in the rain did him good, people rushed home for shelter, leaving the world to him, no one made fun of him, no one chased him away. As he ran he embraced the earth, the air, the water, he felt himself becoming fire, a soul more than a body, in harmony with the universe. His running took him far, that was how he'd ended up in the city. He talked of his daily life, the things he perceived through his ghetto blaster, since he found it, that was a long time ago, he'd never changed the batteries. When they arrived by Amok's car, the early-morning light had driven the darkness away. The passenger door had been opened, the driver's chest was resting on the steering wheel, he'd remained like that all night, Shrapnel felt a twinge of guilt, promised himself not to leave him again. He saw Amok's lips moving, his brother-friend was delirious, his spirit was back inside him, weakened, dazed, but there nonetheless. The ditch whose unknown occupant had impressed him seemed to have never existed, to have been only an illusion in the course of a troubled night; yet he was sure that he'd descended into it, spirits didn't have visions, as far as he knew. He'd penetrated into a land under the earth, a world below, reflecting the one above, it hadn't been the fiery hell of fables, there'd been flowers, trees, a house, a guard. Shrapnel was annoyed with himself, in his haste he hadn't understood, hadn't given himself the time. He was beginning to glimpse the meaning, beyond the images, Kalunga had warned him.

Continent Noir had no need for instructions. He put the ghetto blaster down on the roof of the car, then the book, hoisted Amok's body over his shoulder and picked them up again in one hand. With his shoulders hunched under the weight, he walked ploddingly, his hut was nearby, the man would rest there, he had undoubtedly been the victim of a dazzlement. Continent Noir had built his hut in a garden planted with royal palms and fruit trees. He'd worked on it patiently, with his own hands, with no help from anyone. He was proud of it, he lacked nothing, many wounded people had been welcomed within these walls, all had left healed. It was not Continent Noir who tended the sick, he added, everyone had in them their strengths, they provided what was necessary. All he had to do, for his part, was rescue those who, among the victims of the dazzlements, were still meant to inhabit the world of the living.

A woman was sitting on the threshold of the house, waiting. He recognized her right away, was hardly surprised by her presence, didn't have to question her, this time. Continent Noir's remarks had lifted a corner of the veil, not everything would be put into words, it was up to him to listen. From the woman's gaze, Shrapnel understood that she saw him even in daytime, even upper ground, but she didn't address him. He felt small, he'd fallen short, she wouldn't bother to tell him so. In her presence, he dared not enter the room where Amok was being cared for, he wasn't worthy. Shrapnel thought of the protesting spirits, without whom he wouldn't have attracted the attention of Ras and Kalunga, the strict guardians of passages dedicated to respecting the order of things. He'd join them at the end of his earthly sojourn, spend eternity at their side, if by chance their petition was rejected. This reason alone made him determined to accomplish what he'd been sent to do among the living. As soon as he could, he used Continent Noir's radio, to call his memory to his brother-friend's mind. Seeing the effects, he felt encouraged to continue, he ventured to slip into Continent Noir's body, into his eyes, in order to manifest his presence with greater force. Amok recognized but didn't name him.

He didn't really know what to do, it wasn't thanks to him that Amok wouldn't put an end to his days. Having journeyed through his intimate night, his friend had chosen not to reside there, but to hold onto something that he would transform in the new day. Shrapnel, who pretended to help others, had never done so himself. Proud to possess an ancient knowledge, inherited from his grandmother, he'd neglected to learn in his turn how to add to this heritage lessons from his own journey as a man. What exactly had he been, when his steps, so sure of themselves, had paced the streets of the world so that the nobility and beauty of ostracized peoples would be seen through him? What had he been when he'd taken one woman's body after another, more satisfied with receiving love than eager to give it? He'd enjoyed being a Black man at whose feet the oppressor's women threw themselves, thereby becoming spoils of war. The one who'd arrogated to himself all the rights in the world, whose money bent nations to his will, would at least have his women ravished. One day, on the way to Amok's place, he'd let himself be drawn off his path by a silhouette, a look. That was how an encounter of another kind had taken place, one with a full human being.

Gabrielle had opened a different realm to him, but just as he was about to step inside, it had been snatched away. He'd died at the age of thirty, in the subway one evening, leaving nothing but dreams behind, not even the germ of an achievement. Others, before him, had sung of greatness and beauty. It was up to their successors to endow these forms with content. Death may not make life cease, but it marked the end of a trajectory all the same. It was impossible to go on from the other place where souls resided, which he had somehow hoped he could do. Seeing Amok wrestling with his own shadows, not shying away from the battle even if his mind, disturbed by pointless questions, sometimes turned in circles, Shrapnel understood that he had no business here. He'd wanted to come, but no one had invited him, the dead could not impose themselves on the living.

Shrapnel couldn't resign himself to leaving without saying goodbye to his beloved brother, now a dark fire gradually rising from the abyss. Having embraced his darkness, Amok would discover the light that was attached to it, find a purpose for it all, he had confidence in him. Using once more his attunement with Continent Noir, Shrapnel had provided him with kani pepper to add to his morning coffee. The flavor of the beverage would bring him to Amok's mind. He took his place in the hollow of the rift that opens between night and day, while his brother-friend was busy cleaning the hut. From there he called Kalunga. The passage keeper brought him back to her. The brothers were standing by the side of the road leading to the Spirit, the cries of past idols still filling this part of *misipo*. Not a word was uttered to welcome him back, he greeted those who were there, knowing that nothing of his journey to the other realm had escaped their attention. Shrapnel didn't ask to be taken aside to share his feelings with the one who'd dispatched him among the living. He had no desire to protest, the Spirit would do its will. Maybe, in the endless lamentation of the great men of yesteryears, there was something to reflect upon. All he had to convey now was his acceptance of death. The departed who'd made their way to the end of the road to the higher planes couldn't approach the living, he now knew, without being invoked, convoked. If they weren't, and if they chose not to reincarnate, theirs would be an idle eternity. Heka had only intervened after he'd called her. Many requests, he acknowledged, would go unanswered, when the deceased who were summoned had ended their journey in this desolate region of the universe. Death alone conferred no power. Shrapnel didn't express himself immediately. Instead, he turned to the earth, curious to know how events would unfold over which he'd have no control, tried to remain impassive. Yet a very special emotion warmed him when he saw Amok, in Continent Noir's hut. He listened to his thoughts, heard the first sentences of the text, observed him as he darkened the pages of a spiral notebook with a ballpoint pen. To satisfy those who were hoping for a word from him, Shrapnel said: *To the living, life.*

Notes

PAGE 6. **It was like countering a lie with another lie**: Refrence to Article 17 of the Charter of Kurukan Fuga, also called the Manden Charter, promulgated *c*.1222 and considered the Constitution of the Mandingo Empire. It stipulates that "Lies that have lived for 40 years should be considered like truths." The charter was inscribed in 2009 on the Representative List of the Intangible Cultural Heritage of Humanity kept by UNESCO.

PAGE 6. **The jewel of *Negro Nations***: Reference to Cheikh Anta Diop, *Nations nègres et culture* [Negro Nations and Culture, 1954], which became a classic, even outside Afrocentric circles.

PAGE 7. **In relative opacity, fulfill it or . . .** : Frantz Fanon's famous statement in *The Wretched of the Earth*: "Each generation must discover its mission, fulfill it or betray it, in relative opacity."

PAGE 17. **A library that could burn from one day to the next**: Reference to Amadou Hampâté Bâ's statement that "when an old man dies, a library burns down," which has become a famous dictum extolling the wisdom of the old in sub-Saharan Africa.

PAGE 40. ***Rendez-vous en terre inconnue:*** The TV show *Rendez-vous en terre inconnue* took a celebrity to an unknown destination to live for a couple of weeks with a minority ethnic group whose culture and traditions were threatened by modern lifestyles.

PAGE 115. **Minitel:** A French online network, a precursor of the Web, in service from 1980 until 2012. [Trans.]

PAGE 116. **Sapeurs:** From *saper*, French slang for getting dressed up; *sapeurs* can be compared to dandies, but they are part of a movement that spread beyond its Congolese origins, for which the act of dressing up, often in brightly colored suits, has a broader cultural and political significance. [Trans.]

PAGE 135. **Brightening darkness as in the gathering darkness:** Reference to the following lines from the classic sub-Saharan poem "Souffles" by Birago Diop:

> *Ceux qui sont morts ne sont jamais partis*
> *Ils sont dans l'ombre qui s'éclaire*
> *Et dans l'ombre qui s'épaissit*

> (The dead are never gone
> They're in the brightening darkness
> And in the gathering darkness)

PAGE 135. *Laisse-moi devenir l'ombre de ton ombre:* From Jacques Brel's famous "Ne me quitte pas": "Let me be the shadow of your shadow, the shadow of your hand, the shadow of your dog, but don't leave me." [Trans.]

PAGE 136. **Masculinity undid most men:** The expression is adapted from Junot Díaz's comment "Masculinity will undo most men" made during a talk titled "Art, Race and Capitalism" given at the Americas Latino Festival, in Denver, Colorado, November 17, 2013. Available at: https://bit.ly/3SahzwJ (last accessed on July 27, 2022).

PAGE 176. **Craô's son's quest:** Rahan, Craô's son, is a character from a comics series popular in France. His quest, among others, is to find the sun's lair, the place where it sleeps at night.

PAGE 232. **Film adaptation of *Cry, the Beloved Country*:** The 1982 film titled *Amok* by Souheil Ben Barka was an adaptation of Alan Paton's 1948 novel *Cry, the Beloved Country*.

PAGE 250. *Il est possible de se réconcilier avec le fait*: Original English: "In whose time? One has only one life. One may become reconciled to the ruin of one's children's lives is not reconciliation. It is the sickness unto death."—James Baldwin, "Negroes Are Anti-Semitic Because They're Anti-White," *New York Times Magazine*, April 9, 1967.

PAGE 250. *Nous devons chercher une nouvelle manière d'être au monde*: "We must look for a new way of being in the   world . . ."—Jean-Marc Ela.

PAGE 269. **On the lines of Article 12 of the imperial constitution:** Article 12 of the 1805 Constitution of Haiti stipulates that "No whiteman of whatever nation he may be, shall put his foot on this territory with the title of master or proprietor, neither shall he in future acquire any property therein."

PAGE 270. **Something that was confirmed by Article 14:** Article 14 of the 1905 Haitian Constitution stipulates that "All acceptation of color among the children of one and the same family, of whom the chief magistrate is the father, being necessarily to cease, the Haytians shall hence forward be known only by the generic appellation of Blacks."

PAGE 272. **French guy singing about lying at night and taking trains across the plain:** Lyrics from "La nuit je mens" by Alain Bashung, a French singer-songwriter who was popular in the 1980s and 90s. [Trans.]

Glossary

Camfranglais is a Cameroonian slang, a mixture of French, English, and indigenous languages. The pidgin used in this text is the English-based pidgin spoken in Cameroon.

Akata (Cameroonian slang): people of sub-Saharan type

Ankh: an Egyptian cross, known as a key of life

Balock (pidgin English): from bad luck

Bensikin (Cameroonian slang): motorcycle taxi

Beta falla a mapan to nang: Better find a place to sleep

Carabote (Camfranglais): made of boards, from cardboard

Depso (Cameroonian slang): homosexual

Djed: Egyptian pillar-shaped symbol, known as a pillar of life

Djo (Cameroonian slang, Camfranglais): a guy

Dos (Cameroonian slang, Camfranglais): money, from "dollars"

Feymen (Cameroonian slang, Camfranglais): swindlers, deceivers

Kandakes: Black queens of Meroe

Kombo (Cameroonian slang, Camfranglais): fuck

Lep mon gars (Cameroonian slang, Camfranglais): Leave my guy alone; *mon gars* from French for "my guy" and *lep* is a deformation of the English "leave"

Long pencil: educated person

Massa (pidgin English): boss

Medu neter: ancient Egyptian language

Misipo: the universe; also used in this novel as a character's name

Mwen rele ou koulye (Haitian creole): I am calling you now

Ndeng (Cameroonian slang): male genital

Rythmer (Cameroonian slang, Camfranglais): accompany

Sissia (Cameroonian slang, pidgin English): intimidate

Sky (Cameroonian slang, Camfranglais): whisky, pronounced skī

Tournedos (familiar, Cameroon): makeshift restaurant, from French tourne, turn, dos, back, as customers have their backs turned to the street.

Yuruga: figure in Dogon cosmogony associated with chaos; an Afrocentric reading sees it as representing the Eurocentric action on the world

Places

Alkebulan or Alkebu-Lan: African continent, of disputed origin

Ayiti: Haiti, in Haitian creole

Ityopya: Ethiopia, in Amharic

Katiopa: name for African continent, of Kongo origin

Kemet: Ancient Egypt, also used to refer to the African continent

Nzi we mabwe: Great Zimbabwe in Kalanga

Tin-Buku: Timbuktu in Tamasheq

Soundtrack

Carleen Anderson, "Mama Said"

Alain Bashung, "La nuit je mens"

Alain Bashung, "Gaby oh Gaby"

Jacques Brel, "Ne me quitte pas"

The Brothers Johnson, "Stomp!"

Commodores, "Nightshift"

Dis bonjour à la dame, "Chris'Tal"

Bobby Hebb, "Sunny"

Maître Gazonga, "Les jaloux saboteurs"

Prince Nico Mbarga, "Sweet Mother"

Curtis Mayfield, "Sweet Exorcist"

Maze, "Woman Is a Wonder"

Charles Mingus, "Goodbye Pork Pie Hat"

Lee Moses, "The Dark End of the Street"

Ohio Players, "Skin Tight"

Mica Paris, "Young Soul Rebels"

Greg Perry, "Come On Down (Get Your Head Out of the Clouds)"

Joshua Redman, *MoodSwing* album

The Whispers, "In the Mood"

Cassandra Wilson, "Resurrection Blues (Tutu)"

Bonus: The music of Luther Vandroos, Kid Creole, Billy Strayhorn and TPOK Jazz